Subcortical

JOHNS HOPKINS: POETRY AND FICTION
Wyatt Prunty, General Editor

Subcortical

Stories by Lee Conell

Johns Hopkins University Press
Baltimore

This book has been brought to publication with the generous assistance of the John T. Irwin Poetry and Fiction Endowed Fund.

© 2017 Lee Conell
All rights reserved. Published 2017
Printed in the United States of America on acid-free paper
9 8 7 6 5 4 3 2

Johns Hopkins University Press
2715 North Charles Street
Baltimore, Maryland 21218-4363
www.press.jhu.edu

Library of Congress Cataloging-in-Publication Data

Names: Conell, Lee, 1987– author.
Title: Subcortical / Lee Conell.
Description: Baltimore : Johns Hopkins University Press, 2017. |
    Series: Johns Hopkins: poetry and fiction
Identifiers: LCCN 2017012953 | ISBN 9781421424224 (softcover :
    acid-free paper) | ISBN 1421424223 (softcover : acid-free paper) |
    ISBN 9781421424231 (electronic) | ISBN 1421424231 (electronic)
Subjects: | BISAC: FICTION / General. | FICTION / Short Stories
    (single author). | FICTION / Literary.
Classification: LCC PS3603.O5329 A6 2017 | DDC 813/.6—dc23
    LC record available at https://lccn.loc.gov/2017012953

A catalog record for this book is available from the British Library.

Special discounts are available for bulk purchases of this book.
For more information, please contact Special Sales at 410-516-6936 or
specialsales@press.jhu.edu.

Johns Hopkins University Press uses environmentally friendly book
materials, including recycled text paper that is composed of at least
30 percent post-consumer waste, whenever possible.

Contents

Subcortical

The Lock Factory

When my mother was seventeen, she got a summer job in a lock factory about twenty minutes away from the south Chicago suburb where she grew up. She'd waitressed the summer before at a Howard Johnson's, where she wore pins that said things like "Think strawberry!" Which was just kind of fascist, my mother thought. Telling people what to think? Even if it was only telling people to think about strawberries, it was still a bit fascist. My mother believed her new job would be better. Of course, it didn't pay better, but at least she wouldn't have to wear pins or smile at customers. She was free to wear jeans and frown for eight hours a day if she wanted, so long as she met her quota.

On the drive over to the lock factory, she must have seen cornfields and the occasional water tower and little elevation. When she talked about her childhood to me, what she spoke of most of all was the land's flatness. "It's different for you, Becky," she said, "growing up in Chicago. There's tall buildings breaking things up." Everything my mother had seen had been stubbornly horizontal. For a time, as a child, she even refused to believe the earth was round because she saw no evidence that it was. She supposed she could keep walking straight across those cornfields and reach the end of the earth, and from there? She might step off the earth entirely and float through zero gravity to the moon or to Mars. Imagine her disappointment when she first got a boy to drive her out as far as he could go and instead of the edge of the earth she just found more of the same—more cornfields, more gas stations, more burger joints, and the moon still far away and gravity still present as always.

The lock factory looked like a giant rectangular box. Around the rectangular box was a parking lot and around the parking lot was a tall wire fence and around the tall wire fence were more cornfields. The inside of the factory appeared big and dark, full of different stations. The managers were men, but the other employees consisted mostly of old women, high school girls, and mentally handicapped people of both sexes—the lock factory received government subsidies for hiring within each of these demographics. The different demographics didn't always get along. There was a lot of antagonism especially between the high school girls and the old women, mainly around chairs. All the old women had their favorite chairs. On their favorite chairs they placed donut-shaped blow-up cushions to help them sit comfortably through their shift. They'd turn livid if any of the teenagers sat on their cushions, even in jest. "Get off my donut!" the older workers would shrill. The high school girls would laugh and laugh and finally give the donut-shaped cushion back.

My mother was placed at a station with a pretty blond girl she knew from high school, Donna, and an old woman with short white hair who always wore orange lipstick, called Hatsy. Donna, Hatsy, and my mother spent eight hours a day together. Each of them had been given modified screwdrivers, which they used to stick little springs into small metal pieces called rockers because of the way they rocked back and forth. The pieces Hatsy, Donna, and my mother made went into the combination locks kids used at school, but no one was quite sure what the pieces actually did. One afternoon the three of them passed the time positing theories about the rockers' true purpose. My mother guessed the rockers controlled the latch of the lock. Donna thought the rockers were in some mystical way responsible for generating the numbers for the combination. But when my mother asked Hatsy what she thought the rockers were for, Hatsy just pressed her orange lips together, so that her mouth resembled a sliver of American cheese. Then she shook her head. "We're not meant to unlock the combination lock's secrets," Hatsy said. "That isn't our job here."

Which suggested even Hatsy didn't have a clue what the rockers were for, an especially depressing fact given that Hatsy had been at the lock factory for a long time—though when my mother asked her how many years she'd been there, she just said, "Ages." Hatsy was married, but her husband had hurt his back and couldn't work and that was all Hatsy had to say about him. She never mentioned any children, but the donut cushion she sat on resembled a floatie taken from a kiddie pool. It was translucent except for its pattern of small pink flowers. When Hatsy sank into the donut-hole center of the translucent cushion, her thighs, squashed against the donut's inner ring, seemed covered in a cheerful, floral form of chicken pox.

While the women worked, Donna would often go on and on about how once she saved up enough money from the lock factory, she was headed straight for LA to become an actress. This rankled my mother a little—she, after all, was being practical, saving up for nursing school, while Donna was just being bigheaded—but she never voiced her criticism. Hatsy, though, was not so peaceable. She was usually nice to my mother, but always mean to Donna. Once Hatsy turned to Donna and snorted. "This one—" Hatsy said, pointing a long knobby index finger at Donna—"hasn't had to ask for a thing in her life. Not one thing. You can just tell. See that smirk on her face? Spoiled as sin."

"Sure." Donna tossed her hair behind her shoulders like she was in a shampoo commercial. "I'm really spoiled. That's why I'm spending my summer at a lock factory."

"And then you think you're going to be in the movies."

"Yes."

"There's lots of pretty faces out there," Hatsy said. "Prettier faces than yours."

"I have a cousin with connections." Donna smiled serenely. "He works in the movies. Well, a second cousin. He works in lighting."

"What does that mean," Hatsy said, "to work in lighting? He shine flashlights on famous people? That's no connection. You're not going to be in the movies."

Donna would keep up the serene smile and say, "Get back to your rockers, Hatsy."

Putting the springs in the rockers was tougher than it seemed. It took a good amount of pressure to get the springs in there; if you didn't do it right, the ends of the springs might fly up and knick your fingers. Sometimes when the women left work, their hands would be flecked with small cuts. And frequently their hands cramped up. Every thirty minutes or so, Hatsy would stretch out her arms and flap them up and down, to prevent what she called her "circulation complications." When she did this, Donna would grin and say things like, "What, do you think you're a bird?" Or, "Hoping to fly away? You're too old for that, Hatsy!" Then Hatsy would mutter under her breath and sit back down and shift her buttocks on the blow-up cushion in a little wiggly dance of fury.

When the shift was finally done, my mother would leap up from her non-cushioned seat, eager to escape the voices of Hatsy and Donna both. "I'd literally run to the parking lot," she told me. *Literally* as in she was able, then, to literally run. She and a friend of hers (not Donna, but another friend who was at a different station) would race across the parking lot, pretending someone was after them, their lungs hurting sweetly from their running and their laughter. This image from my mother's lock factory stories stayed with me even more than her descriptions of rockers or translucent cushions or her imitations of Hatsy or Donna. My mother running. When she was only in her early thirties, and when I was just learning to walk, she developed rheumatoid arthritis. Her feet and fingers became twisted up with constant aches and she needed to do a series of stretches just to swing herself out of bed in the morning. She'd had to quit her job as a nurse and find a sedentary office job instead. The arthritis flared up around the time her own mother died.

Only once in my life had I seen my mother really run: I was five years old and I decided to escape from the playground, just to prove that I could. With my mother calling after me, I sprinted. I was tall for my age and my legs already knew how to race. I crossed out of the park, my light-up sneakers smacking against the sidewalk. Until then, I'd always imagined an invisible tether linking me to my mother—if I got too far away, I was sure that tether would snap me back to her through some kind of mysterious maternal physics. But no. My legs were powering me far and fast and farther still. Then I was on the street, with taxis halting before me, honking, and delivery boys on bikes swerving around me, cursing, and a city bus breathing hot exhaust right into my face. The bus driver slammed on the brakes.

And there, coming after me, was my mother. But not my mother like I knew her. I had never seen her run so fast. I had never seen her move with such strength. She caught me up in the middle of the street. The bus driver shouted soundlessly behind his windshield. My mother lifted me up and shook me so that my teeth rattled in my head. She kept me lifted high like that until the adrenaline wore off, until we had crossed the street, and then she put me down on the sidewalk and said, her voice quaking, that we needed to go back home.

She was so sore the next day, she couldn't get out of bed and couldn't go into work. I said I was sick too—I *felt* sick—and stayed home from school. Around dinnertime my mother had to crawl out of bed to heat up some soup for the both of us. The cans of soups were up on a high shelf. Normally she didn't have trouble reaching that shelf, but that day, because of her soreness, she grimaced. I willed myself then to grow up, to grow tall, so that I could reach the high cabinets where the cans of soup were kept. I vowed that once I was tall enough to reach those cabinets, I would stick around always, so that my mother would have someone to help her, to keep her from grimacing like that. This vow allowed me to imagine that tether between us again. It made me feel less sick.

I go into this only to stress how remarkable that earlier image was—the one of my mother, young and running with no consequence, no care for the state of her bones the following day. But this is not something my mother herself would stress when she talked about the lock factory. She'd only say that, when work was out, she and Patti from sixth-period algebra would run, *literally* run, through the parking lot, gasping for air. Pretending they were being chased.

"By what?" I asked once.

She said, "Something invisible."

■ ■ ■

Whatever caused Hatsy to despise Donna started getting worse. While Donna would maunder on and on about her future stardom with her special brand of yackety blitheness, Hatsy would seethe in silence, sometimes biting her lower lip, sometimes smiling meanly to herself. One day, when Donna had left the station to grab more rockers, Hatsy leaned close to my mother and said, "I know you can't stand her either. The way she acts like no bad thing's ever touched her!" Hatsy placed her hand on my mother's shoulder. It was less a hand than a collection of knuckles. "Listen," Hatsy said. "Are you listening? There's something you should know."

My mother put down her modified screwdriver and flexed her fingers. "What?"

"I'm in trial for more of a management position." Hatsy leaned back again into her chair, her translucent cushion squeaking a little. "Management trusts me, you see. I've been here the third longest, and the first two longest aren't quite right in the head. A couple of days a week for the last couple of weeks, I've been in charge of locking the lock factory up. I'm not an ambitious woman anymore," Hatsy continued, now sitting up very straight. "It's not something I'd let get to my head—all the trust they put in me. But I wanted to let you know. I might be leaving you little girls at the rocker station soon enough."

My mother congratulated Hatsy. Hatsy smiled, but then leaned in again. "Just don't tell that Donna character about the change in my fortunes, okay? She'd find a way to ruin it. Even if she said 'Ohhh Hatsy, ohhh, that's great,' in that tiny baby way she's got, even still I'd know she was laughing at me somehow. Everything's a big joke with her."

Then the manager, a short man with a gut, came over and said someone at the box station was out sick. It was my mother's turn to fill in. She hesitated. The social dynamics at the rocker station were delicate and she was a mediating force between Donna and Hatsy, kept them from insulting each other too directly. But the boxing station was one of the easiest stations in the factory and my mother's right hand was cramping up a lot that day. So she told Hatsy she'd see her later, and went with the manager.

All that my mother had to do at the boxing station was fold up the boxes for the combination locks. At first it was wonderfully easy.

But after three hours, even wonderful easiness turned dull. The mentally handicapped demographic was heavily represented here at the boxing station, and none of the men or women around the table would look my mother in the eye or speak at all. In fairness, she didn't look them in the eye or speak to them either. Instead, to entertain herself, she started to write little messages on what would be the inside flap of the box—"Escape while you still can!" and "School is hell!!!!"—things like that. Then she would fold the box up so that the message was concealed. Maybe someone would open the box she folded on the first day of school, reach for their lock, and find her words. They might be forever inspired. They might break out of whatever prison they were in. Because of her!

When I was in middle school and got a combination lock for my first locker, I opened the box and looked for a message just like that, a message from my mother or someone like my mother urging me to break free. But there was just a strip of paper, like you'd find in a fortune cookie, telling me the numbers that would release the lock.

. . .

My mother's absence from the rocker station did, in fact, escalate tensions between Hatsy and Donna. At the start of her shift the next day, when Hatsy was in the bathroom, Donna tossed her hair and told my mother, "She's so bold without you here. And much more vile. You should have heard the awful things Hatsy said to me when you were in boxing. About my brains, about my attitude. Even about my hair. She said it's too flat looking. Do you think it's too flat looking?"

"You have beautiful hair, Donna," my mother said.

Donna hummed, "Thank you." She tossed her hair again, then added, "But really, someone needs to teach her a lesson."

My mother raised her eyebrows. "Leave Hatsy alone. She's just an old woman, Donna. Also, I think she's a little crazy."

"If she was crazy, she'd be a permanent in boxing. She's sane enough for rockers, right?"

"Still," my mother said. "Still. You should leave her alone. Look, she's coming back. Be good, okay?"

But instead of being good, Donna stole Hatsy's translucent blow-up cushion. She snatched it off Hatsy's chair just as Hatsy was about to sit back down.

"My donut!" Hatsy cried.

Donna put the cushion on her chair and sat on it and giggled. She thought she was being a real original.

"My donut! Give it back!"

But Donna didn't budge. After a while, seeing how red Hatsy's face was becoming, my mother said, "All right, Donna."

"All right, Donna" was code for get off the cushion. It was code for have some pity. It was code for we need to keep working. They had their quota, didn't they? The whole assembly line could get backed up if Hatsy and Donna kept fighting. But Donna refused to budge. She cooed over the cushion's coziness and cute little flower pattern, even though Hatsy was starting to quiver.

Finally Hatsy got right up in Donna's face. She was so close her breath lifted the soft gold tendrils that curled around Donna's temples. Hatsy hissed: "Give. Me. Back. My. Donut."

Donna just gripped the edge of the table. What was Hatsy going to do? Push Donna off her chair? Donna was stronger and heavier and Donna, now, was grinning, daring Hatsy to give her a push.

Hatsy took a deep breath.

She lifted her arms.

She was actually going to try. Hatsy was actually going to try to push Donna off her cushion.

"You can't do it," Donna said then, her voice movie-star smooth. "You're not strong enough to budge me even an inch, Hatsy."

And somehow that was it. After all the time Hatsy spent trying to insult Donna, after all the time she spent rolling her eyes at the girl, that was all it took to deflate Hatsy. A smooth, young voice telling Hatsy she wasn't strong enough. Hatsy's shoulders slumped. She backed off. She sat down. She was shorter without the boost of her cushion. Donna began chattering about her weekend plans like nothing had happened, going on first about her date the next night, then about the foothills around Los Angeles. Her second cousin in lighting had told her about those foothills. It wasn't flat in LA, not like here, Donna said. You could stand on the top of a mountain and look down at the whole world, more or less. She told Hatsy, very sweetly, that she'd send her a postcard when she made it big. Hatsy could tell her grandkids or whatever that she knew Donna when.

Hatsy said nothing in reply. She wouldn't meet Donna's eyes.

Finally Donna tossed her hair and announced that she didn't need Hatsy's cushion anymore. Her butt was so big, it was a cushion all its own, haha! She handed Hatsy the cushion back and Hatsy, very pale, sat back down on it.

Even with the extra boost, she didn't seem any taller.

. . .

The day after the cushion incident, a Saturday, Donna telephoned my mother. It was morning but it was hot and humid outside already; the phone, cradled under my mother's chin, felt sticky. "What is it, Donna?" my mother asked, keeping her voice low, because her own mother was still asleep.

"Did Hatsy call you, too?" Donna asked.

"No."

Apparently Hatsy had been asked by management to telephone Donna. Hatsy and Donna, Hatsy had said, needed to come into the factory that weekend because management decided they hadn't done their rockers right.

"I'm positive I didn't mess mine up," Donna told my mother. "I'm very detail-oriented. My theory is Hatsy was upset about my little cushion joke. She probably messed up her rockers on purpose and told management I was to blame, too, just so I'd have to come in on a weekend."

"I'm sure that's not true. Hatsy's not that conniving."

"She sounded way too happy on the phone. Just tickled to be ruining my Saturday. I don't know if you've noticed, but Hatsy? Hatsy has it in for me."

. . .

Every Saturday when I was a kid, my mother and I would walk to the grocery store. She'd tell me stories about her growing up to pass the time on the way over there and also on the way back, when we each carried heavy plastic bags. As I got older, I took more and more bags on, since their plastic handles hurt my mother's hands. But even when I carried most of the weight, we always walked home pretty slowly. That must have been how I first heard about the lock factory, and about what happened there. My mother would do the voices of Hatsy and of Donna, transforming an anecdote from the past into a play that seemed to be unfolding right that moment. Hatsy and Donna didn't always say the exact same thing from telling to telling, but the outlines of the narrative didn't change. Donna always tossed her hair in a shampoo commercial way. Hatsy always called Donna to tell her she needed to come into the lock factory that weekend to make quota.

I liked the lock factory story from a young age, because it seemed to me my mother was telling a variation on an animated fairy tale:

Hatsy, the wicked witch, and Donna, the beautiful blond Disney princess, singing songs about how someday her dreams would come true. The one plotting against the other. And there was something fairy-tale-like, too, about the idea of my mother as a young girl, not too much older than me, about to begin her life.

Sometimes, particularly at night if I wasn't able to get to sleep, I'd take the frame of my mother's story and fill in new dialogue. Once I imagined Hatsy actually pushed Donna after Donna stole her cushion. Another time Hatsy and Donna got into a fight on the floor of the lock factory and my mother dove in between them, kept them from hurting one another. Another time I had Hatsy chase Donna around with the modified screwdriver and my mother had to run after Hatsy and tackle her while Donna watched, pretending to be shocked but actually smiling behind her hands. Really, I was just composing new stories. My mother's material gave me the limits I somehow needed to imagine more freely.

But what made the lock factory story especially memorable was that it also ended up being weirder than I could ever have imagined on my own. Because in real life—by which I mean in the story my mother told me—when Donna showed up at that lock factory to fix the rockers that Saturday, she didn't come out again. At least, she didn't come out for the rest of the weekend. No one saw Donna or heard from Donna.

For several days, the girl vanished.

What had happened was this: Hatsy used her copy of the lock factory's keys to open the factory. She had then lured Donna inside to the rocker station, telling her to redo a batch. When Donna started working on the rockers, Hatsy excused herself to the ladies' room, then left the factory, locking Donna back inside. Donna didn't even realize she was locked in for a good while. Finally she wondered if Hatsy was all right. Maybe she had had a heart attack on the toilet?

She crept to the ladies' room, called, "Hatsy?" Her own call echoed back to her. The bathroom stalls were empty. Donna tried to open the factory's main door, the side doors, her hands starting to tremble a little more as she realized. Trapped. The only phones were in the managers' offices, which were locked.

She threw boxes of locks against the wall in a rage. She hurled modified screwdrivers up at the high windows, hoping somebody would see the shattered glass. After a while, she sat down in her chair at the rocker station and just listened. The racket of machinery usually made the place sound like a railroad station. And even during the rare moments the machinery was turned off, the lock factory was always filled with the murmuring of the old women and the young women in conversation. What disturbed Donna most must have been the silence, even though her own breath was surely heavy in her ears.

In the women's bathroom, she sluiced her face in cool water, listened as the drops she missed slipped down the drain and through some pipes, going somewhere else—who knew where? She went back to the rocker station. She tried to think about Los Angeles but instead she thought about the parking lot around the lock factory and the tall wire fence around the parking lot and then about the cornfields around the parking lot, which I like to pretend was as far as her imagination would stretch. Did Donna cry that day, locked in the lock factory? She must have cried. Right at the rocker station. Rocking back and forth. Later that night, she slept on a makeshift bed of blow-up cushions. She left Hatsy's donut on Hatsy's chair. The next day, she cried some more. Then she ate the ancient off-brand candy bars in the factory's vending machines until she ran out of change.

The following Monday morning, when the doors to the lock factory were opened, Donna tumbled out, her hair a greasy tawny tangle, dark blue circles under her light blue eyes. The tale of her weekend emerged—she told it in between sobs. "How terrible," everyone, including my mother, said. "How terrible."

But what I thought was really terrible was that no one had even noticed Donna had vanished. Her father lived with a woman in Indiana, her mother had been out of town with her new husband. Her brother she hardly ever heard from. Donna had been a missing girl that nobody knew was missing.

Once Donna had been found, Hatsy claimed the whole thing was an accident—she said she'd thought Donna had left the factory already. Management chose to believe Hatsy had made a mistake. She was old. Muddled. Probably she just got mixed up about who was in there and anyway, did the younger girl really have to shatter a window like that, damaging company property? Still, even though Hatsy wasn't accused of anything, she resigned her position immediately. No one was quite sure where she went afterward. "Maybe Los Angeles!" my mother joked once.

Donna quit the lock factory too, because she decided she didn't need to be there anymore. She had gotten briefly famous from the episode. The newspaper picked up the story—a girl locked in a lock factory, even accidentally, made for an entertaining "weird news" headline—and a Chicago news station actually interviewed her. My mother said Donna looked stunning on TV, and had a very charming on-camera cry about her trauma: a single tear got caught in her eyelashes and meandered, during the course of the interview, down her cheek. For a while everybody was coming up to Donna, telling her they'd cried watching her cry. It was the last push Donna needed. The next weekend she called my mother.

"I'm going to strike while the iron is hot!" she sang. "I can't wait any longer, I really can't. I've got just enough savings and I'm going to do it. I'm going to LA."

My mother told Donna she was happy for her. She told her the new girls at the rocker station were nice, but it wasn't the same, and my mother was looking forward to quitting soon herself for nursing school. "Good!" Donna said. "Get out of that place!"

Then both of them fell silent. There was nothing much more to say, actually. Finally, my mother wished Donna the best of luck in Los Angeles. And Donna said, "Have the best time in nursing school!"

So Donna left and, to the shock of everyone, she was cast in a movie. The film was about an out-of-work actor who had once been a Hollywood heartthrob, and was now trying to escape his failed celebrity past by romancing a young shop girl or something. It was called *Too Late for True Love?* Donna played Girl Fan #3. She walked down the street and, upon spotting the seriously jawed former heartthrob taking a stroll with the shop girl, seized his lapels. Girl Fan #3 cried, "Christ, weren't you in the movies? Jesus! I used to be such a fan!" The former heartthrob—who wanted to keep the shop girl innocent of his past in order to make sure her attraction to him was pure of heart—worked his serious jaw to and fro, then denied that he had ever been in cinema. Girl Fan #3 tilted her head doubtfully. The actor playing an actor shrugged Donna off, grabbed the shop girl's hand, and rushed past. The camera followed him and the shop girl, without a second glance in Donna's direction.

"What was *that* about?" the young and pure-of-heart shop girl costar asked.

"Oh, you know," said the heartthrob, with a nervous laugh. "People just see what they want to see in this town."

But in the end the scene was cut. Donna took this very, very hard, took this as a sort of sign. Or maybe she was just lonely. Or maybe she missed flat land. In any case, she moved back home and married some guy. They bought a house not far from the lock factory. They had some kids. And that, said my mother, was that.

As I got older I didn't totally believe what my mother told me, about Donna going to Los Angeles after all (I couldn't find a hint of *Too Late for True Love?* on IMBD), but I didn't question her to her face. I figured she might have added the detail in so the story would have more drama, a better arc. She wanted it to seem less simplistic, maybe.

My own understanding of Hatsy and Donna remained simplistic for some time. Hatsy stayed the unhappy witch, Donna stayed the unhappy princess, my mother stayed the neutral narrator. But my mother had a more complicated take, which she shared with me when I was older. It was early in my senior year at the time and I was trying to finalize where to apply to college. My mother wanted me to cast a wide net, apply to schools on the East Coast. She said I should go places now, before something—my body or some man, some change I couldn't yet see—got me stuck. But I felt strange about being so far from her, and from home. What if she needed my help? What if the arthritis got worse?

"Not a valid concern," my mother replied when I brought these questions up one night before bed.

We didn't argue too much more about where I'd apply for school after that, but one morning in the living room, a little bit before applications were due, she told me the lock factory story again.

"You see," she said, doing her morning toe-touching stretches, "the reason that Hatsy disliked us—two, three, four—I mean the real reason the old women didn't like the high school girls, it wasn't because we were stealing and sitting on their donuts. It was because we weren't stuck there, at the lock factory, and they were. It's not like I expected to go onto better things. But I expected to go onto different things, at least. I was young enough to get out. Eighteen, nineteen, twenty." And she stood up straight and stretched her fingers to the ceiling.

Yet something in her Hatsy and Donna theory didn't ring quite true to me. Because Hatsy had never seemed jealous of or angry at my mother. And my mother, like Donna, had plans to get out of the lock factory. Why, then, would Hatsy focus all of her rage on Donna? Maybe it came back to the perception of Donna as a girl without a care in the world. "The way she acts like no bad thing's ever touched her!" Maybe Hatsy had locked up Donna for the weekend because she couldn't stand that the girl seemed already completely free. Her appearance, her smiles, her little jokes, her attitude—Donna was so confident, already, in her upcoming liberation, and that unearned confidence and happiness was what irritated Hatsy the most, perhaps.

But then there was the fact that the whole weekend, no one had noticed Donna was missing. She could not have been as happy as she pretended. No, I don't think Donna was very happy. But probably she was very free. Free to leave the state, free to disappear, because nobody would really notice or care. And what if Hatsy had sensed all that lonesome freedom, all that possibility, wasn't, actually, what Donna really wanted? Maybe, by locking Donna in the lock factory, by causing a stir, Hatsy wanted to alert other people to Donna's existence, so they could interview her and notice her and snare her in a way that would be good for her, in a way she maybe even secretly desired.

. . .

One late night, the summer after I finished high school, I looked up the lock factory online. I thought it'd be fun to go on a road trip with my mother, to drive to the place where she grew up, to see the setting for one of her stories, especially because in a few weeks I'd be going to a college nearly a thousand miles away, in a place where I knew no one, and I would not see my mother again until winter break. I had never been away from her for longer than a week and I was already half-convinced that I would leave school for good after a month and come back home. Every morning that summer, I woke up from dreams that left a fluttering feeling of anxiety in my stomach. I thought a road trip with my mother might distract me a little.

But after a quick search, I discovered the factory had been shut down in the late nineties, acquired by a bigger lock company. Some of the jobs had gone overseas, some of the jobs had gone to robots, some of the jobs had gone to a factory in Milwaukee. (A few years after that, I would read an article about President Obama visiting that same lock factory in Milwaukee to show his support for American manufacturing.)

In the morning, over breakfast, I told my mother about what I'd found. She blinked, then said, "Why on earth do you think I'd want to go visit the lock factory, anyway?"

To my own surprise, I wasn't sure. "I thought we could find Donna," I tried. "Find out what happened to Donna."

"I told you what happened to Donna," my mother said. "Donna went back. Donna stayed put. I know just what happened to Donna."

I hated how she said that, hated how quickly she stripped Donna of all mystery, hated that she was trying to tell me how to think about Donna just because Donna hadn't managed to permanently leave her hometown. And maybe my mother saw that I hated it and wanted to provoke me into telling her why. Because she said it again: "Yes, I know just what happened to Donna."

I looked down at the fibrous slush of my cereal. "Maybe you do, maybe you don't."

My mother drummed her fingertips along the edge of the table. Then she stood up, even though she was in the middle of eating her cereal too, and began to do her stretches, reaching first high in the air and then all the way down to her toes. She said, "You should stretch too, you know. Okay? It's good for you. It doesn't matter that your body is healthy still. It's good for anybody at any time in life."

I made a show of rolling my eyes. But then I remembered that she did these stretches to feel less trapped by her body, by her illness, and after a minute, I got out of my seat and stood in front of my mother. We had the same dark eyes and thin shoulders, but I was taller than her and my hair wasn't turning gray. She smiled at me. We reached down together, toward the floor, and up together, mirroring one another. "Three," my mother said, "four, five. Get into the rhythm of it!"

I touched my toes a few times. Then I said, "How about Hatsy?"

"Huh?"

"We could find out what happened to Hatsy."

My mother stopped stretching. She stared at me. "Don't you know how to think? And they let you into college?"

"Huh?" I said.

"Do the math, honey! Hatsy?" She laughed. "Hatsy's free."

And then my mother looked away from me and began to move again. She stretched the tips of her fingers toward the overhead light.

A Suggestion

One summer afternoon, in a bar in Hell's Kitchen, I met a guy who looked pretty normal. I mean, he looked pretty much like me: receding hairline, dark eyes. But when I asked him what he did for a living, he said, "Don't laugh, man. I'll tell you what I do, but don't laugh."

I promised I wouldn't.

"I dress up as Elmo." He grinned. "You know, the Muppet? The red one?" He said, "That's my job."

Impersonating Elmo, the man said, was tougher than it looked. Not only was the Elmo suit itself pricey, but you competed against a phalanx of Elmo impersonators dressed just like you, all hustling for tourist dollars. You had to not only gain tourists' attention, but hold their attention long enough for them to take a photograph with you. After the photograph, you asked for money, working a fine strain of aggression into the request. The tourists were usually too embarrassed to refuse a Muppet, their kids being right there and all.

"You got kids?" the man asked me. "A wife?"

"I have an ex-wife." I thought about her shiny hair and added, "She's in computers."

"I should have gone into computers."

"She makes a lot of money." I turned my drink around on its coaster.

"Hey, man. It's okay to be mad."

"I'm not mad," I said.

"Where do you work?"

I'd lost my job in the recession. Why else would I be here, I asked, in the middle of the afternoon?

The man downed his beer and looked at me. "Maybe you should think about buying a suit."

"I have a suit."

He said, "You know what I mean."

. . .

After another drink I left the bar and walked east, into the heart of Times Square—just for curiosity's sake, I told myself. The mayor had banned cars from 42nd to 47th on Broadway to relieve crowd congestion. Now there were rubber lounge chairs and food stands and tourists and hustling, rollicking Elmos. I'd noticed the men in Muppet suits before in passing, but today I sat in a lounge chair to make some observations. The Elmos skipped up to families, kids squealed, photos got taken, cash changed hands.

After a few minutes my eyes wandered to an only partially garbed Elmo sitting in a chair close to mine. He'd removed his Elmo head, which sat on his still-furry Elmo lap. He was a man/Muppet hybrid. Trails of sweat ran down his exposed bald scalp. The sun gleamed hard. He bounced the costume's head on his lap the way a mother might dandle a toddler. He didn't notice me staring.

One of the big plastic Elmo eyeballs had a hairline crack.

After another minute, he reached into the head and pulled out a pack of cigarettes. He smoked one, then another. A little boy passed, staring, and the man lifted his red Elmo hand and waved at the kid. The boy started to cry. The boy's mother grabbed the boy's hand and pulled him past.

Finally the man put the head on and, fully Muppeted once more, rose to his feet. I thought my Elmo—somehow in my mind this fractured-eye Muppet had become my own—would go toward a group of kids, but he moved instead toward a woman walking by herself, a big leather tote bag under her arm, low-heeled black shoes glinting. She wore a blazer with shoulder pads despite the heat and her hair shone glossy. She looked a lot like my ex-wife, actually.

The woman smiled tolerantly when she noticed my Elmo, and shook her head. She mouthed, "No thanks, no photos," as my Elmo approached, but my Elmo just skipped right toward her, whispered into the whorl of her ear. I watched the big permanent smile on my Elmo's face and I watched the woman's own small smile vanish. I didn't hear what he said but I understood. He'd made a proposition, he'd suggested she do something vulgar, he'd said something to make this woman feel lesser. Her shoulder pads seemed to deflate, and she slumped, not like a Muppet but a marionette, one whose strings had been suddenly released. Then she shook herself and walked away very quickly. I saw her take out her phone and hiss something into it and then she disappeared.

When the woman was totally out of sight, my Elmo sat in a lounge chair and looked down at his own red mitts. Even though the Elmo head was perpetually smiling, my Elmo seemed mad. A jackhammer further down Broadway rattled the air but no one around me even flinched. I pretended to stare at the NASDAQ building, blazing with market quotes in LED lights. Down the street I spied bright red pelts of other Elmos at work, doing furious little jigs.

A few minutes later, two policemen arrived. They went straight to my Elmo. How they knew him from the others I couldn't say. Maybe he'd been identified by the crack in his plastic eye. My Elmo removed his Elmo head, placed it beneath the lounge chair. He said something to the police and his scalp looked too fleshy in all that August light, a pale white grub pushing up from the ruddy body of his suit. A jackhammer battered away in the distance. I heard the phrase "a series of complaints." I heard the word "disturbance" many times. Then one of the police took my Elmo by the elbow. He was led away.

When he was gone, I walked back to his lounge chair. Beneath the chair sat my Elmo's head.

It sits now on a shelf over my desk at home. When I'm supposed to look for jobs online, I often look at the empty head instead. Some days I like to pretend it's a trophy. An animal I slayed. But other days the head transforms, seems less like an animal and more like a suggestion. Its plastic eyes catch the light of my computer screen and take on their own hard gleam. Then I stand up, reach for the head, try it on. Just to see if it fits me.

Unit Cell

On a Saturday afternoon in the lab, Sheila looks through her microscope and does not see the contents of her crystal trays, does not see drops of precipitant or protein sample. Instead she sees her dead twin sister.

She blinks. Steps back from the microscope. Okay. She should breathe. So she breathes. She turns around. Nobody here.

Her trays, clearly, are contaminated.

A crystal is formed from repetition: the unit cell, translated over and over again in three dimensions, forms a crystal lattice, makes a higher-order thing. Every well in the tray contains different conditions—varying pH, salts, buffering components, precipitants—designed to elicit crystallization in the protein Sheila's studying. The protein plays a role in DNA replication, and if Sheila's attempts at crystallizing it are successful, she can analyze the protein's structure, see how it's put together, see how it does what it does. The process is not perfect. Sometimes gunk gets caught in the tray. A piece of hair, a shard of plastic. An eyelash, occasionally.

But not a memory of your dead identical twin.

Yet when Sheila looks into the microscope again, there's June as a little kid, running toward waves. Sheila leans in, examines the moment. She recognizes this memory: there's the ocean, there's the lifeguard. It's as if Sheila's crystal trays don't hold precipitant and droplets of protein at all, but little particles of past time. What if a ghost has decided to haunt Sheila's crystal trays? No. Ghosts—if ghosts exist—haunt old houses and abandoned towns. They don't hang out in Greiner CrystalQuick sitting drop protein crystallization plates. Which means Sheila's hallucinating. She leans back from the microscope again. It's almost six. In one hour she has to meet Marcus for tacos. What she should do is let the trays sit overnight. Clear her head. Sometimes trays sit for years and there's no sign of crystallization and then one day, there is one. A sign. After years.

It's been years since Sheila last saw Marcus, who was dating June at the time of June's death. A couple of days ago he messaged Sheila, told her he was in Nashville for business, did she have time for dinner? The dinner will be awkward and Marcus, probably, will small-talk aggressively to make up for that awkwardness, the way he did the last time he saw Sheila, when she came by to collect some of June's stuff: how was your drive here, how much work are you missing, was it this hot this time last year? His hands had flapped helplessly at his sides. He'd stared hard at her face, then blushed.

She knows why he wants to see her today. He's recently become engaged—she got an e-mail from one of June's old friends freaking out about it—and her guess is he needs Sheila to say it's okay he's moved on. Probably he needs her to say this because she has June's face. But she isn't sure what she's going to tell him when he brings up the engagement. She isn't sure if she'll say it's okay or if she'll throw a drink in his face.

Sheila looks through the microscope at another sample, sees June, alive, at the ocean again. Another sample, the ocean again. If she's going to be haunted by a memory in this way, shouldn't it at least be her memory of June's death? Shouldn't it be the feeling of her phone buzzing against her thigh, the scrambled-sounding soft-ness in her mother's voice, the way the bright fluorescent lights in the lab had seemed to dim?

. . .

When they were small, Sheila and June shared a secret language. A private grammar of blinks, a classified vocabulary of shrugs and specifically timed vowel ululations. But then Sheila and June went to school, were placed in separate classes, corralled into a more collective grammar. Is that what caused them to forget their shared language?

Their mother, when Sheila asked as an adult, after June's death, said yes, that was what caused it.

But Sheila—looking through her microscope—develops a different theory. She decides they forgot their secret language for good around age five, after the incident at the ocean that has crystallized inside her trays. It was their first family vacation. One parent vanished to pee, one parent was focused on their fat golden retriever, Ninja, and June headed for the waves, doggy-paddled too far out and got swept up in a current. Sheila, terrified of the water, turned away from her sand castle, stood up, stood straight, watching.

Something like sand sucked at her feet—she couldn't move them.

Something like sand stuck in her throat—she couldn't speak.

June saw Sheila watching and cried out to Sheila, just once, in their language. Sheila, later, would remember the word she cried as their word for help, but she would not remember the actual word's structure, if there were blinks or shrugs or a lot of vowels involved, and when Sheila did not act, did not move, June, drifting farther and farther from shore, managed to thrust her head above the waves and cry out—not in the secret language, but in the language of Everybody Else—"Help!"

She did not cry out this word just once. She repeated the word over and over again and was finally heard by someone who could act. A lifeguard dove in and saved her.

Sheila hadn't lost June that day on the beach, but after she had failed to respond to June's first cry, they never spoke in shrugs and blinks and vowel-howls again.

. . .

A door slams and Sheila jumps. The lab's usually quiet at this time. There's a loud slapping sound accompanied by a faint buzzing. Sheila gulps in air. The source of the sound emerges: Amber, one of the undergraduates. She sometimes helps out in the lab because she thinks the service will improve her med school applications. The buzzing sound comes from Amber's MP3 player, going full blast. The slapping sound comes from Amber's pink flip-flops.

The first time June visited Sheila in her new job, in her new lab, June wore flip-flops, too, and the big forced smile of a despairing tourist who can't remember how to ask for directions. June stared at the graphs on the walls, at the lists of procedures, gazed at Sheila's lab coat with her name on it. She pointed out the window by Sheila's desk and said, "Pretty trees!"

June dropped out of college when she got pregnant, and even after she lost the baby, she didn't go back to school. She and a friend moved to Asheville and started a small shop, Cosmic Core, selling precious aura-cleansing stones and incense and clearing bells and flower essences. June was convinced that, in the new recession economy, people would be clamoring for aura-cleansing stones. They'd want a new beginning; they'd want to clear away past debts.

When June visited the lab, Sheila knew her sister was nervous. Nervous about all the tasks Sheila performed at work that June didn't understand. Nervous about the terminology she didn't know. Sheila tried to explain the images and graphs around her desk. She explained about X-ray diffraction. The X-ray through the crystallized protein is the event, she said, and the resultant image, a series of points of varying intensities, are called a diffraction pattern. She showed June a diffraction pattern on her computer: black spots radiating outward against a white background. June said, "It looks like lace."

Sheila said, "You figure out information about the unit cell of the crystal from this image. And the arrangement of the atoms in the protein."

"I don't understand a word you're saying, Sheila." June was still smiling, but the smile had twisted up in this wrung-sock way.

Sheila told herself to stop lecturing. But then, unable to help herself, she spoke about sending the crystals to the synchrotron just outside of Chicago, where someone would shoot an X-ray beam through the crystal. (Her voice went a little breathy here, because she still found herself excited by her work, the weirdness of it, the wildness.) After the X-ray beam went through the crystal, the resultant image—the diffraction pattern—would be converted to an electron density map. This map would help Sheila better understand the atomic structure of the protein she was trying to crystallize. She explained to June that when she looked at the image sent to her from the synchrotron, she wasn't even seeing the nuclei of the atoms, the core of what was really there. She was seeing, instead, signs of the electron cloud around each atom.

June's eyes, by this point, clouded over with disinterest. Sheila looked away. She'd chosen to study the tiny pieces inside most every human being, and yet, outside of a lab, most every human being squinted at her when she explained her work.

Later, after June returned to Asheville, Sheila sent June a copy of an expensive textbook, *Introduction to Crystallography*. When June got the package, she didn't call Sheila, she e-mailed. "Well She-She, I made it through precisely ONE paragraph of that book. Did you know the word crystallography derives from the Greek 'crystallon' (cold drop OR frozen drop) and 'grapho' ('I write'). Maybe I'll give the textbook another try tomorrow. Do the words make more sense as you go along?"

. . .

When Amber flip-flops past, Sheila bows her head to the microscope again. The ocean is still there. She lifts her head, walks over to Amber, who is starting up the computer at an absent postdoc's desk. Amber doesn't nod hello to Sheila, which isn't unusual, but which does for some reason, today, piss Sheila off. She says, loudly, "Hi, Amber."

Amber doesn't hear her over the electronic beat her earbuds emit.

"Amber," Sheila says. "Hi."

Nothing.

"Hi," Sheila shouts.

Amber blinks. She takes her earbuds out. "Whoops!" She turns toward Sheila. "Did you say something?"

"You're supposed to wear closed-toe shoes in the lab," Sheila says.

Amber looks down at her feet. "I'm just here because my laptop is broken." She shrugs. "So I'm using Jason's. I'm not, like, doing experiments."

"You still need to wear closed-toe shoes. It's the policy."

"Gotcha," Amber says. "Next time." She puts her headphones on.

"Amber," Sheila says, but Amber's music is turned all the way up, the same beat going over and over. The girl can't hear a thing outside that sound.

A crystal is formed from repetition. The unit cell translated over and over again, in three dimensions, to make a higher-order thing. What if a story from childhood is translated into the present, over and over and over again? What if the reason Sheila's microscope is showing her the memory over and over again is that the memory is trying to grow into something of a higher order? Will June's death become structured into some form Sheila can analyze, maybe even understand?

What a relief that would be. Maybe, instead of trying to keep the memory back, she should allow it to repeat until that higher-order structure emerges. Then she will meet Marcus and tell him she understands June now, she understands the reasons for what happened, and there's no need to talk about it anymore, all these years later, okay? She will tell Marcus this and then she will walk out. She will let Marcus pay for her tacos. She will not let him project his fantasies onto her face just because some parts of her repeat his memories of June.

. . .

Marcus and June had been together for almost three years when a gigantic fight between them erupted—an argument over who was responsible for a houseplant's death managed to spiral into a declaration, by June, of deep unhappiness. This was several weeks after June visited Sheila's lab and maybe that visit had made June unhappy. Or maybe June was tense because of the shop—Cosmic Core wasn't doing well, might have to close. After the fight with Marcus, June had gone out to a bar and had a vodka tonic, and then another vodka tonic. Another drink same type another same type another same type another same type. The bartender, after the fact, had told June's family this. Had there been cries for help? No one had heard them. Who had let her drive? No one was watching.

Sheila shouldn't imagine that scene, June failing to turn in time. Shouldn't try to imagine what June was thinking, feeling. She is using her work as metaphor for a personal tragedy, for feelings inside of herself, and that's not the point of what she does. The point of what she does is to feel the world outside of herself. Its vastness, its beauty, its unknowability.

Yet Sheila can't help it. As she looks through her microscope at another sample in another well, Sheila thinks she can spy the lime green of the lifeguard's swimming trunks and the bright pink diamond pattern on June's white bathing suit. She doesn't see any angels through the microscope, though. After the incident, June told them all she saw an angel when she was underwater. She talked about the angel at church, she talked about the angel at the playground. June turned loquacious with all the attention. And Sheila, remembering how quickly her sister had turned into a small, drenched, lifeless-looking thing, turned quieter. "The observer!" her father called her, still calls her.

Sheila looks down at her white coat with her name stitched on it. She takes it off and drapes the coat over the back of her chair. Placed there, the coat seems like it's being worn by someone with rounder, looser shoulders, a straighter spine. What if she had never sent June *Introduction to Crystallography*? What if instead she had sent her a sweater? No, not a sweater. A scented candle for her bathroom? Something useful to June.

She walks to the exit and goes down a spiral staircase. Nobody in sight. Around her are the windows of other labs, some of the windows lit up, some of the windows weekend-dark. In a hall sits a whiteboard on which somebody has written, "JP Morgan ROX, Goldman Sachs SUX." She hopes Marcus won't look at her face and say seeing Sheila is like seeing the ghost of June. As soon as he brings up the engagement, she will leave. She'll eat a taco, take stock of the changes to his face, wait for his announcement, and then leave. She'll make him pay for what she eats and what she drinks.

Outside, the air smells like honeysuckle and car exhaust. The taco place is close enough to walk. Down Edgehill Avenue, Sheila passes music studios and parking garages. A young man with a guitar on his back leans against a wall and doesn't look up at her and doesn't hum anything. Sheila can tell, just from the tight way he holds his shoulders, that he wants something.

. . .

Marcus is already at the restaurant, at a booth in the back with a bottle of Dos Equis. He's cut his hair very close to his head. The pinkish nubby tips of his ears are now visible. He gnaws on his lower lip with his big teeth and clutches a beer. When he sees Sheila he stops chewing his lower lip and gives her a big, shaky smile.

Sheila sits down across from him. She says, "Hi, Marcus."

"Hey, Sheila!" Right away he begins to scratch at the label on his beer bottle. The bottle is labeled with two red X's. His neat square fingernail digs around until a corner flaps free. "Hey!" he says again. "So amazing to see you."

A waiter comes. Sheila orders a margarita and tacos. Marcus stares at her. Sheila feels a sharp stabbing sensation in her stomach and looks away. Bring up the engagement, she thinks. Just do it, so I can tell you I can't give you the permission you need, so that I can deny you, so that I can leave.

But Marcus doesn't bring up the engagement. He says, "How's Nashville treating you these days?" He says, "Have you seen any country music stars yet?"

Sheila says she wouldn't recognize a country music star if one fell from the sky, and Marcus laughs way too hard. She tells him she can't even read musical notation, and he says that's not really what country music's all about, and her margarita arrives. It comes with a little umbrella. Sheila has a big gulp and when she puts the glass down, she doesn't look Marcus in the eye. She looks him in the teeth. Marcus begins to talk about his favorite bands, before asking how Sheila's work is going and what is it exactly she studies again?

The tacos arrive. Some shredded lettuce has already fallen out of Sheila's and she stabs at the loosed taco innards.

Sheila says, "I study structures."

Marcus nods. Sheila focuses on maintaining the integrity of the taco as she eats. There are no follow-up questions about her work. The shredded lettuce spills all over the place, as do gobbets of ground beef. Sheila reassembles the taco in silence. It seems a great deal of time passes before Marcus, at last, says, "So, Sheila. So."

From the weight in that second "so" Sheila knows the moment has arrived. Finally. The point of the dinner—the announcement, the engagement. She is ready to tell him she thinks he's a coward for needing to come to her. She is ready to throw down her napkin, if not her drink, and make a dramatic exit. She looks Marcus in the eye again. Then swallows with surprise.

Wet drops have formed just above his eyelids. She's imagined what this dinner would be like many times, but she never imagined tears.

She sits up straighter.

Marcus rambles: this new woman is important, he thinks maybe he's ready, he hopes he is ready, he's scared, he's wondering if it's inappropriate but it's not inappropriate, right, it's been years, but he's scared, it's been years, he's looking for a sign that moving on now is the right thing to do. His fingernails start scrabbling at the tattered remains of the beer bottle label. Sheila almost recognizes meaning in the way his fingers are scrabbling—this is some word in the language of sustained grief, this is a language she and Marcus secretly share. A weird warmth floods her head. She doesn't get up and leave. Instead, staring at the drops that have now moved to Marcus's eyelashes, she feels she is back at the lab, looking through the microscope, searching for the shape of something that will clarify a deep-inside form, the cloud of a structure, if not its core.

The restaurant smells like salt and limes and frying grease. Sheila's nostrils flare as she breathes in deeply, knowing she is responsible for her half of the meal, knowing she'll pay for it after all, knowing that any second now, she will need to respond to what Marcus is really trying to say. She leans forward. She is listening for something in Marcus's voice, something like the sound of June calling from the sea.

Finally, finally, Marcus asks the question he has been building to: "Is it okay I've fallen in love again?"

Which actually, maybe, is the same thing as crying out "Help." And in the crowded, noisy restaurant, she almost hears it, what June shouted that day at the beach—the word June cried in their private language, the word June cried not to everybody else, but to Sheila, and to Sheila alone.

What the Blob Said to Me

When I was a girl, I helped build the atomic bomb. I traveled from New York to Knoxville by train and was driven to a secret town with a group of other girls, none of us older than twenty. The secret town had been built over other lives: the government had seized farms and homes and tore down houses and tore up the land—all for our country's good. At the time I arrived, the town they'd created still seemed more like a construction site than a place to live. Buildings sat surrounded by what looked to me like nothingness, and the streets were muddy and rutted with tire tracks. When I stepped out of the car and began to walk toward the administration building for my papers, my right foot got stuck. The blobby muck of earth sucked at my high-heeled shoe and what else could I do? I pulled my foot free.

The shoe, still wedged in the mud, was ruined.

I did not scream. I hopped forward, silently. I was very quiet back then. My job was mostly taking dictation. All day long, I listened to men talk. I listened to what important men said and I wrote down their important words and I reminded myself that I was here to help this town and to help our country and to help my boyfriend, Alfred, who always smelled like minty chewing gum and who was overseas.

I was not allowed to talk about my work even in my letters to Alfred. We'd all signed contracts promising our silence, promising to report anyone who talked too much about what they did—enemies were everywhere, we were told. The billboards around town, instead of advertising Coca-Cola or pest control, advertised secrecy: *Your Pen and Tongue can be Enemy WEAPONS*. Or: *Loose talk HELPS our enemy so let's keep our trap shut*. The billboard that frightened me the most said, *What you see here, what you do here, what you hear here, when you leave here, let it stay here*. With a picture of three monkeys. One monkey covering its eyes. One monkey covering its ears. One monkey with a single shushing finger over its coil of monkey mouth.

We all knew we were here for the war effort, but we didn't know one of the ultimate aims of this town was to figure out how to enrich uranium for the atomic bomb. Or at least I didn't know about that, even with all my dictation work. I didn't really understand what we were doing in the Appalachian foothills. I didn't know about irradiated slugs of uranium, I didn't know about electromagnetic isotope separation, I didn't know about mass spectrometry, I didn't know what was being tested in buildings bigger than football fields, and none of the men were going to tell me what was going on, what was being made.

I made love to Alfred in my sleep back then, in my dreams, most every night. I'd never actually had sex with Alfred, and so maybe that was why the dreams seemed so much like science fiction. In one dream, Alfred's fingers felt cold as ice. In another, his penis was an actual metal probe and I ran from him until he vanished from sight. When I'd wake from these dreams, the first thing I'd hear would be the steady breathing of my roommate, Mae, a skinny girl whose fat freckles seemed at war with the rest of her face. Mae's family had lived in this area for generations until the government forced them out to make way for the secret site, paying them poorly for their land. "You want to know something?" Mae said when she met me. "They destroyed her grave."

"What?"

"My grandmother's grave. The cemetery we used to go to. That's gone now. They destroyed that cemetery to build this town we work in."

"Oh," I said.

And then of course Mae had to come back here, had to ask the very same people who had thrown her family's life into turmoil for a job so her little brothers could eat. The jobs here paid well, better than anything else Mae could get, so really, she told me, she shouldn't complain, she knew she shouldn't complain, her grandmother always told her not to complain.

I knew all about Mae's troubles because she shared them with me all the time. However, she mostly didn't ask me a single question about myself, except for the one night she wanted to hear how I met Alfred. We'd known each other since childhood was what I told Mae. For some reason I didn't tell her that our families belonged to the same synagogue. I guess I was worried she'd ask me a lot of questions about being Jewish, like some of the girls in the car from Knoxville had done. Or maybe I sensed, even at the beginning, that there was something strange about Mae.

Of course, nothing about Mae seemed especially peculiar until this one night when I woke from one of my Alfred dreams to find her standing at our window.

"Something is out there," she said.

"Nothing is out there, Mae." I sat up. "We're in the middle of nowhere."

"This isn't the middle of nowhere. It's only the middle of nowhere to you because you're from New York City." She gestured out our window, to the sky. "A monster is out there. They are making a monster. I hear it."

She began to talk about voices. About how the world was full of unheard voices trying to find vessels. About how voices were forever trying to pair up with visions so the voices could be not only heard but seen. About how her grandmother had had capital-v Visions, had heard all sorts of lost souls and monstrous forms through these Visions, and Mae herself maybe had inherited this skill. "They're making prophetic potential out there," Mae said. "They're making a monster." Although she was babbling, Mae's voice stayed low and dreamy. She seemed not crazy so much as steeped in somnolence, like maybe she was sleep-talking.

"You're having a nightmare, Mae," I told her. "A waking night-mare. There are no monsters."

"Have you ever had a Vision, Ruth?"

"There are no monsters. Monsters don't exist. Go back to bed, Mae. Listen to me."

And she listened to me. She went back to bed, folded all those freckled limbs beneath the sheets. I felt a small puff of power, the kind of power that comes from acting like a big sister to a relative stranger, from forcing intimacy through a condescending command.

As the weeks passed, my dreams about Alfred changed. I wasn't dreaming about him naked anymore. I was dreaming that he had died. I never knew how he had died in the dreams, just that he was gone, and then all these other dream-men, with flabby arms and a simian gait, began asking me questions. I woke up each time scared that by dreaming Alfred's death, I'd make it happen. I worried that the materials the scientists around us were working with really might contain small particles of prophetic potential, like Mae had said.

Then one day I heard. Not about Alfred. About this place. About what we had done, exactly, in this place. About what we had made fall from the sky.

Soon Alfred returned to New York and I left Tennessee and joined him. We talked about our lives apart in careful, controlled terms. I never told him about Mae, about how she'd stand at the window at night, claiming some monster was out there. He never told me about what he'd seen, either. Blind to each other's wartime lives, we pretended to envision a clear future together, and in fact, what we envisioned turned out to be mostly true. We got married, I left my job, we had a kid, we had another kid, happily ever etcetera. The end.

. . .

The end is how I'd like to think about the story, anyway, except time keeps trundling past and Alfred is dead from pancreatic cancer and my children are in other states and I am okay, I am okay with my book club and my circle of friends, I am okay until my grandson, Brandon, who never calls me, calls me. He wants to come to New York and do an in-person interview with me for one of his college classes. He wants to interview me about my role in World War II. My Role in World War II. The stiff way he phrases it makes me laugh and he laughs too, nervously, before he says, "What do you think?"

The truth is the idea of making some sense out of my life, presenting my life's story to my grandson like a gift, seems exhausting, akin to climbing up a mountain and then being forced immediately to do a landscape painting of the damn view when all I want is some water and a nice pastry.

But I say okay, yes, he can interview me.

Over the phone, Brandon recites a list of questions about war to think over before he comes to visit. *Did you take any part in the war effort? Where did you live during WWII?* He knows the answers but he tells me he wants to hear the answers in my own words. He uses that phrase a lot during our phone call, "in your own words," and those words do not sound like his own words but like the words his professor has told him to say. He'll get a bus from Boston to interview me and stay with me for the night, if that's okay, of course. I tell him I guess I can clear off the day bed in Alfred's old office.

"Great," Brandon says. "Fantastic."

He adds that he will take me out for dinner and a movie in thanks for all my help, asks me how do I feel about seeing the movie *The Blob*, the one from the fifties of course, it's playing at an art-house theater near me, and would that be kind of fun? He thinks it'd be kind of fun. To see something I saw when I was young. And maybe it'd trigger some memories that would help for our interview.

Yes, fine, I say. I don't tell him that I'd never even seen the movie when it came out, had been too busy raising his father. I also don't tell him that I am surprised the movie is playing in such an artsy-fartsy theater because *The Blob* always looked pretty schlocky. Do monster movies ferment into art, then, given enough decades?

. . .

Mae was a heavy mouth-breather the whole time she was my roommate at Oak Ridge, but she was truly wheezing one evening after our dorm mother came to our door and said there were three men waiting downstairs for me.

I thought, "Alfred is dead. They are here to tell me that Alfred is dead."

The three men downstairs were not much older than me. They seemed to speak all in unison, although surely only one of them was speaking, surely only one of them asked me to step outside with them. I stepped outside with them. Behind us the administration building seemed to breathe. I waited for the men to tell me about Alfred.

But the three men had a request. They wanted me to listen to what people said. What the other people who worked in this town said.

So: none of this had anything to do with Alfred.

Which meant Alfred was probably alive.

I did not smile. I tried to keep looking solemnly up at the men and the men kept talking. They not only wanted me to listen to what people said, but to write down anything strange they might say. Anything strange said in the dorm, anything strange said in the cafeteria, anything strange said on the bus, anything strange that women said to their boyfriends, anything strange that men said behind their hands. Enemies were everywhere. I was to report on all unusual behavior and mail my reports to an address in Knoxville.

I imagined listening to people meeting behind trees, eavesdropping on cooks in the kitchen, or lovers burbling love-words back and forth to one another on the bus, or baby-heavy mothers waiting on line for food together, their feet aching.

I knew if I said no, my refusal itself would be reported on as unusual, suspicious. Maybe I would be fired, sent back home, without the money I needed to bring to my parents and without helping Alfred in any way. I stood up straighter. I was smart enough at listening that I could tell when I was being commanded to do something, even if the command was camouflaged as a question, a request. I nodded to the men. I said yes, I would listen, I would write down strange and suspicious things.

I went back upstairs. Alfred still was not dead. Mae still was sitting on the edge of her bed, so pale that her freckles seemed rash-like. I told her I'd been called down by mistake, that the men had been looking for another Ruth, that everybody was fine and alive and nobody wanted anything of me.

. . .

My grandson shows up at my apartment with a backpack. He will be staying tonight with me, tomorrow night with other friends in the city. He seems even taller, beardier than when I last saw him, and when he hugs me he softly presses his hands down on my back and cups my shoulder blades in his palms, like my shoulder blades are not bones at all but birds in danger of flying off. The gesture is so unexpectedly tender, I don't know what to say to him when he releases me. I say, at last, "Let's go see *The Blob*."

The movie begins with a meteor hitting the earth, no beating around the bush, and with the meteor comes the Blob. The Blob eats doctors and old people. Although doctors and old people are the primary populations I spend time with these days, I do not find myself scared. I close my eyes for a second and picture the images a doctor showed me once, the lumps on Alfred's pancreas. I open my eyes again. I am wearing my Casual Clogs and despite all the orthopedic support they are supposed to offer, the heels suddenly seem to dig into my foot-skin.

Why is the Blob so silent? When the monsters don't speak in these sorts of movies, they still usually roar. Godzilla roars. King Kong roars. Even the monster that Mae believed in made sound that she heard. But the Blob is an oozing hush of havoc, a mucousy muteness surrounded by the sounds of others, by human screaming. I close my eyes and see those lumps on Alfred's pancreas again. I know it is stupid but I feel suddenly, sitting next to my grandson in that art-house theater, like the Blob, through its silence, is trying to speak to me.

I listen.

And what does the Blob say?

Well, that's between me and my Blob.

Haha. Just kidding.

I don't hear anything.

Okay, that's not quite true either. I hear some things. Things such as: The actors' voices and the movie's soundtrack. Also my grandson's breath as it rushes in and out of the pocket of open mouth buried beneath the burls of his beard.

. . .

The night I agreed to spy on people at Oak Ridge, I couldn't sleep. Was Alfred awake, too, wherever he was right now? Alfred, overseas. Overseas. If you repeated the word enough, "overseas" started to sound like the name of another galaxy. Alfred was in another galaxy and all the people he was fighting weren't people, were aliens, were aliens in movies, were not quite real.

"Did you hear that?" So Mae was awake too. "Did you *hear* that, Ruth?"

"Did I hear what?"

"That sound."

"Your monsters again?"

"Maybe the monster I'm hearing is her. Is my grandmother. They built over my grandmother's grave."

"I know."

"How do you know, Ruth?"

"You told me, Mae. You're just having nightmares."

"No. I'm not. I'm awake. Just *listen*."

We both fell silent. We breathed in and out through our mouths, noisy, together. And then Mae said, "I really don't know anything about you, Ruth."

"Well," I said, "ask."

So for the first time Mae began to ask me about my life, about myself, about my father and my mother and my siblings and how I grew up and what I thought about religion and God and what we were doing here. When I told her I was Jewish she said, like the girls in the car from Knoxville, "I've never met a Jewish girl before."

"That's okay," I said.

She breathed noisy again through her mouth and I shifted in bed.

"My uncle had to go to an accountant once." Mae's voice was now bell-clear. "And his name was Rubenstein."

"Oh."

"And my uncle said he got swindled."

I didn't say anything. Mae sat up in her bed.

"You don't look Jewish," she said. "I mean, that hair. You've got really beautiful hair. I thought so the very first time I saw you."

I folded my arms over my chest and studied the darkness above my head, studied the way the darkness could take on shapes if I stared long enough. Shapes like clouds, mostly. Real clouds outside must have moved because some moonlight entered the room, slanted over me. I kept staring up.

Mae cleared her throat. She seemed calmer now. "Do you ever feel…"

"What?"

"I don't know." Mae shifted on her bed. "Do you have family over there? Overseas."

"Nobody I ever met. Mostly we're all in New York. A few in Chicago."

"Well, gosh. What a relief." She leaned forward. "So what does it feel like? Knowing part of the reason all this exists—" she waved her hand around vaguely—"is for you?"

"What?"

"To protect your people."

"Is there something in particular you want me to say, Mae?" I wished "say" and "Mae" didn't rhyme. I didn't want anything child-like or playful in my words. I wanted stiffness, no fluidity.

She did not respond. I let my breathing go steady. But I woke up early, before Mae, full of different things I should have said to her, comebacks, questions. What did it mean that I didn't look Jewish and did she somehow blame me for the fact that her family had lost their home and why did she mention Rubenstein, her uncle's accountant, exactly what point was she trying to make?

I didn't say or ask any of these things when Mae woke up. I didn't say anything to her all day long. Instead, the next morning, I reported on Mae. I wrote down what she'd said about the monster outside, about her grandmother and the cemetery, the tinge of resentment. Those men had asked for me to report on the loose-lipped and the suspicious and the strange. Well, fine, here was the loose-lipped and here was the suspicious and here was the strange, here was a girl who was mentally unfit and who talked far too much.

I slipped my letter into the box they told me about.

Soon Mae was gone. No goodbye, no note, or anything.

Silence.

I got a new roommate who sang hymn-bits to herself in the morning, but who did not speak much. She came from Nashville, from hours away. "I'm a city girl, too!" she said to me. A cheerful girl whose name I have forgotten, a girl who snored hard in her sleep but who could sleep through everything, thunderstorms, firecrackers, someone else's crying. A bomb could fall and she'd sleep through it, I joked once to the dorm mother, after the bomb did fall, just before I went back to New York, and the dorm mother was very kind—she made for me a sound much like laughter.

. . .

The Blob is not that funny a movie but because it looks so hokey in the present day, the audience keeps laughing at the scary parts. My grandson is laughing hardest of all, it seems to me, right until the end of the movie, when Steve McQueen and his girlfriend played by Aneta Corsaut and some other man stand and stare at the Blob. The Blob has finally been neutralized after terrorizing their town, after glooping along and eating people alive and almost killing Steve and Aneta too. They have just figured out how to freeze the Blob, and now what will happen to it? The other guy tells Steve it will be sent to the Arctic by the Air Force. "It's not dead, is it?" (Steve asks that.) "No," says the other guy, "it's not, just frozen. I don't think it can be killed. But at least we've got it stopped." "Yeah," says Steve. "As long as the Arctic stays cold."

Aneta is there in those final moments with the two men, but she does not have any lines. She stands silently in her blue dress with her matching blue headband and matching blue eyes—her eyes seem more like an accessory to the dress than the other way around.

As the men talk, the camera cuts to a shot of a clear blue sky, of a clear blue ocean, and three white balloons carrying the Blob descend and I guess plop it in there. Letters that look like clouds appear on the screen. "THE END." Triumphant music plays. But then the cloud letters clot together into a single line and reform as a question mark. The sky and the ocean and the Blob all vanish, the screen goes entirely black, except for that single cloud-white question mark, which hangs around a moment longer before finally vanishing too.

My back hurts.

When I sit for too long like this, my back hurts.

The place Brandon takes me for dinner is not like the theater. Most of the people here are very young. For some reason I'm missing Alfred now, a lot, more than usual, and I am not hungry but I could really use a drink, so I order a Merlot. Brandon gets an expensive cocktail, what the waiter calls an "altered Manhattan." On the walls there are animal heads. Deer, a moose.

Brandon starts to talk about the movie not as a movie but as a *film*, a film that is almost *too obviously* about the Cold War. "The Blob is red," he says. "It is a red and all-consuming mass."

His whiskey-coated voice becomes confident, bold, and also boring. He talks for a while about the Cold War. He asks me to remind him where I'd gone to college. When I tell him I haven't gone to college, he says, "Oh, well, things were different in those days, huh?" His voice transforms even further, turns into a towering turreted thing, a giant penis of a voice. Which is a horrible way to think about your grandson's voice, but there, the thought is there in my mind while Brandon goes on and on about *The Blob* and I sit sipping my drink, with nothing intelligent to say.

"The whole film, actually, is really a refraction," Brandon tells me. "A refraction of the fear Americans had of a third world war. Of the atomic bomb."

Maybe the Merlot has muddled up my mind, or maybe I am embarrassed by how I've started to slouch in the cold, crisp shadow of my grandson's expertise, but when he says the word "bomb" I sit up straighter.

I say, "You know I helped build it?"

"Yes!" His eyes are bright. "Dad was telling me. We need to get to that. I mean, in the spirit of full disclosure, that was partially why I wanted to see that movie with you."

"Because of the bomb?"

"Yes. Well, because the movie is so *very much* about that. You know?"

He takes out a notebook, a recorder. He is going to write something up on me. An essay, an article, an ode, who knows. So I explain about Oak Ridge, I talk on and on about the place, about the mud in the streets, about the billboard with the three monkeys. I do not tell him about Mae. When I am done speaking, he says, "Wow." He strokes his beard. "It's funny."

"It is?"

"I mean, funny-strange. You seem almost proud. But do you ever feel guilty?"

"What?"

"I'm just thinking about directions I can take this paper. I don't want it to be another person alive during World War II going on about sacrifice, greatest generation, blah blah blah. You know? We have a unique opportunity here. We have an original angle."

We. That word "we." What a lie. He. He means "he."

"You're not responsible for the bomb in any linear way, of course. I'm not saying you really did anything, gave the go-ahead for mass murder."

"It was war. Also, I just took dictation. For a man in charge of transit, mostly."

"But you see it as more than that. Right? You see it like you built the bomb. I mean, I know you didn't actually build anything. But do you feel guilty ever? And how do you cope with that?"

"I don't."

"You don't cope?"

"Feel guilty. I don't feel guilty. My husband's life was at risk. What do you want me to say?"

He says nothing.

"I don't want to talk about this anymore, Brandon."

"Do you not want to talk about it because of trauma?" His eyes are wide. He isn't listening for what I say. He is listening for what he wants me to say. He is hearing whatever he wants to hear in my silence.

The rim of my wine glass is shiny and wet. A drop of drink hangs off the edge. A blob. A small red blob. It quivers, seems almost to be winking at me.

If it could speak to me, what would it say?

It can't speak. It's a drop of liquid.

I lift the glass to my lips, catch the drop. Cool, cool.

. . .

When I was a girl, I helped build the atomic bomb. I said this sentence to Brandon and I say this sentence in my head sometimes because it makes me feel like I have done something that has changed the world. *When I was a girl, I helped build the atomic bomb.* Alfred might take issue with me saying that. Alfred might say no, you didn't build anything, you sweet deluded creature, you didn't build anything at Oak Ridge, did you know about irradiated slugs of uranium at Oak Ridge, did you know about electromagnetic isotope separation at Oak Ridge, did you know about mass spectrometry at Oak Ridge, no, you *know* you were only eighteen, you were a virgin at Oak Ridge, a virgin with no college education, you took dictation at Oak Ridge for the man in charge of transit, sweetheart, I don't mean to be harsh but don't be so dramatic, don't say things you don't mean about building bombs or making bombs, at eighteen you didn't make bombs, you were a bomb*shell*, haha, at least to me, remember that photo of you in the white blouse, those seams near to bursting, god, where is that photo, but listen, you want real war stories, let me tell you about my time in the trenches, let me tell you that, not that it's a competition but I *heard* bombs going off during the war, and what did you hear, Ruthy, sweetheart?

I heard men talking. That was what I heard.

I don't mean to paint Alfred in the wrong light. He was actually very loving and respectful, just also a little bit haunted and irritable when it came to certain topics. Anyway, Alfred, if he rose from the dead, if he said all those things? Alfred would be a little bit right. I'd say, Alfred, it's so good to see you, darling, and you are a little bit right. But I'd still argue that all of us there, in that new government town, we all built the bomb a little bit, whether we knew we did or not, whether we worked in the cafeteria or drove a bus or monitored machines we didn't understand or collected waste buckets or were dorm mothers or took dictation, we were still all a part of building the bomb, even if we had no idea it existed until it went off.

Many people died because of the bomb, yes. But I refuse to spend my last years feeling bad about their vanishing, feeling bad about something that now feels like it took place not just in another life, but in some other solar system. My grandson comes in and thinks he can dictate how I feel about my own past. He thinks that, in doing so, he can change my past. The young believe they have this power. But they cannot change the past. They can only make up new stories about it, with different heroes and different monsters.

. . .

After Mae vanished from Oak Ridge, I started listening for the sounds she heard at night. For the sounds she heard at night outside our window. Like I mentioned, the new roommate was a snorer, so it was difficult sometimes to hear much of anything else. Once, though, when I couldn't sleep and was standing at the window, staring out at the administration building, I did hear something. A low humming. The low humming was followed by a creaky old voice calling, "Where's Mae, hey hey, where's Mae, hey, hey."

It was Mae's grandmother's ghost, maybe? A rhyming phantom? Or my own mind generating sound? I didn't care to find out what was real or what was monster or what was alien or what was dream. I ran back to bed. I hid under the covers. I closed my eyes and covered my ears and shut my mouth.

. . .

Back at my apartment, I tell Brandon I need to lie down because my back hurts. I go into my bedroom and sit up very straight as I look out the window, my fine view of fire escape and brick. It is raining. I hear something. Rain is what I hear. I remember Mae's galvanic stride toward our window in Oak Ridge, her movements electric, the hairs on my arms standing on end as I listened to her listening.

Suddenly thirsty, I leave my bedroom. There is mumbling from Alfred's old office. The door's ajar. I stop, listen. Brandon is talking about me, about my denial, about how sad it is. He is talking to a girl. I can hear it in his voice. And I try extremely hard to understand that his pitying tone about me probably has little to do with me and more to do with sex. He is telling this girl that he asked the questions nobody else dared ask of me all my life, the questions I didn't even dare ask myself. He is saying to this pretty girl something like *I made my own grandmother uncomfortable with my questions but I just wanted to get to the truth but is it really worth it that is what I want to know what did I do* and who knows, he is maybe even shaking a little behind that door, genuinely upset but also genuinely needing for this girl to look at him as a complex, morally present person, needing her eyes to bulge big for him when he returns to Boston, needing her eyes to shine on his in that beautiful blobby way of young love, and hearing all that youth and need in my grandson's voice, remembering also the weirdness of young love, it is much too much, I am almost breathless with the aching weight of it all.

I sit down in the paunchy soft of the couch, what had been Alfred's couch spot, and then sitting there it happens.

I have what Mae's grandmother had, what maybe Mae had.

A Vision.

The Blob drops on New York City. I see it enter from the river, which it probably reached from the ocean (it has traveled here from the melting Arctic, from overseas!), and I see it blob up a houseboat on the Hudson, and I see it blob down some gulls, all of this silently, silently. It consumes buses into its blob shape, and bus shelters, consumes parks, parked and moving cars, it moves toward the Metropolitan Museum of Art and consumes all the Monets and Manets and monuments of the Mesopotamian dead and the Vermeers I've recently become so rapturous about.

If monster movies ferment into art, then yes, art can morph into a monster.

But it is not done, not the Blob, not my Vision: there go bodegas, pretzel stands, boutiques. One moment, the Blob is like a great viscous moon that has crashed down onto the city. The next, it is like a balloon from the Macy's Thanksgiving Day Parade, a balloon that has gained its own sentience and momentum and has escaped its handlers and now is floating upward, upward to my fourth-story window. People run and people flee and the Vision-Blob comes right up to me.

It says, through the window, "My voice is the voice Mae was hearing."

I want to answer "That's impossible" because the movie *The Blob* didn't come out until the fifties and Mae could not hear the future.

Unless she could. Prophetic potential. Hadn't I wondered about that when I was in Oak Ridge? Hadn't I worried my dreams of Alfred dead might be a little prophetic? And weren't they prophetic in the end? Alfred is dead. I foresaw Alfred's death. Who knows what future monsters Mae herself might have foreseen? Now one of Mae's visions is here to get its revenge, to consume me.

But then the Blob does something surprising. It does not enter my apartment and consume me. It seems to look at me for a while, and then, like it has decided I am not tasty or nutritious enough, it leaves. It just vanishes.

Which is almost worse than it crashing in and blobbing me up for good.

When the Vision clears I am still sitting on the couch, looking at the slick-wet fire escape outside the window, and Brandon is still talking behind that door, talking about all the things I will not tell him, the guilt he says I will not admit to.

I am shivering all over from my Vision. Also, my Casual Clogs are hurting my feet again. I take off one of the shoes and I look at in my hand. It is heavy with its orthopedic features: A dual-density footbed. Antimicrobial microfiber. Convertible straps that look like padlocks. I feel a new strength in my arm, a lingering gift, perhaps, from whatever I just saw.

Through the door I hear Brandon say, "And what, actually, does she regret?"

I lift the shoe in my hand and throw it at the door of what was once Alfred's office. I throw that Casual Clog so hard, harder than I could have ever predicted, harder than I've thrown anything in years.

And Brandon stops talking. He opens the door, confused.

"Did you just knock?" he asks.

I take off my other shoe and throw that at him too. He ducks. He curses.

Wow!

What must he be thinking? He must be thinking I am crazy, cruel, and mean.

Okay. And maybe now I am crazy and cruel and mean enough to speak truthfully to him, maybe now I am ready to really speak to my grandson. Maybe I will tell him to listen to me and to please for the love of God ask no questions. Maybe I will tell him my capacity for shame is only so big as one human life. Maybe I will tell him I feel no regret over the vanished dead in other lands, the only thing I feel regret over is Mae, the girl I had reported to those men, the girl I had sent back home, the girl who I had not spoken of since, the girl who'd heard monsters and who I pretended I hadn't believed although I knew even then that yes, yes, of course monsters exist.

My Four Stomachs

RUMEN

On our first date, we went to see the fistulated cow. The fistulated cow had feather-soft eyes, had a hole cut into her side, had a plastic plug placed over that hole, had a name. The fistulated cow's name was Buttercup. My date's name was Jack. During gym, while we stretched together on sticky blue mats, Jack had described Buttercup to me as a cow with a window surgically placed into her hide so you could see right through to her guts. The inside of a cow, Jack said, is out of this world.

When we walked up to Buttercup in a field, I did not yet know about Jack's theories concerning things out of this world, concerning alien-directed climate change and a dying planet and selenotropic plants from other solar systems. I knew Jack went around school reading science fiction books and I knew he wasn't very good at basketball and I knew his family had come to the United States on the Mayflower. I knew his father worked at the university and was an expert in large-animal surgery. I knew a year from now, next fall, Jack would probably go to a far-off private college and I would probably stay home with my mother who'd just lost her job. I would probably stay home with my mother's sadness and my mother's coupons and my mother's talk shows. I knew—or thought I knew—what would happen to both of us: Jack would become a professional in a distant city while I'd work at a fast food place in Raleigh, grilling up Buttercup's poor sisters.

But I tried not to think about all that I knew when Jack and I approached the cow. Instead I concentrated on how the moon was out and full, although it was still just early evening. Jack shone a flashlight through the plastic plug covering the hole that had been cut in Buttercup's body, and under the flashlight's beam I saw something shifting around in there, hay and grass being digested. Sort of gross. And sort of lovely.

A fistula, Jack explained, was a permanent hole surgically placed between the external world and an internal organ. The plastic plug covering up the hole in Buttercup's side was generally removed only for reasons educational and scientific: Surgeons reached into Buttercup and pulled out useful healing juices. Veterinary students observed the digestion process in Buttercup as it was happening in real time. I thought about that phrase. Real time.

Cows have four stomachs, I said finally. Don't they?

Jack said no, I didn't really have it right, it wasn't that cows had four stomachs, but a single complicated stomach, a stomach with four compartments, four chambers, very different from human stomachs. I wanted to know the names of the four chambers. But Jack said he was no expert on the ruminant digestive system, could only remember the name of the chamber we were looking at now—the rumen.

It's the hugest part of the cow's stomach, he said. All those enzymes are in there, simplifying the complex stuff. The rumen is where things begin to break down.

He took my hand. He told me about gut flora. How the fistulated cow was fed well so it'd have great gut flora. And how when other cows were in surgery, Jack's father would reach into Buttercup and pull out some of Buttercup's gut flora and put that gut flora into the bodies of sick animals, helping them to recover more quickly. This process was called transfaunation.

Inside Buttercup, I imagined a field of flowers. I imagined Jack reaching into Buttercup and pulling out a healing bouquet of Queen Anne's lace and giving the Queen Anne's lace to me with a romantic flourish of his hand. I looked at him sidelong.

Do you want me to remove her plug? Jack asked.

Will things spill out of her?

No. She'll be fine. They do this all the time for the transfaunation stuff.

When Jack unplugged the plug at Buttercup's side, I was sure he would reach into her stomach first. But instead Jack grabbed my hand and pulled it into Buttercup's side without asking either Buttercup or me if we were ready. The warmth of her insides was so startling, I jumped a little bit, the slightest convulsion, and Jack smiled really smugly as if he'd just made me come or something, although he hadn't. I was pretty sure he hadn't.

I removed my hand from Buttercup. Jack said my cheeks were red and I said how could he tell, it was dark. He shone the flashlight right on my face and I cursed at him, told him where he could stick that flashlight. He grinned. He said he'd always appreciated my honesty.

He was reaching around inside Buttercup's stomach himself now. I didn't want to watch. After a while, he plugged her hole back up and told me to close my eyes and open my hand. I did. I was envisioning it again—that bouquet of Queen Anne's lace. Instead he put a hard seed into my waiting palm. I opened my eyes. Jack said this seed had come from Buttercup, from when he reached into Buttercup just now. I said no way. He said yes way. He said it wasn't the first time he'd found a seed like this in her rumen.

Listen, Carley, he said. Plant this seed and put it on your windowsill but only at night, okay? When the sun is out, move the plant into the shadows. The closet. Wherever. I'm telling you, the thing will grow in the night. It'll bear fruit. Based off the moon's light. It's the first step those alien fuckers are taking.

Taking to what?

To take our planet away. Duh, Carley.

Then he laughed, so I figured he wasn't serious but was just flirting. He had floppy hair that he kept pushing out of his eyes. On the drive home, he said plant life was moving from a mostly heliotropic model to a purely selenotropic one, and soon the whole earth would respond more to the movements of the moon than the sun. This shift was all the work of lunar aliens who were slowly colonizing the planet, changing it bit by bit to fit their temperament.

Global warming isn't caused solely by us, he said, but is being helped along by outside forces. As soon as we really get to destroying this planet, other life forms from other planets will make themselves more fully known, will take advantage of our weakness. They'll square off sections of our skin, too, will fistulate *us*, will try to see inside us that way, to understand how we grow, function, process.

He spoke in such a dreamy tone, I thought he was just telling me fiction ripped off the books he read. I thought this was all just some weird-dude whimsy, thought he was showing off his imagination. Presenting me with little love poems of science fiction. Maybe I thought this because he had more money and so I believed he was smarter than me. Or maybe I thought this because to my own surprise I so badly wanted to kiss him. The other guys I dated hadn't talked to me, had just tried to take off my shirt, to pull down my pants, to expose me.

But Jack? Jack was telling me stories.

Before he dropped me off at home, I recited some lines from the nursery rhyme where the cow jumps over the moon and Jack nodded, said yes, exactly, and where do you think that rhyme comes from?

I don't know, Jack. Where?

The aliens wrote that rhyme.

I smiled. And he kissed me. Very gently.

When I got home, I didn't plant that seed he gave me, didn't bury it in dirt. I put it in my underwear drawer. And we didn't talk about the seed again. He never asked me about it. We became busy with other things, each other's bodies, brains, etc. At least for a while.

When Jack was hospitalized, my mother seized my hands. Compartmentalize, she said (regurgitating Dr. Phil, Oprah). Trust me, Carley, compartmentalize. Don't let this derail you. Your grades in school have just shot up. You're on *a path* now, I can tell, I've always had a sense for these matters.

It's the opposite, I said. Aren't you actually supposed to do the very opposite when things like this happen, *do not* compartmentalize, isn't that what they say?

My mother shook her head. No, no, nope, the way you digest a tragedy, a broken relationship, anything bad and unexpected, is compartmentalization. Trust me. I have a sense for these matters, too.

The rumen is where things begin to break down. If you have the right view, if the right hollow space has been made between the outer and inner world, you can see that breakdown start to happen in real time.

RETICULUM

After my first date with Jack, I looked up the other compartments of a cow's digestive system. The reticulum is the second stomach, or the second compartment. It's simultaneously the place of trapping and the place of softening. If the cow eats part of a fence, the reticulum will trap that fence part, prevent it from going forward, prevent it from potentially working its way into the cow's heart. At the same time, the reticulum is also where the grass that a cow eats softens, turns to cud.

A place of entrapment, a place of softening. All at once. As if entrapment and softening were synonyms.

They're not synonyms.

What maybe trapped Jack: His own mind. The story he created. The selenotropic system. The idea of alien colonizers to this earth. The idea of colonizing my thoughts with his specific alien/cow beliefs. The idea of his own ancestors colonizing this country with their specific god/Christ beliefs. The sun moving closer to the earth. The greenhouse effect. Wildfires. Ultraviolet rays. Maybe an imbalance in dopamine and glutamate. Maybe growing up with cows like Buttercup whose insides he could see at too young an age.

What nearly trapped me: My mother's unemployment. My father and his weekend calls ("Hello and how's school"). The pictures of women I'd found in my father's studio apartment. Long, lengthy, rail-thin, no clothes, women more see-through than Buttercup. My father's look when he saw me looking at these women and the way I heard him talking about my mother on the phone once, calling her "the bitch." Jack. The way I so blindly believed in Jack and how he looked at me. Like there should be more of me, not just more of my body, but more of my words in the world. (He said to me once, write me a love poem. I wrote him a sequence of terrible sonnets. He said what about free verse? I told him I liked having a form to follow—it allowed me somehow to be both weirder and more truthful. To both soften words and to trap them quicker, too.)

What maybe softened Jack: The florid poems about gut flora I finally wrote for him. His father's eyes when he talked to Jack about the farm he'd grown up on. Buttercup's eyes. The softness of the inside of Buttercup. All those photographs of polar bears on shrinking glaciers. When I told him I was falling in love with him and we had both cracked up, like, how did we get in this genre, and he called me Meg Ryan.

What definitely softened me: When Jack got hard. The books Jack lent me. The warmth of the inside of Buttercup. The smoothness of the inner wrist of Jack. Sex. The skylight in Jack's bedroom through which the sun shone most. The idea of a stomach with four compartments to sort everything out. Researching ruminant stomachs at the same time I began to look into colleges. The way the third compartment of a cow's stomach, "omasum," sounded in my mind: an exotic brain-massage of a word. Omasum, omasum, omasum.

The descriptions of "omasum" I found online: a compartment with many folds.

A water-absorbing thing.

A filter.

OMASUM

For months, Jack didn't talk about aliens or selenotropism. But then all of a sudden, around the time college apps were due, he started mentioning them again, all the time. He'd call me up and ask me if I'd seen the latest statistics, if I'd read that article he'd sent me about the new thermal stresses being placed on mussels, about how stunned even the scientists were at the swiftness of melting things, about a new study indicating that the water in the brain was affected by the moon just like the tides of the sea, and of course, the alien colonizers knew that.

And then, for two weeks, he stopped talking to me all together because I told him he needed to relax with the alien colonizer thing. He told me I was a bitch and that he'd thought I, of all people, would understand, and I told him he sounded dumber even than a rom-com dude, he sounded like a whiny wannabe songwriter, all angst and entitlement, no substance. Then? No dates, no texts. I cried at night sometimes, yeah, but mostly I was mad. He had talked to me like other guys I'd dated had talked to me, had called me the name my father called my mother, and I felt like I'd gotten fooled.

Then I got a call. Jack had tried and failed to kill himself in his parents' bathtub because nobody believed his visions of rising oceans and extraterrestrial invasion. He was placed for a time in a psychiatric hospital. His mother was the one who called me. His mother did not like me very much—barely spoke to me when I went over to their house—but her voice on the phone was so hushed and sad, I felt a new lurching intimacy with her. After she'd delivered the news, I was not sure what to say or do. Should I send her family a bouquet of flowers? What kind of flowers? I didn't send anything. I didn't say anything. No, that's not true. I said, on the phone, "I'm so, so sorry."

Which was the same as saying nothing, really.

. . .

To compartmentalize as my mother wishes, to digest more properly, I must filter this next part of the story by taking on a different perspective, one with some necessary distance: Let's say it wasn't me who refused to visit Jack for several weeks, but some other girl. Let's say this other girl finally received another call from Jack's mother, a shaming call about how Jack had been asking after her, and let's say this other girl agreed to make a visit.

This other girl showed up in the psychiatric hospital, found Jack perched on the edge of a marshy green sofa. His torso had become much skinnier, his stomach shrunken, and his head tilted in a funny way. He looked like a boy who had tried to turn into a bird, but changed his mind halfway through. When he saw his girlfriend walking up to him, he jumped a little.

Oh, wow. Hi, Carley. Wow.

This other-Carley, this girl, said, You grew a beard.

Jack lifted his hand to his chin, as if in doubt. Yeah, he said at last. I haven't shaved in a while. No razors allowed in here.

A blue hospital bracelet dangled from his bandaged wrist. The girl looked down at her own naked arm, the fine serpentine squiggle of a vein. Jack continued to rub his fingers along the bottom of his chin. The girl tried not to be shocked at the way a person's mind *and* chin could transform so quickly into something beyond recognition.

The girl said, It doesn't look bad.

What doesn't?

The beard.

Okay.

The girl looked away from him and examined the visitors' lounge, which was painted a pastel pinkish shade seen primarily in Easter egg dye and women's cotton underwear. The walls were covered in framed macro photographs of flowers: pixelated petunias, monstrously massive marigolds, red roses like large wounds. A chess table sat in one corner of the ward, and a bookshelf filled with old encyclopedia sat in the opposite corner. There were also other people in the room, but the girl could not bring herself to focus on them.

Jack moved closer to her on the couch, and the silence between them changed abruptly, acquired an animal stillness. The girl saw the beard on his face as a slow-breathing beast, creeping past his cheekbones, readying itself to smother his mouth and cover his eyes until he was speechless and blind. The beard became a filter for the real Jack, the funny Jack, the sexy Jack, the weird-but-charmingly-so Jack, the Jack who told stories.

His body, warm, crept very close to the girl. He was inching toward her. The beard transformed again. It turned into the steel mesh of a radio speaker emitting a kind of desperate bleating. Jack was crying? She moved away from him on the couch, although she knew the right reaction was to betray no terror, to stay calm, to simply change the topic to something compassionately ordinary.

He moved again, closer to her than before. He apologized for not being more honest with her about how much his fears had seized onto him. He was trying to protect her. But he saw now he shouldn't have hidden anything from her. He wanted to kiss her. His hand rested on her arm, the fingers recollecting. The girl stood up abruptly, looked first to the nursing station, then to the exit.

My mother's waiting downstairs. I have to go, said the girl.

No response.

But I'll come back soon, she added, like a child remembering manners.

Jack seemed suddenly totally disinterested in her. She walked away without kissing the person who had been her lover, who had done nothing wrong, only gotten lost in his mind. The girl's mouth had gone totally dry. Was she actually maybe grateful to the beard? It had made it easier to treat Jack like a stranger.

The doors leading outside the hospital were glass. She had barely noticed them, coming in, but now she saw there were many doors in a long line, as if the hospital anticipated a great rush. The glass was smudged with the prints of people trying to push their way in and out. The girl stopped in front of one of the doors and examined the pattern of smudges, tried to see past them. She felt for a moment that she should go back upstairs and apologize. Then she leaned forward and let the pads of her fingers smear the glass.

That night she dreamed about the fistulated cow. But instead of a little plastic porthole into its murky insides, a large plate of glass covered all four compartments of Buttercup's stomach. The large plate of glass was like a window, a skylight, and each of the cow's four stomachs were lit up like small glowing suns. That sheet of glass turned the cow's stomachs into some brand of bovine solar system, the cattle becoming cosmic. The filter of the girl's subconscious, the complicated folds in the girl's mind, re-saw Buttercup as something else, something otherworldly, something alien and, in fact, spectacular.

ABOMASUM

The final compartment, where the food is at last digested, where the nutrients are at last sucked up, and where all that remains is at last allowed to turn to shit. After Jack was released from the hospital, I met him at the Starbucks in the mall. Jack ordered something without caffeine. He was drugged up on all these new medications, not twitchy, just dead-eyed and dull. He didn't mention the moon or aliens or colonizers or anything. He was clean-shaven but it didn't matter. I still didn't want to kiss him. I was so ashamed about how much I didn't want to kiss him that I could hardly look at his face. Looking at his face would expose something horrible in me, something intolerant, fearful. I didn't want to see any of that shit. Not in myself.

I made an excuse about having to leave the mall early. I stopped talking to him, even in school. I stopped thinking about him much. Was I scared I might catch his despair? Was I scared his ideas were already too deeply planted in me? The word "transfaunation" would blossom in my mind sometimes, out of nowhere, and make me cold. I blamed that word, somehow, for sending Jack to the hospital. And I worried that word might send me to the hospital in the future, too.

. . .

I'd decided to apply to a wide range of colleges and I got into a place that gave me what I thought at the time was a decent scholarship. My mother sobbed with terror and with pride. But once I was at school, away from home, I couldn't seem to concentrate anymore. My grades fell. The scholarship was retracted. I returned to my mother after one year with a horrible academic record and a mess of student loans. I told her I was taking a little time off and she said yes, okay, she understood.

. . .

I visited the fistulated cow once on my own after I went back to my mother's. It was a different cow now. Named Blossom. Blossom!

. . .

I didn't work in a fast food place but I did start waitressing and one day, at the diner, I met Brad, handsome, funny, firmly rom-com material. He'd just gotten some tourist industry job on the Outer Banks. Brad didn't tell me stories about a future of aliens but he did tell me stories about the future we'd have together, a dog that we'd teach to shake hands, a nice house near the ocean, a kid or two even. Because I wanted to get out of my mother's apartment, Brad and I moved in together fast, not into the house he had described, but into a first-floor apartment that yes, was near the sea.

Too near the sea. As the months passed, the ocean moved closer and closer to our home, and I spent a lot of time arguing with Brad about how we might get flooded out. Brad said I was being paranoid. Paranoid like Jack had been paranoid? I wondered. Jack's parents could afford to put him into a nice hospital but me? If I lost it like Jack, what would happen to me?

After a while longer, Brad said he was just not feeling it. He just was not. And, also, he was sleeping with someone else. He moved in with this person and said I could stay in our apartment until the end of the month, or longer, of course, if I wanted to pay the whole rent myself.

I visited my mother, just to get away for a few days, and in my childhood bedroom, I found the seed Jack had given me, still in my underwear drawer. I took the seed back to the Outer Banks with me and I planted it in a small pot on my windowsill and I moved it out of the sunlight during the day and let it bask in the moonlight at night. I told nobody what I was doing because I did not want to seem crazy like Jack and because I mostly didn't think anything would happen.

Except that seed sucked up all those lunar nutrients and *grew*. Grew fast and fat and beautiful. Grew not into a flower, but into something kind of like a tomato plant and kind of not. Like something from another planet? Yes. Sure. Or at least like something redder than anything you'd see in the supermarket. Spindly vines running amok. I lost my appetite. My stomach shrunk. I watched the new plant grow.

Alone in my apartment, with the ocean at my door and debt piling up, I started thinking about Jack more and more, about how I was pretty sure he really had performed some sort of transfaunation of ideas on me, thinking he was enlightening me, healing me, when he was actually making me feel sick.

And I started thinking about how the temperatures this summer were the hottest ever.

And I started thinking about how close the waves sounded.

And I started thinking about the way the maybe-tomato plant grew with the moon.

If Jack had been proven right about those things, who was to say he was not right about the rest? The earth scorching up for good, the colonizers testing our planet, planting alien seeds into our livestock, then coming for us when they'd decided we'd pushed ourselves close enough to our own destruction.

One night when I couldn't sleep, when the wind was really howling outside, I picked up the spindly plant on the windowsill and looked at its red fruits hungrily.

I told myself I didn't want to eat one of the plant's fruits. If I did eat one of those maybe-tomatoes, another seed might be planted in me. Eating the fruit might be acknowledging something real in Jack's vision and that was dangerous. If I ate the maybe-tomato, I was conceding that maybe soon I might open my eyes onto a new world. I might find myself with a glass plate installed over my chest, just like Jack predicted. The fistulated woman the alien colonizers kept for purposes educational and scientific.

A rhyme forced itself into my thoughts: *Hey, diddle, diddle. The cat and the fiddle. The cow jumped over the moon.* I was ravenous. I ate one of the maybe-tomatoes out of many different types of fierce hunger.

And almost immediately everything looked stranger. The moonlight in the room brightened like a veil over the night had been lifted. The black sky looked like a frothing sea, the stars like a naval flotilla. My stomach hurt. My stomach really hurt.

The vomit should have tasted like that sour fruit I'd just eaten but it didn't. It tasted like grass, like the sweet way grass smells, like a field.

I wanted to call up Jack. He was right. I would tell him that over the phone. And I would tell him that the alien colonizers, when they came (which, yes, they were coming), would put me in a desiccated pasture scorched by wildfire.

They would peer into my insides, into the real seal-slick muck of me.

There's her heart, they would say, and through the window they'd installed they would study my heart's chambers, its compartments, its universe of flaws and degradations, its perpetual failure at digesting loss, sadness, shame, pride, because a heart is not a stomach, because digestion (the colonizers would decide) is not what this particular and singular hollow organ was ever designed to do. No, it had its own uses.

The Rent-Controlled Ghost

Big, rich, important men were waiting for the old lady in 4C to die. She lived in a rent-controlled apartment for which she paid not very much a month. Only when the apartment was vacant could the real estate company that owned the place finally sell it for the millions of dollars it was worth. At first the company had planned to wait the tenant out, but the old lady kept not dying. Finally one of their managing agents paid the lady in 4C a visit, offering her a large sum of money to move.

"Where would I move to?" the old lady asked. She gestured at the leggy houseplants around the windows, the piles of videocassettes on her bookshelf. "Where on this actual earth would you suggest I go?"

New Jersey, maybe, the managing agent said, his eyes settling on a large iridescent fly hovering near the plants. The real estate company, he added, would cover all her relocation costs. The managing agent was much younger than the old lady, but he forced what he hoped seemed a paternal smile. He said he knew she'd lived in the apartment for decades and wanted to make this transition as easy as possible. His company so valued their partnership with her.

The old lady coughed. She suspected the managing agent saw her as a dried-out husk of a human being with no connections to the world of the living, but in fact she had a son who had grown up in 4C, a boy who, when he was young, would go to Central Park and feed pigeons from the palm of his hand. He'd turned into a teenager when the neighborhood was full of drugs instead of fine denim, and soon he began spending much of his time in the area by the subway station known as Needle Park. For a while, his comings and goings were fairly regular. But as his heroin addiction grew worse, the distance between his departures from home and his returns also grew. Now it had been decades since the old lady in 4C had seen her boy. She didn't know what had happened to him, but she didn't want to lose the apartment because what if he tried to find her again? She hated the idea of him coming back in his late middle age—perhaps with a wife, with kids—only to find his childhood home full of strangers. She herself had been forced out of her home as a small girl, a home in another country, and if she returned there, no relative would remain to welcome her. But as long as she was alive, her boy would be able to return to his childhood home and find at least one familiar face.

So the old lady told the managing agent, "No."

"No?"

"I'm not moving."

"You're aware that my company owns this unit? That we're responsible for any upgrades, any repairs in this apartment, any complaints?"

"So?"

He pointed at the plants by the window. "I'm going to need you to get rid of those." The paternal smile again. "The super's saying there's been complaints." He scanned the apartment. The large housefly had plastered itself to the old lady's window. "Complaints about bugs."

"My plants don't have bugs."

"I'm telling you that if you want us to make repairs in the future, you'll need to follow through on this one. You'll need to get rid of your plants. If it's found you're not complying—"

"Okay." She held up a thin hand. The word "complying" had a

powerful bureaucratic weight that rested heavily on her shoulders, exhausting her utterly. "I'll get rid of the plants."

And she did. She dumped the plants, and adapted to their absence by hanging pictures from her old Botanical Treasures twelve-month calendars all over the walls. Where the living plants had been there were now images of Japanese maples and hydrangea blossoms and dew-fringed red roses with brachial thorns.

. . .

The managing agent's battle against the old lady did not stop there. When the ancient springs on the top sash of her bedroom window began to fail and opening the window proved challenging, the managing agent never got around to sending over a repairman. The old lady in 4C was forced to adapt again: she bought a new three-speed fan. A few weeks later, when her stove would not work, the managing agent did not put in a request to replace it. And so she started eating frozen food dinners. She ate chicken-flavored cheesy rice and sometimes she mixed in microwavable bags of peas and carrots. Several months after that, when her refrigerator began to make a new groaning sound, she did not even bother to call the managing agent. She listened to the groan almost cheerfully, as if the fridge had turned into an empathetic friend.

In spite of all she'd learned to put up with, the old lady in 4C was no saint. Most mornings she would complain loudly to Miguel, the porter, as he mopped the fourth-floor foyer. She would kvetch about her troubles with the apartment owner, or with the broken stove, never asking Miguel a thing about himself. Miguel—feeling sorry for the lady, and also conscious of his Christmas tip—would nod and say, "That's too bad, ma'am."

"You're damn right. You're damn right that's too bad. You don't understand real hardship," she'd tell Miguel, shaking her head, "until you get to be my age." She would then sigh heavily, wave goodbye, and take the elevator downstairs. Outside the building she ran errands, went to the doctor to see about changes in her heart and lungs, sat in coffee shops and looked out the window at the always-changing city. The neighborhood was safer than ever, but there were more young white homeless people now, squatting in doorways with scruffy dogs. She thought often of her son. Sometimes she nodded to other old ladies she knew, but mostly she kept to herself. Before dinner she usually took a brisk twenty-minute walk from Columbus Avenue westward to the Hudson River. Some decades before, it had been a terrible idea to walk here, but these days there were joggers everywhere, neon blurs crisscrossing around her. When she finally reached the long pier, the joggers diminished. Behind her rose the West Side Highway and the Trump Place towers. Before her, the car-garage skyline of New Jersey and the rush of the river.

For nearly an hour, she would stare at the river and whisper messages to her deceased loved ones: to her husband, who had died of a heart attack years ago, and to her mother and father, who had died in another country. If Henry Hudson could find this river, she guessed the dead, even the international dead, could find this river, too. The deceased must travel lightly.

She did not whisper messages to her son because she was sure he was still alive. Instead she worried about what might happen if she died and he came back here too late. If she kicked the bucket, she'd have to find a way to stick around until her son's return. She'd have to haunt the damn place. How did you put in such a request with a higher power, a request for a haunting, if nobody would even follow through on your request for a functioning stove?

When she'd spilled enough memories and words for one river to handle, she walked home, heated up her chicken-flavored cheesy rice, and watched a taped episode of *Days of Our Lives*. After the episode was over, she usually went to her window and spooned out whatever remained of her meal onto the windowsill. The pigeons fluttered near her ledge, ate her offerings.

Her routine seemed like it could go on in just this way for years and years. But one day, during an especially cold week in February, the radiator in her bedroom started to leak. Some maintenance people came by and blocked the radiator off, plugged the pipe. They said as soon as the payment from the unit owner went through, they'd get a new radiator for 4C. In the meantime, the apartment was freezing. The old lady bought space heaters, made lots of Lipton tea, and wandered the rooms in her winter coat. Sometimes she would listen to the refrigerator's groan, which had evolved into a sound like *galumph galumph galumph*. She called the maintenance people about the radiator again. They told her they were still waiting for a part to come through: the unit owner had only just placed the order. Only just placed the order! When the real estate company knew about the cold all week, when they knew all week, too, about the radiator, and still, knowing all of that, still—only just!

That night in her dreams she saw her boy as a child, saw the pink of his palms upturned as he waited for pigeons in the park. While she dreamed this dream, one of the space heaters shorted out and the temperature in the apartment sank. In the morning, she awoke to a coo-cooing sound. A rangy pigeon sat on her window ledge, as if it had flown in right out of her dream. The old lady pushed herself out of bed and, shivering hard, dug around in her kitchen trash until she found a leftover glob of Green Giant from the night before. She took a spoonful of chicken-flavored cheesy rice to her bedroom window, which she opened with great effort.

"How do you feel about chicken?" she panted to the pigeon. "How do you feel about bird eating bird? But it isn't really cannibalism if it's just chicken-*flavored*, is it? No. Flavoring is a different thing altogether. Thank goodness for flavoring." The pigeon bobbed its head. "Are you listening? Listen. What would life be without flavoring?" She placed the spoon on the windowsill. But when she tried to shut the window again, the ancient springs in the window's top sash failed and the top part of the window fell open. She could not close it. A cold burst of wind covered her face with a spattering of snow. She went back to bed and began to have wild thoughts, halfway hallucinations. In the hallucinations, she forgot her own name and the name of her son and the face of her son and saw little besides a constant blur of voices and how could you see voices, anyway?

Later that same week, the old lady in 4C came down with pneumonia and was taken to the hospital, where she died.

. . .

Once the old lady was gone, the apartment was renovated. Granite counters were installed in 4C. New marble tile was put into the bathroom. The radiator? Replaced. Most of the old lady's stuff was thrown in the alleyway by the courtyard. Afterward, Miguel showed up in the alleyway with a dolly, put the old lady's TV on the dolly. Miguel lived in New Jersey and so did Miguel's mother. He was going to give the TV to her and he knew that when he did this thing, she would clap her hands and beam at him.

. . .

Less than a year later, at the start of another cold winter, a man and his son moved into 4C. The man was tall and in his forties. His wife had died a few years before in a car accident. Their son, Cooper, was eleven, though he looked younger. He had thin arms, a slightly rounded belly, and flushed cheeks. He possessed, still, the highly focused stare of an infant. Cooper had never wanted to leave their old apartment. But Cooper's father had told him that this new apartment was in a better location, a good investment for the future, while the old apartment was in a less great location, plus also freighted with memories of loss. "It's hard for me to be there, Coop," Cooper's father said. "It reminds me of your mom."

That was exactly why Cooper had loved the old apartment. In the old apartment, he was able to believe in the possibility of his mother's reappearance. On his birthdays, he could almost hear her voice, could almost see her hands. On her birthdays, he could almost smell her lavender shampoo, could almost feel her hair falling over his face as she held him to her. Now, here, in this new place, his mother—the sounds and smells of her—had never felt so distant from him, as if they were slipping away over the edge of a tall building, vanishing.

This sense of distance became especially strong one morning, shortly after they had finally settled into the new place. Cooper's father sat his son down and told him he had a friend coming over for dinner that night, a friend named Julia. Julia was bringing a dessert that involved gelato and chocolate and how did Cooper like the sound of *that*?

Cooper was silent. His father touched his arm, said he had to head to work, and Cooper should hurry up, too, he didn't want to be late for Academic Winter Day Camp, did he? His father told Cooper to wear boots because they were expecting snow. Then Cooper's father left. Cooper tried to bury the idea of Julia.

Academic Winter Day Camp was just a couple blocks away, easy to walk to. Slowly, he put on his coat and the wool knit hat with the red hanging pom-pom at the top. Cooper's father had warned him in advance not to wear the hat to Academic Winter Day Camp, had said the hat was meant for a little kid. "You're a little bit asking to be beat up, buddy." His father was always telling him to be "more of an adult," but Cooper clung to his childlike ways for very adolescent reasons: to irritate his father. He pulled the hat down far over his ears. When

Cooper stepped out of the apartment, Miguel stood there, mopping the floor. Miguel's earbuds were hanging around his neck, but his MP3 player was still playing something, filling the fourth-floor foyer with an apian drone punctured only by the radiator's occasional hiss. Cooper nodded to Miguel and walked to the elevator. He watched Miguel move the mop, hoping Miguel would strike up conversation, although that had never happened before. Finally Cooper cleared his throat, as his father sometimes did. "I don't want to go to Academic Winter Day Camp," Cooper said.

To Cooper's surprise, Miguel grinned. He said, "I get that. You should see my sister's kid. He never wants to go to school. Anyway, aren't you supposed to be on break?"

"Yes," Cooper said. "Exactly."

Miguel continued to mop. Cooper tried to think of a new topic of conversation. Then Miguel said, casually but in a low voice, "You seen her yet?"

"Seen who?"

Miguel began to mop faster. "Never mind. Forget I mentioned her."

"Who? Who did you mention?"

"I shouldn't tell you. I could get in trouble. Talking about a ghost."

"You're making fun of me," Cooper said. "I know when people are making fun of me."

"I swear I'm not messing with you, kid." Miguel lowered his voice even more. "The woman who lived in 4C before you and your dad? She was the last rent-controlled resident in this whole building."

Cooper tugged his hat down further around his ears. "What's rent-controlled mean?"

"Rent-controlled means 4C was paying hardly anything to rent an apartment worth a whole lot of money. That's what your dad paid for the apartment, you know. A whole lot of money." Miguel's smile turned toothier. "Probably thinks it's a great investment. Probably when you're older, he'll move somewhere else and rent the place for even more cash."

Cooper's ears grew hot under his wool-knit cap. Who did Miguel think he was, going on about Cooper's father, and Cooper's father's plans, and Cooper's father's cash?

"4C was one strange old lady," Miguel said. "I used to see her on her walk to the river. She'd go every day, rain sleet snow whatever, like she was a mailman only her messages were all addressed to water. She thought she could talk to dead spirits on the Hudson. She told me about it, lots of times. And I'd say, right to her face, 4C, you are one strange old lady. Which was true. But I tried to be nice to her because it's no easy thing, to be a woman living alone, you know? My mother is a woman living alone, and she needs me over all the time for help with this or that. 4C was like her but much older, plus no one ever came to visit 4C, plus my mother's much younger and her voice is much less annoying."

"What was her name?" Cooper pulled up his backpack straps. "The woman who lived in our apartment?"

"Nobody called her by her name. Everyone called her either the old lady in 4C, or just 4C. The maintenance people, the super, the renters, the owners, all of them. Though I guess we can't call her that anymore, huh?" Miguel smiled. "I guess your name is 4C now."

Cooper said, "My name is Cooper."

"Right," Miguel said. "I got it, 4C." Then he added quickly, "I'm just kidding."

Cooper looked at the door to the new apartment. The letters "4C" were written on a shiny gold plate, positioned just beneath the door's peephole.

"What I definitely can't tell you, though," Miguel said, "under any circumstance? Is how 4C died."

"Tell me," Cooper said.

"I can't. Isn't your dad a lawyer? He might decide the building had done something illegal, he might find some way to sue, and maybe I'd lose my job for shooting off my mouth."

"He's not that kind of lawyer," Cooper said. "He's intellectual property."

"Still. He might find a way to sue. People always find ways to sue in this building."

Cooper's frown puffed up his cheeks. "You can't start to tell me a story and then *not* tell me. That's not fair. That's not fair, Miguel."

Miguel cocked his head when Cooper said his name. "Fine," he said at last. "I'm all about fairness. When I commute in here and have that hour or two to think before I start mopping all these floors, you know what I think about? I think about fairness."

He moved the mop back and forth and back and Cooper said, "So you'll tell?"

. . .

Miguel told Cooper all the things the old lady in 4c had divulged and complained to him about in her life. He told Cooper about the broken window sash. He told Cooper about how nobody fixed the window sash for a long while. He told Cooper about the old woman's missing son. He told Cooper about the woman leaving warmed-up chunks of chicken-flavored frozen food for the pigeons, and about the piles of *Days of Our Lives* on VHS. He told Cooper about the broken radiator. He told Cooper the old 4c had been, in his opinion, a little bit murdered. He told Cooper yes, he did believe people could be only a little bit murdered. He told Cooper about how the old 4c's son had fed pigeons too, when he was a boy, and how the old 4c's son had disappeared, and how the old 4c had dreamed about her boy right up until the end.

When Miguel finished the story of the old lady in 4c, he looked at the bell-shaped light fixture above his head, his chin propped on the nub of the mop. For a good minute the two stood there without speaking, the only sound coming from the earbuds around Miguel's neck. Finally Cooper asked how Miguel knew all these details about 4C, anyway. Not the broken radiator stuff, but the other stuff. Like how did he know she'd dreamed about her son right until the end?

"I'll tell you a secret," Miguel said. "You can't tell anyone. I talk to 4C sometimes. I mean the old 4C."

"What do you mean, you talk to her?"

Miguel shrugged. "It gets boring, mopping all the foyers in the building. Sometimes the building spirits take pity on me, share their life stories with me." He smiled. "Or maybe I just have a good imagination. How good's your imagination?"

Cooper had once had a tutor who told him that he needed to learn to think longitudinally as well as latitudinally. Cooper wasn't sure what that meant, but he guessed it had something to do with his own imagination's failures. He scratched the tip of his nose, regarded Miguel. He said, "I don't believe you."

"You don't believe in ghosts?"

"I don't believe you."

"Good thing is I don't care who you believe. I know what's real and what's not."

Cooper breathed in deeply. Was that lavender he smelled? No, cleaning products. But did cleaning products ever really smell that floral? Maybe it was lavender. Maybe it was lavender shampoo. Cooper said, quietly, "Why would the old 4C talk to you and not to me? I've been here for weeks and I haven't heard anything weird."

"Maybe she's not talking to you because she wants to speak to someone sympathetic."

"I'm sympathetic." Cooper glared at Miguel. "I've been here for weeks and I'm sympathetic and she hasn't talked to me."

"You haven't lived what she lived. Not even close. You just can't be sympathetic, not truly. If she decides to haunt you, it's not going to be in the gentle, talky way. I'd be careful if I were you. She's hanging around that apartment because she's still angry about what they did to her, how they forced her out so you could move in." Miguel shook his head. "She's pissed."

Cooper looked down at the tile. He could see the arcs from where Miguel had mopped. Even after Miguel had gone to the fifth floor, even after Miguel had gone all the way down to the basement to leave the mop and bucket in his alcove off of the laundry room, even then a person on the fourth floor could look down and see those arcs and picture the way Miguel's arms had moved the mop while he waited for his shift to wind down.

Cooper's face suddenly lit up. "What if she's not hanging around because she's angry? Maybe she's hanging around because she's waiting. She's still waiting for her son to show up. Maybe she wants to see him again."

"I thought you didn't believe in ghosts."

"I don't feel too well." Bright-eyed, Cooper backed away from the elevator door, to the door that said 4C. "I'm not going to Academic Winter Day Camp," he announced. He took out his keys. "I'm sick." Without another word for Miguel, he went back into the apartment.

Cooper knew his former tutor would tell him he was behaving in a childish manner. He knew his father would sigh and say, "Oh, Coop," and lecture him about meeting developmental benchmarks. He was too old to try to speak to ghosts, definitely. Yet something in Miguel's story had rung true, had made him yearn for a sighting of the old 4C. If Cooper made himself more sympathetic, she might show up and talk to him. And he wanted her to talk to him very badly. He would ask her to tell him about her life in the same way she told Miguel, and he would say comforting things to her, and maybe he would tell her his mother was dead and maybe she would say comforting things back to Cooper, or at least fly through walls for him, which would also be cool to see.

First, though, Cooper called his father and told him he had not gone to Academic Winter Day Camp. "I'm sorry, Dad," he said into the phone. "I got really nervous about the other kids."

"Coop. Come on."

"Dad." He lowered his voice. "It was social anxiety."

Cooper's father excused him of almost anything if he could name it in a grownup sounding way. And, indeed, his father sighed and said they'd talk about it later, after dinner with Julia. Julia. Cooper now felt sick for real. He hung up the phone. Forget Julia.

He spent the morning watching old episodes of *Days of Our Lives* he downloaded online. Initially, Cooper watched the show because he thought it might draw out the ghost of the old 4C. Maybe she'd want to catch up on the plot twists she'd missed since heading for the afterlife. But soon he watched just for his own pleasure. The show was really wonderful! The women were all pretty and all the women seemed to be mothers and all the mothers seemed roughly the same age as all the children, and this was strangely soothing. Every now and then he would look around his room, still full of cardboard boxes. He was glad he hadn't listened to his father about unpacking right away. This space didn't feel like his to claim yet.

After a few hours of TV, Cooper heard a sound on the window-sill. A pigeon had landed there and was rustling its feathers, like it wanted to get Cooper's attention. Cooper shot up fast and ran to the kitchen. The cabinets and drawers were new and smooth and still smelled a little like forest. He opened the top left cabinet, fully stocked with microwavable meals for when his father worked late. He took out Brown Rice Risotto with Butternut Squash. Not exactly chicken-flavored cheesy rice, but perhaps close enough that the old 4C might relate to him, might respond to the way Cooper's actions in the apartment rhymed with hers. The stainless steel microwave hummed for a while, finally chirped. Cooper grabbed the meal, spooned some out onto a square-shaped porcelain plate, and ran to his room.

The pigeon had flown away. Still, Cooper opened the window and put a glob of risotto on the sill as an offering. When he closed the window again, it shut smoothly, effortlessly. It had been fixed, of course, before Cooper and his father moved in. It was now airtight.

And yet Cooper thought he felt something. A breath on the back of his neck. He spun around. Nobody. But the air smelled of chicken flavoring. Goosebumps ran down Cooper's finely haired arms. "I'm sympathetic," he called out, and the words did not sound childish to his ears, but newly deep and resonant. He felt a hard pounding against his shoulder blades. "I'm sympathetic." His voice quavered. He needed to seem more commanding. "Reveal yourself," he tried. "Now. Talk to me. Now."

Silence except for the radiator hiss. The apartment suddenly felt extremely hot, almost unbearable. He needed air.

. . .

Miguel was no longer in the foyer. But when Cooper took the elevator downstairs to the lobby, Miguel was there, running a gray rag over the gold frames of the lobby's mirrors.

"I tried to talk to 4C," Cooper said. "I told her I was sympathetic. And I told her to show up and talk to me. But she didn't show up. So."

"So, what?" Miguel bunched the rag up in his left hand. "You calling me a liar? She's not going to just show up because you demand her to. She's not your servant, you know. Or maybe the problem is you don't know. Maybe that's why she's not showing up."

Cooper's expression—a collapsing look of anger and hurt—maybe made Miguel a little nervous, because he quickly added, "You get that I'm just messing with you, kid, right? I'm fooling around. Don't take my story too seriously. I'm always just joking around."

"I'm going out," Cooper said.

Miguel said, "Stay warm."

It was freezing outside. The wind, gusting hard against Cooper's face, was coming from the west, from the river, from the very direction he was heading, but Cooper didn't let that deter him. He passed a McDonald's and a vitamin store, a pizza place and an organic bakery, a shop that sold luxury jackets for men. The closer he got to the river, the fewer commercial buildings he saw, and the more residential the streets became. Many of the buildings here were old and had strange details on them: Above a first-floor window, a flowing relief of dragons. An angry bearded man wearing a lion skin. Griffins sharing a joke together. Gargoyles and grotesqueries. He imagined the old 4C looking at these mythological beings, too, every day, on her walk.

As he neared Riverside Drive, the buildings changed. Huge condo towers loomed. "TRUMP PLACE" the towers said. Cooper heard the whir of the West Side Highway and smelled the river's stink. He crossed the street and descended the ramp to the narrow walkway. Off of the walkway stretched a long recreational pier with steel chairs looking out onto rotting Hudson River piers and the ruins of the New York Central Railroad 69th Street Transfer Bridge. Cooper's father had once taken him around here to ride bikes and told him this area had been a hub of ships and piers and docks and trains, but now it was a historic landmark, a privately funded public park.

In the summer they would play movies here. Every year, Cooper's father said, new improvements were made.

There was only one other person on the pier right now, a man stretched out on a row of steel chairs, asleep, as if it were not winter but a hot day in July. Cooper walked to the end of the pier, didn't look at the man but instead looked out at the water, which in places had turned into slushy ice. A bright red streak in the ice caught his eye. A rose. Someone had tossed a red rose into the river and the river had frozen around it so that now it floated there as if encased in glass. If that wasn't a sign of ghosts, what was? There might after all be spirits on the river. And he, like the 4C before him, should try to speak to them. Cooper closed his eyes. He thought he'd talk to his mother but he couldn't think of anything to say to her besides, "I cut Academic Winter Day Camp and I'm sorry."

Which was a lie. He wasn't sorry. Even when he tried to speak to his own dead mother, he spoke in lies. Who on this earth could ever sympathize with him? Certainly not the old lady in 4C. Why had he expected she would reach out to him? He leaned against the rail, his fingers numb. He looked at the rose.

Instead of saying another word to his mother, Cooper started to talk to the old lady in 4C. It was easier talking to the old 4C than it was talking to his dead mother who he hadn't spoken to in years—a mother-flavored ghost, rather than his actual mother, was somehow less intimidating. He told the old lady in 4C that his father was going to introduce Cooper to a woman named Julia tonight. His father had dated before but never anyone he liked enough to introduce to Cooper. And what if Cooper's mother was replaced by this other woman bringing gelato? This new woman and his father might then have another child and that child might replace Cooper, even though Cooper's father would pretend nothing like that could happen. A new child. A good investment for the future. Cooper himself might become a ghost in the new apartment.

This, right here, was the closest to praying that Cooper had ever come. What did people do when they prayed? They asked for favors, didn't they? For a second he thought about asking the old lady in 4C to use her ghost powers to kill Julia, but then he softened. He told her instead, "Make it so Julia doesn't show up tonight. I don't want to meet her. Please make it so I don't have to meet her."

It was too bad he didn't even know the old 4C's name. His plea felt flimsy and cheap without a clear personal address.

A police officer sauntered down the dock. Cooper's shoulders stiffened. The officer might approach him and ask, "Shouldn't you be in Academic Winter Day Camp?" What would Cooper say? Something like, "I'm privately tutored. My tutor wants me to expand my longitudinal thinking by pretending to see dead spirits in the Hudson." But the officer did not approach Cooper, or even glance his way. Instead he started talking to the guy lying on the chairs. It was cold, it was going to be freezing, it wasn't safe to sleep at this spot. The cop told the man he should get out of here. He didn't ask the man his name. He asked him did he have a place to go.

■ ■ ■

By the time Cooper returned to his building, it had begun to snow. Miguel was no longer in the lobby, but the mailman was there—a short man with a moustache and wide reddish hands. He was sorting envelopes and magazines into individual boxes. The mailman said, without looking at Cooper, "What apartment?"

"4C."

"Nothing yet," said the mailman. "But I just got started."

Cooper stood there unmoving. He had an idea. To the mailman

he said, "I was wondering." The mailman kept sorting. "I was wondering what's the name of the woman who lived in 4C before me? Her first name?"

The mailman stopped sorting. "You been getting some of her mail?"

"I don't think so."

"You shouldn't be getting her mail."

"We're not."

"So why do you want to know her name?"

Cooper shifted from one foot to the other, the red pom-pom on his hat swaying from side to side. He tried to look as hopeful and innocent and pathetic as he could. He said, in a soft voice, "I just want to know."

The mailman sighed. The old 4C's last name was long and confusing, he told Cooper. He couldn't quite recall it anymore, which was saying something, because he was *great* with names and he didn't want Cooper thinking anything different. But her first name wasn't hard to remember. It sounded like Helena, only 4C didn't spell it that way. She spelled it Halina, and the mailman spelled it out for Cooper, his eyes raised to the ceiling so that he resembled a child at a spelling bee, mentally groping for the right concoction of vowels, H-A-L-I-N-A. When the mailman finished spelling, Cooper felt he was holding the spoken letters inside his own brain tissue, as if the name was now something he owned.

"Did you ever meet her?" Cooper asked.

"Once or twice."

"What was she like?"

"Just an old lady."

In the elevator, as Cooper was pulled upward by cables invisible to him, he allowed himself to think the old 4C's name again and felt a new intimacy with her. The rooms he inhabited were Halina's rooms. The same plumbing carried his pee away as had carried Halina's. The view from his window had been Halina's view, too. And the Julia-woman coming to the apartment tonight, she would try to make those rooms and pipes and views her own.

I don't want her in our apartment, Halina, Cooper thought, very fiercely. He whispered her name out loud, closed his eyes. And he believed he felt a hand holding his shoulder, gently, maternally, maybe, until the elevator doors opened onto the fourth floor.

Back inside 4C, Cooper stood in front of their brand new refrigerator and listened to its quiet burbling. Then he sprawled out on the couch with his laptop and watched more episodes of *Days of Our Lives* and waited.

. . .

When Cooper's father returned home, he was carrying a long red rose. A zombie rose, Cooper thought for a second, remembering the rose he had seen frozen in the river. But no, he had bought it at the corner bodega, and the flower was for Julia. "Unfortunately," Cooper's father said, "right after I bought this for her, I found out she won't be joining us for dinner."

Cooper sat straight up. "Julia's not coming for dinner?"

"No. Sorry, Coop."

A miracle.

"She's worried about this blizzard," his father continued. "They might suspend some subway service in a couple hours."

A miracle!

"It's supposed to turn into a really bad one. Came sorta out of nowhere. Global warming, I guess."

"How can it be global warming, Dad? It's *cold*."

"It's all connected up, Coop."

Ghosts or global warming? Cooper thought the real culprit behind the blizzard was pretty clear. He had underestimated the old lady in 4C to such a degree, it was almost insulting. When he had told the 4C river spirit "Make it so she doesn't show up tonight," he had guessed maybe Julia would get caught in traffic or come down with a sore throat. The old 4C had gone above and beyond in her service to him. She had turned an expected flurry into a blizzard. She had pulled cold air toward the equator and pulled warm air toward the poles. She had brought strange currents together. She might even create whiteout conditions!

Plus, as a bonus, Academic Winter Day Camp would probably be cancelled tomorrow.

His father did not feel like cooking now that Julia wasn't coming over, so they heated up one of the remaining risotto frozen foods. Cooper described some of the *Days of Our Lives* plots to his father, which took a while. When he was done, his father said, "I wish you had spent your day doing something besides consuming television. Have you even gotten any fresh air?"

"A little."

"Well, get a little more. Why don't you go around the corner and pick up some ice cream from the deli before it gets really bad out there? I'm craving dessert." He reached for his wallet and handed Cooper twenty dollars. "Don't go crazy, Coop. Bring back some change."

Cooper put on his coat and scarf and pom-pom hat. As soon as he had left 4C, he allowed himself one brief, broad smile, and headed downstairs. Of course, his father would try to orchestrate another occasion to meet Julia, but now someone else was on Cooper's side. A secret weapon. And who knew what could happen when you had the support of local ghosts? Perhaps Julia would never cross 4C's threshold. Perhaps Julia would in fact disappear.

A black rubber mat had been put out in the lobby, to soak up the snow and slush people might bring in. At the end of the black rubber mat, outside under the building's long awning, stood Miguel. Cooper couldn't wait to tell him what had happened. Miguel was texting on his phone. When Cooper neared, Miguel didn't say anything. He kept texting.

"Don't you leave in the evenings?" Cooper asked Miguel. "Aren't you going home?"

Miguel exhaled. The steam from his breath seemed to drift past the awning's little string of lights. "They're not letting me go today." Miguel shrugged. "They want me on hand to shovel snow when it gets bad. I'm sleeping in a cot next to the boiler room."

"I'm sorry," Cooper said, but he was beaming as he said it, bursting to tell his news. "Guess what? 4C helped me."

Miguel looked at him sideways. "What?"

Cooper told him about his mother and about Julia coming over and about how he'd spoken to the old lady in 4C down by the river and in the elevator, too. "I was really sympathetic. And then I asked her to do whatever she could to keep the woman from visiting."

Miguel shook his head. "So you think you got a ghost to be your servant."

Cooper didn't think that was fair. It was not servitude, if she had done what Cooper had asked. It was love. Or if not love, then at least some cousin to love.

"My mom might be snowed in." Miguel turned his eyes back to his phone. "She's got no one to shovel her out because I won't be there, because I gotta stay here to shovel out you and your dad and everyone else, or I'll lose my job. She's waiting for me right now because she's not strong enough to shovel herself out." He sneered at Cooper. "What do you think about that? You think your ghost made it so I couldn't check up on my mom, too?" Miguel was shivering a little. He wore a long sleeved shirt and jeans and sneakers and no scarf and no hat. Despite Miguel's sneer, Cooper felt a warming surge of pity. He took off his own hat then.

"Here," Cooper said. He held out the hat to Miguel, an offering. "You can wear my hat if you want. So you don't get cold."

And then Miguel's sneer turned very quickly into something else, something much worse. Something like rage. He grabbed the hat and put it back on Cooper's head. He pulled it down hard on Cooper's head so that the hat covered Cooper's eyebrows, which were raised high on his forehead with hurt and surprise. Miguel pulled the hat down past Cooper's eyes so that Cooper couldn't see.

And Miguel laughed at him. He laughed soft and long. Cooper stood there blindly, feeling the wool against his eyelids, feeling, too, that many eyes were now upon him. But when he lifted the hat back up over his eyes, it was still just Miguel standing there. Well. Who else had he expected?

"Oh, man," Miguel said then. "Don't cry. Shit. I was just kidding, pulling the hat down like that. Look. Don't cry. That's the kind of trick I play on my nephew all the time."

"I'm not crying."

"You going to tell your dad about this? Please don't cry. Please. Please don't tell."

"I'm not crying." Cooper stepped out from under the awning. "You don't get to tell me what to do," he said to Miguel. "I'll tell my dad whatever I want."

And he began to head west down the street, without waiting for Miguel to argue or apologize again. I *am* sympathetic, he thought. I am. He looked up. When the snowflakes passed under the streetlamps, they resembled buzzing bugs, living things, flying in directions both longitudinal and latitudinal. He lifted his hands to the sky and felt a few cool flakes on his upturned palms. All over the city, it was snowing. And in New Jersey, too. Cooper took a deep breath and said defiantly, but quietly, so that Miguel couldn't hear, "Thank you, Halina." His breath turned steamy in the air, and for a second it seemed as if he could see his own voice—a visible pocket of condensation. He stopped and watched the steam disperse and tried to forget about Miguel, about the way Miguel had seemed to see right through Cooper, straight to something Cooper couldn't yet name. *So you think you got a ghost to be your servant.* Cooper shivered. Well, it was cold.

He pulled his hat down further over his ears and continued walking toward the corner store, his father's twenty dollars warm in his pocket, the snow just beginning to swirl more swiftly around him.

Subcortical

In the early seventies, I began sleeping with a married doctor who wanted to cure homosexuality. I was twenty-one. In our hotel room, he showed me black-and-white photographs of patients' brains like they were Kodak color snapshots of his own children at play: cooing over the cerebellum's left lobe, marveling over the funniest reaction some area had had to electrical stimulation. I'm exaggerating a little, but not much. He pointed out, very tenderly, the deep brain and surface electrodes, his finger pads leaving sheeny traces of grease on the photograph.

I'd admitted to the doctor that when I was a little girl, I myself had wanted to be a doctor. I wanted to save lives, to rewire hearts and brains. My mother had laughed at me. She'd told me to marry a doctor instead, or a dentist at least. She'd told me I was going to be beautiful and shouldn't waste nature's gifts and where would the money come from, anyway, and don't be silly. The doctor, though, saw that I genuinely wanted to learn and he knew I didn't have money for college. So he tried to explain things to me. What the different parts of the brain might do. How memory worked. I don't remember much from his lessons now. What I do remember is that during the second week of our affair, before we left the hotel, he talked to me about the action of electroshock at subcortical levels and then he held out some money for me. He said he knew my mother had medical debt, he said he knew I didn't make much waitressing.

But I knew really he was trying to tell me something about this transaction, trying to define it himself before I could have a say in labeling the thing between us.

When he held out the money to me, I breathed in deeply. The hotel smelled like apples. Outside were rooftops, a collection of water towers. It was a nice hotel room, though the drapes were an ugly Paleozoic brown. Central Park was not far away. Sometimes, after I saw the doctor, I took walks there.

I took the money. I placed the bills carefully into my wallet. I thought *subcortical subcortical subcortical.* A new word to understand. A new understanding.

We left the hotel and walked in separate directions: he to his apartment overlooking the park, I to the subway tunneled under the street. I did not feel dirty, not even on the subway. I felt clean with new knowledge. *Subcortical,* I whispered to myself, to help with remembering.

. . .

I met the doctor again and again and again. I was learning about bodies, about brains, I was learning the names for different regions of the parts of myself I couldn't see. I was learning more about the medical world than I'd ever known before. If I had to play up my own sexuality, my own girl-ness, in order to keep the doctor interested, to gain this knowledge, well, fine. The doctor was a broad-shouldered man and not unattractive. When we were apart, I'd sometimes think about his patients, I'd wonder how they were doing. I wondered about them more than I wondered about the doctor or even myself.

The doctor's favorite patient, the one he always told me about, was a twenty-one-year-old homosexual male who wanted to be a woman. "You're the same age as he is!" the doctor exclaimed to me sometimes. Of course the patient and I (the doctor said) were very different. The patient—the doctor told me we'd call him Patient C—suffered from depression, drug and alcohol abuse, and suicidal rumination. Under the doctor's direction, stainless steel electrodes were implanted into a number of subcortical sites in the patient's head. Soon, the doctor told me, his team of researchers would begin to passively stimulate these implanted sites. They were going to determine which region of the brain was associated with pleasure.

"You figure that out, you program the boy back the way nature intended, stimulate the subcortical sites while you show him pictures of pretty women, and the alcohol and the drugs and the thoughts of suicide and the dick-loving?" The doctor touched my side. "All that goes away. Name in the history books."

"Whose name? Patient C?"

"Don't tease. My name." He put his hairy hands on my stomach and examined my belly's flesh through the interstices of his fingers. "My name in the history books. And you can say 'I knew him when.' Just don't tell my wife about all that knowing."

He laughed. I didn't. I said, "Do you respect me much less than your wife?" I had half hoped the words would come out sounding insecure—even guilty—so that the situation between the two of us might start to seem more normal, less deviant, so that our exchanges could return to a more regular script, like something that might be on TV. But my question came out flat and cold; I sounded more like I was posing a scientific hypothesis, speaking about myself with dispassionate interest.

"Joyce," the doctor said. "Don't be silly."

. . .

Every time we met after that, I heard a little more about Patient C's progress. I was interested in learning about the inside of Patient C's brain, in learning the names for all the parts, in understanding my own brain better through his, in understanding all brains better. As far as Patient C's homosexuality went, I had no strong feelings one way or another. I'd gone to a conservative church every Sunday as a kid and I won't pretend I was some wildly open-minded person. Nor was I particularly interested in being wildly open-minded. I was interested in opening up a brain and cataloguing the wildness there.

But, to my own surprise, I developed a kind of attachment to Patient C. I supposed Patient C, like me, was sinning and so felt myself in company with him and liked him better than most men, even though I'd never met him. Sometimes I thought about what the doctor said, about how the patient and I were the same age. I didn't know his birthday, but I enjoyed imagining the two of us as babies screaming in the same hospital at the same time. We wouldn't just be screaming *in* the hospital, we'd be screaming *at* the hospital, at its borders and walls, we'd be screaming at how someone had checked boxes already saying what we were, what we should be shaped into, what we were allowed to become. He could not become a woman. I could not become a doctor. To deviate from these ideas was silly. I knew this fantasy was mostly based in fiction, but I couldn't help thinking about it sometimes. The two of us screaming together.

The doctor must have sensed the frisson I felt thinking about Patient C, because he had taken to telling me about the patient's progress always before sex, so that the updates began to seem like a kind of foreplay. One day, he told me his team had determined that the septal region alone was associated with pleasure. That day, during sex, I thought over and over, "Septal region septal region septal region." I was conducting an experiment, trying to see if calling to that space, articulating it in language, might somehow make my feelings more intense. It worked. I know it's not scientific, but it worked. I shuddered all over. I broke out in a fresh sweat. I didn't moan more loudly, but the sounds I did make seemed to come from a more centralized place, caused vibrations in not just my spine, but the doctor's—I could feel those vibrations in my finger pads. The doctor thought he alone had triggered this reaction in me, and he looked inordinately pleased. He ordered two gigantic meals from room service.

We sat for a time, silently gnawing at pastrami sandwiches. Then I asked, "What happens next?"

"Dessert? You want pie?"

"You know that's not what I mean."

"Do you mean what happens next with us?"

"No." I laughed. "I mean with Patient C."

"I kind of want pie."

"Tell me what happens next to Patient C. Are you close to curing him?"

"Well." The doctor looked down at his sandwich as if the pastrami would show him the words he needed. "Well, now that we've determined the region of pleasure, we'll start up regular periods of septal area stimulation. You understand that?"

"I understand that."

"The patient himself will at times be allowed to take the initiative, to stimulate this area himself with the push of a button. Joyce."

"And then?"

"You're not like normal girls."

"You mean I'm not what you *think* a normal girl should be. In the surface parts of your brain."

"Joyce. Put down the food and come here."

The whole way home, even though the doctor's pastrami smell was all over me, I could not stop thinking about Patient C. I struggled to imagine his face, but I could easily imagine his hands: thin and hairless and hovering over a button that I decided would be big and colored green like a streetlight saying *go go go go go*.

. . .

Not too long after that the doctor made an announcement. Fingering the thick brown draperies in the hotel, he told me that Patient C had reported increased interest in female personnel and feelings of sexual arousal.

"You mean he's starting to like girls?"

"He's starting to like girls. We even showed him a film."

"A film."

The doctor came close to me and whispered about it into my ear. I'm sure he didn't use the clinical language I remember now. What I remember now is his telling me the subject had watched the film, become aroused, and masturbated to orgasm. The whole time, the doctor's researchers had recorded the electrical activity in the patient's brain. I wanted to know if the doctor had watched. Was there a screen or something? Was Patient C alone? How did it work?

"We didn't watch," the doctor said. "We watched the electrical activity, Joyce."

"So is he cured? When does it count as he's cured?"

"Not yet. We're getting close."

Before we parted ways that day, he left me an envelope full of more cash than he'd ever left before. He had to rush out for work and was already gone by the time I counted it. I had a funny feeling some of the money was a kind of down payment on some future favor, some new transaction I didn't yet have the education to predict. And I was right. The next time I met the doctor, he told me he had a request for me.

"It's a little illicit, but I didn't think you'd mind. I thought maybe you'd actually like it. Because actually it's for the good of medical science. Hell, of humanity."

"What is it?"

"Patient C is progressing," said the doctor.

"What's the request?"

. . .

Central Park, once, had contained slaughterhouses. Then it contained robber barons and their offspring, strolling the park's paths, commenting on the way a new white bridge was in dialogue with the birch trees around it. Now the place had made its pendulous move back to its old slaughterhouse roots, its greenish insides full of young kids coming through here to mug and shoot one another, at least according to the news. I walked through the park's paths only in broad daylight, and even then I kept my pocketbook clutched close to my chest, which had the added advantage of concealing my chest. Still, despite these safety precautions, I found the park a real inspiration that day. If a place could contain multiple pasts within its perimeters, play multiple roles, could a person? And how different could those roles be from one another?

Patient C had vocalized a desire to be with a woman. It was a major breakthrough, or in the doctor's words, "a potentially key pavestone on the path to an historical achievement."

He said he remembered what I said about wanting to be a doctor. He said despite what I thought, despite what my mother said, it wasn't too late. He wanted it to be me with him, with Patient C. He wanted me to sleep with Patient C. He wanted that so much. He could not think of anything that would turn him on more.

"If you say no," the doctor added, "that's okay too. We'll go with someone else. A professional."

"A professional."

"But I want it to be you. You're articulate. You're engaged with the patient. You know his story. You can tell us, truthfully, how it went, after. Whether it seemed...genuine." He smiled at me. "And I'll know I can trust what you say."

I still hadn't said anything.

"You can use the money for school," he went on. "It will be a lot of money and I'm going to ask that you use it for school." When I was still silent, he added, "You've already been doing this, Joyce. Taking the money from me after we're together. A little bit more each time. It's not that different."

Had he been training me for this? Probably there was a psychological term for what he'd done, something to do with incremental steps toward rising stakes.

"Joyce, if this works, he's potentially cured. Do you know what that means?"

Alone in the park, after, I felt like someone was following me. I walked more quickly, to get out of the park and re-enter the grid. Still, once I was out of the park, once I was again on Central Park West, I turned around and looked back. I was curious about what had followed me.

■ ■ ■

I don't want to go into any details about what happened. There are only a few facts to know:

1. Patient C was tall and skinny and his ankles were bony and red. Electrodes snaked from his shaved head. He said, "They put these extension cord things on my electrodes. They said it would give me more mobility." And I said, "Oh." And he looked toward a wall of glass—a two-way mirror, I realized—and said to the mirror, "I like your skirt."

2. I wore a very short skirt and a very shiny shirt covered in sequins because I thought if I wore something very different from

what I usually wore—if I wore a costume—everything might seem more like a play instead of real.

3. Patient C wore nothing but a hospital gown and a big grin the whole time. The grin seemed like a costume, also. When he came, he made some signal with his hand, and I realized the doctor was watching us, and the electrical activity between us.

4. The doctor, afterward, wore a big grin too—not a costume grin. I was surprised at the time because I'd thought he'd be at least a little jealous. But he was in control, in charge, never more than that day. He had gotten me to obey, to come here, dressed like this, he had put two deviants together and, in his mind, placed them firmly in the roles he thought they truly occupied. He had authored this situation and he loved it. After all, the doctor loved his work.

The doctor gave me the money. I told him I didn't want to see him anymore and he said he understood. Probably he had thought he'd cured me of something. But several months later, he called me and asked me to meet him in the park. He was sitting just outside the entrance to the Central Park Zoo. When I sat down next to him, he turned around and told me Patient C had vanished. They had released him too soon, the doctor said. He had not done enough. He had failed Patient C and now Patient C had disappeared. Then the doctor began to cry. His tears were large and shiny and reminded me of glistening fat. I didn't touch him. I got up from the bench and left without another word.

Shortly afterward, the doctor's work became well known—not for its achievements, but for its ethical impropriety. Patient C had kept a diary, written his story down. The diary was found, even though Patient C was not. While the treatment he'd received might not have been seen as unethical in the fifties or the sixties, opinion was starting to shift. Soon the doctor's name was in the history books as an example of the way the medical field could become twisted in ways that were pernicious to life and dignity. One of the articles actually said that. Pernicious.

For a while I was sick of the human brain and had no faith in my ability to understand it. But I got over that. I used the doctor's money and went to college. I did very well. I went to medical school and did very well, there, too. I was especially driven because I knew that if I didn't succeed after what I'd already done, I couldn't say for sure what I would do next. Maybe end things. Maybe disappear. Maybe hurt someone. But it didn't come to that. I have my own practice now. I have a husband, also, and a child, a girl, who grew into a woman and fell in love with another woman. They recently were married. They are happy.

But for whatever reason, since they were married, I think of Patient C again, constantly. I think about all he wasn't afforded. I think about what we did together and why we did those things and about where my own responsibility was limited and where it wasn't. I think about his red ankles. Deviant. That word gets snagged onto something in my brain and repeats in my thoughts again and again until I'm wide awake and shivery and sweaty with anxiety.

The only way for me to fall asleep after that is to fantasize. I pretend that I have tracked down Patient C and am watching him from the observation side of a two-way mirror. The mirror looks out onto a strange green place, one that I have never seen before, a place that exists just beneath the surface of my waking mind. It looks like Central Park, a little, but it is not Central Park. It's in another country entirely, I am sure of it, and Patient C walks down its paths with an abstracted expression on his face. My eyelids are growing heavy, but I manage to watch as Patient C spots the two-way mirror. He looks into the mirror hard. Then he looks happy. He grins, finally recognizing the person on the other side.

A Guide to Sirens

Frank's island tour—offered free to hotel guests—is described by the Paradise Inn's brochure as a brief excursion into the island's myths, mysteries, and mermaids, its selkies and sirens. What the brochure fails to mention is that most of the tour is aimed at selling extra-cost amenities. Frank has today's group look at the hotel's spa, the sea-themed restaurant, the saltwater pool, and some pinkish seashells with purported medicinal properties. Only after that does he finally gather the handful of patrons inside a thatched pavilion on the beach. This group stands in pairs, their blinking the sole movement in their flushed faces.

Frank clears his throat and says that long before the hospitality industry became king here, this small island housed an order of Franciscan monks. (The members of the group—mostly honeymooners—look slightly guilty at the news.) During World War II, the monastery was converted into a small naval base. Frank paints touching portraits of soldiers under big church bells, gripping guns. The bells now are lost. So are the soldiers, so are the monks. But to up his tour's lyricism, Frank talks mostly about the bells. The story goes that the monastery bells were dismantled and thrown into the sea by a formerly devout soldier, turned deaf by the booms of bomb explosions and turned atheist by the bomb explosions themselves.

"The bells were never heard again," Frank tells today's group, "until one day a woman at the hotel, unhappy on her honeymoon, tried to drown herself in the ocean. Coincidentally, just as she'd tucked herself into a soft bed of seaweed, she heard a church bell ringing. She opened her eyes and thought she saw a cathedral rising up from the ocean floor. It was a sign, she thought. She came up for air. She swam to shore. She went back to her hotel room. Yes, she lived. Nevertheless, legend has it…"

Frank takes a deep breath. The crowd stares at him. Then Frank offers up his best puckish grin. "Legend has it she still wound up getting a divorce."

The couples always titter at this, give each other knowing glances. Only today when Frank says the line about divorce, a woman gives *him* a knowing glance. Frank, fifty years old, wears shirts with prints of silver swordfish on them, or sometimes rainbow trout. This woman, who appears to be in her twenties, wears a tight-fitting bright blue shirt and white shorts. She looks exactly like his ex-wife looked twenty years ago.

The divorce was her fault. She cheated. He pushed her once, with both his hands, but she was the one who cheated. Frank has packed all his memories of her away in what he likes to think of as the cerebral cellar of his brain. He imagines those memories decomposing down to their more basic bits, fusing to other forms: fairy tales, myths, legends, the stuff of tacky tours, the stuff that makes his living, the stuff that allows him to live.

"Well," he says, after several moments of looking at the woman in the blue shirt. "Well, yes, I guess we're going to conclude now."

He thanks the group, then leads them back to the lobby, where he reminds them their hotel contains five different restaurants specializing in different cuisines: French, vegetarian, Asian fusion, sustainable seafood, and Mexican. The guests disperse.

But the woman who gave him a look, the woman who looks like his wife, she lingers for a moment. Of course, she is not his wife.

His wife is now his former wife, lives in New York, is in her forties. This woman is Something Else. And now the Something Else waves to Frank, before walking into an elevator.

Frank sweats.

. . .

Frank honeymooned at this hotel, on this island, too. They were on the third floor with a partial ocean view, their room covered in pictures of mermaids with Miss America smiles. "So tacky," his wife had said, but she had said so while grinning, while removing her bright blue shirt.

For a while, after the divorce, Frank worked as a guide in all sorts of different museums and cities. Then he came back to this island. He likes his arrangement with the hotel and he likes the ahistorical attitude of the hotel's visitors. They're fine with ignoring troubling cultural pasts, because their honeymoons are designed around ignoring their own pasts, infidelities, prenuptial doubts. When he led tours at a natural history museum, there was someone always trying to out-PC someone else, or asking Frank where the museum had retrieved those skulls, what native tribe they slaughtered with guns to swipe up and preserve those arrowheads. Now, working for the hotel, all he has to do is try to sell seashells and tell stories. No one cares if they're true or not. The group always seems relieved just to be there. His tours offer a break from the physically and emotionally exhaustive work of honeymooning.

Although Frank stays at a discounted rate in a small room on the first floor of the hotel, he doesn't interact much with the guests. He doesn't interact much with the hotel staff, either. Most of the staff, the ones not from the island, are teenagers and early-twentysomethings. They have come to intern here, which means fold towels, wash tables, work in one of the five restaurants. They receive nothing for their time but room and board. For a while they're all smiles about it. The way they see it, they're on a free vacation in paradise. Eventually they realize they're being exploited and they leave. They typically don't last more than a couple of weeks.

. . .

Sometimes, at night, Frank goes to the hotel bar and watches people there. The bartenders serve cocktails that glow a radioactive pink or a radioactive orange, lighting up women's faces. Tonight the woman in the blue shirt just so happens to be sitting at the bar, alone. It's the kind of coincidence that seems like a set-up. Still, Frank slides into the seat next to her. She looks up and smiles.

She says, "I really like your shirt, just so much. What kind of fish are those?"

"Swordfish."

"Oh. Obviously. They do look just like swords." She laughs. The laugh is familiar, high-pitched, unhesitating. A memory, a fragment of forgotten sound, floats out from Frank's cerebral cellar.

"Listen," the woman says, when the little show of a laugh is over. She is leaning forward, her hair spooling on the bar's counter. "I guess you noticed I was staring at you before, during the tour. It's because there's something you should know."

"Yeah?"

"She was me."

"Who was you?" She is still wearing that blue shirt.

"I was that woman? The one who tried to drown herself and heard the bells."

"Hah. No," he says. "It's just a legend."

"Hah. No," she says. "It was me in the story."

"Okay," says Frank. "Totally."

"Really. I came back to see if I'd hear them again. I promise you."

She might be crazy. Of course, he's the one who thinks she looks just like his former wife from twenty years back. So maybe he is crazy. Maybe he's talking to one of his own stories.

"Let's go for a swim," the woman says. "I'll guide you to where the bells are."

"I made them up." Frank tries a flirtatious grin on, feels a little like his face is being sawed in half. "The monastery part is true, but the bell part I made up. They don't exist."

"They do, too," she says. "Let's meet in one hour. On the beach."

"How could you even hear a bell sound underwater?"

"Above land, we hear through air conduction. Under the sea, bone conduction." The woman smiles warmly at him. "People can hear sounds under the sea that they can't hear on land. Sounds at higher frequencies. Isn't that something?" The way she delivers the information, in a smooth, yet friendly sort of voice, she sounds like a host on NPR or something. Not like anyone Frank really knows, but like someone he might half listen to on a long drive, just to distract himself from the slow passing of the seconds.

Then she gets up and is gone. Frank buys a beer and starts to think. He wants to think about the woman, but he ends up thinking about his former wife and his former wife's laugh. What kind of medium conducted the sound of her laugh back into his head just now? Not air, not bone. Can sound be conducted purely by memory?

The time he pushed her: He had been angry. He had pushed hard. This was even before she had cheated. Twice he had pushed her, actually. True? A certain wobbly expression on her face each time. The light in her eyes seemed off-balanced, diffracted, like sun filtering through beveled glass. Her skin rainbow-flushed.

One hour. The woman had not been smiling when she said that.

. . .

If the woman is a hallucination, she's a punctual one: she's already there when Frank arrives at the beach. He wears nautical blue swimming trunks. She wears a sleek black Speedo, a one-piece, all business, her hair pulled back in a ponytail now. There are other couples on the beach but they're very much occupied with one another. The woman waves to him as he comes nearer. Her toenails are painted gold. The ocean is black. The water will be colder than he likes.

"Why don't we sit on the beach for a while first?" Frank asks. "Talk a little?"

"This isn't about talking. It's about listening. I'm *guiding* you, Frank."

She starts to turn away. He reaches for her arm, but she flinches and snakes her body from him like he's hit her. Now the woman is running to the water.

"Come on," she calls to Frank. She dives down, so he takes a deep breath and dives down, too. He doesn't hear bells. Instead, in the underwater darkness, he remembers the look on the woman's face when he grabbed for her arm. He remembers pushing his wife. The small sound she made afterward, steady and quiet and nothing like bells. He goes up again to the surface for air.

He sees some of the interns, down on the beach.

Treading water, the woman forgotten, he watches the interns.

They're supposed to be working, but instead they're lying in the sand, teenagers trying to tan under the cinereal light of the moon. They let loose peals of laughter, even though their bodies have to be heavy with ache from dishwashing, waiting tables, mopping. Pieces of their conversation drift his way. They're talking about opening their own hotel, all of the interns together, right here, right on this spot, free from that bastard of a manager they're working under. They say they will be business partners. By that, they mean they will be friends forever.

But in two weeks, Frank predicts, they will be gone from this place, the whole experience a story they will tell to the new people they meet, the new friends forever that they see on new islands, in new internships.

Where is the woman? Instead of looking for her, he looks some more at the interns, the beautiful young kids glowing with lunar tans. Maybe he will leave with them, even though he seems too old to change. He will go to a new and unhaunted island. The ocean's full of islands.

Someone is grabbing his legs, trying to pull him down under the surface. Probably the woman, joking around. If he ducks his head under the waves, he will hear her highest-frequency laugh, the sound conducted through his bones, and he will know her, what she is exactly, what story to tell to get her to let him go.

Hart Island

When I was fifteen, my heart was broken. Probably that sounds a little maudlin. I know Mr. Berger, my high-school English teacher, would give his disappointed sigh if he read that first line, his big forehead going wrinkly. In the margins of this page, using his green ink (chosen to make his more malicious comments look mother-earthy and benign), he'd scrawl, "Danger! Danger! Can you spot a possible melodramatic cliché here? Why don't you create an image cluster chart. See what other visuals are attached to heartbreak (i.e., wilted roses, stomped-on box of chocolates). Point is this: Do not name 'heart.' *Suggest* in other ways. Can this be shown/dramatized? Scene/setting?"

But fifteen-year-old James—that's the name of my heartbreaker—would probably like it better the way I just wrote it.

"Go ahead," he'd tell me, if he had the chance. "Name it. Elena? Say heart. Talk about it. What does yours sound like before it breaks? Badumbadum? So write badum-ba-fucking-dum, okay?" He would relish that he got to sneak a "fuck" in there, but he would try to play it cool, to hide his pleasure, would try to act like it was no big deal. Then he would maybe lean in close, all gaunt cheekbones and big brown eyes and long pale eyelashes. His skin, in my mind, is zitlessly smooth, time being the great unclogger of pores.

"Go sentimental, go melodramatic, I don't care," he'd say. "Just describe the goopy living things for me."

James is dead, so he'd have a real nostalgia-driven interest in goopy living things, I'd imagine. Still at the end of the day—and maybe I'm only saying this because I'm not in high school anymore, because I'm trying to become a teacher now myself—Mr. Berger is likely right. Broken heart is a cliché and probably an image cluster chart would help.

. . .

When I first laid eyes on James at an assembly in the high school auditorium, he was fast asleep. He wore a green windbreaker and stuffed in the windbreaker's mesh kangaroo pocket was a fat paperback of *Moby-Dick*—a nice, new copy, which told me he was reading it on his own, and not for class. Even though I went to one of the most competitive public high schools in New York City, the tomes the teachers handed out were almost always ugly hardcovers from the early nineties, covered in pen marks. I'd spend an hour with an author trying to goad me into envisioning the Fertile Crescent or polynomials or the world's invisible particles or Gatsby's wild parties or the intricacies of a boneless moon jellyfish. Then I'd close the book and there, on the back cover, would be etchings of genitals as envisioned by my peers, like some kind of peevish reviewer's blurb.

James's book had no marks on it. His nice, new copy of *Moby-Dick* rose and fell with his sleep-breath. I hadn't read *Moby-Dick*, but my father said it was the greatest novel ever written—although he, also, hadn't read all of it. "No time," he claimed. He worked weekdays and weekends, managing a series of laundromats in Astoria, where we lived. Even though my father was a laundromat guy, he said that if he'd been able to finish college, he'd have become an architect. "Do you think you'd want to do something like that yourself, sweetie?"

he asked me once, hopefully, and I said yes. I didn't really know what being an architect involved. However, I liked the idea of building something and I liked the idea of pleasing my father.

The lady introducing the principal walked off the stage, and the principal strutted up to the podium. He opened his speech by telling us that one of the high school's alums had just won a Nobel Prize. My mother had shown me an article about it that morning in the paper, so I already knew. "You see, Elena," my mother had said, "what a good public magnet school can achieve?" I'd studied the alum's picture in the paper: a seventy-year-old white-bearded physicist. I could imagine the odor of his breath—cornflakes mingling with spearmint, probably—but I couldn't discern even the ghost of a teenager in the man's face.

Still, the principal beamed out at all of us in the auditorium like we'd each known this physicist personally, like we'd shared a locker with him or something. "This is the first day of your sophomore year," the principal said, scanning the auditorium as if he believed he could make eye contact with all 700 of us. "And yet, early as it is in your academic lives, I say with total confidence: Any one of you could be destined for greatness." The principal lifted his hands toward the vaulted ceiling. "You each contain within you a wee little Nobel Prize winner that this school can help nurture and grow. That tiny potential winner, that homunculus reaching with stunted fingers for the stars, can be molded into a form that will bring you respect from your peers, honor from the Swedes, and accolades from the entire world."

At least that's how I remember the speech now.

When the principal walked off, and we all applauded half-heartedly, James's eyes finally opened. He looked right at me. I tried to think up something charming to say. In fifth grade I'd gone through a phase where I'd been obsessed with whales and dolphins. So I searched my brain for a *Moby-Dick*–related whale fact I might share. But then James spoke to me first.

"What the hell are we clapping about?"

Before I could figure out how to respond to James's question, April from AP World tapped my shoulder and asked if the first in-class quiz tomorrow covered Iran and Iraq or just Iran. "We'll have only done one day on Iran," she said, swaying in distress. "And Iraq barely comes up in the textbook reading for tonight. I looked. It's just supremely messed up if she's planning to test us on stuff we only read about a little in the textbook. We haven't even discussed it in class yet. You know?"

I said I knew. Then I turned and James was gone.

I raced out of the auditorium, into the hallway, hoping to spot him again. The new glass-protected photograph of our Nobel Prize–winning alum hung in a gleaming gilt frame outside the library, across from a fluorescent-lit alcove where couples were already congregating and kissing, their twined bodies dimly reflected in the physicist's black-and-white portrait. On the same wall as the physicist were the yearbook pictures of members of the most recent graduating class, arranged not alphabetically, but by the university the students went on to attend. You knew, upon graduating, that the younger classes would see exactly where you ended up.

I looked down the hall. I couldn't see James anywhere.

. . .

I ate lunch that afternoon with the girls of AP World, most of whom I'd met previously in Freshman Honors History. The girls all did lots of volunteer work with old people and puppies and soup and the homeless. They talked to me about my too-thin resume. April told me I should volunteer now, so colleges didn't get suspicious about the true nature of my goodwill when all the community service work on my resume occurred the summer before my senior year. I wasn't even sure what kind of shelter April volunteered at, human or animal. Mostly she complained about how her supervisor yelled at her when she showed up late. "I don't know what she expects," April would say. "It's *volunteer*. That means *voluntary*." A couple of times, April had asked me to come to the shelter with her. But I usually helped my father at work on weekends. He paid me to clean out lint.

After lunch with the AP World girls, I went to tech drawing, a course on drafting meant to make us all stand out (together) from college applicants at other schools. Because of my interest in being an architect, I was excited. I'd talked to this older girl, a junior, and she said mostly they'd messed around with CAD software on computers. I was good at computers, so I figured the class would be easy. But the tech drawing teacher I'd ended up with was ancient. A tall, lean man with white hair. He announced that first day that he did not believe in computers.

"I believe in the TANGIBLE," Hoffman barked. "I believe in what we can touch. You will be doing all plates by hand. If you can't draw a straight line by the end of this course, you will fail."

That was when I noticed James, straight across the room from me. Hoffman called attendance. Eventually he said James's name, and that was the first time I knew James was called James. Instead of saying "here" or "present," James grunted and took his copy of *Moby-Dick* out of his windbreaker's pocket. He read silently while Hoffman talked.

"If you want to become an architect," Hoffman said, "this class will be extremely useful to you. If you don't want to become an architect, this class will still be extremely useful to you, because there are certain aspects of logic, dimensions, and design that are applicable to nearly every field of human existence, including, but not limited to, breathing."

I exhaled hard.

When the period was over, I followed James out of the classroom. I was getting ready to walk a little faster, so that I could actually talk to him. (I'd come up with the perfect whale fact, one about their limbic systems.) But then a pale girl with electric blue hair raced down the hall and grabbed the floppy collar of his windbreaker. Maybe five seconds later, she and James started to kiss against the lockers. His spine curved toward her and away again.

I should've been crushed, and I was for a minute. But I kept watching them kiss until the bell rang.

I was three minutes late for English with Mr. Berger. James was not in the class; the other students were mostly girls. Mr. Berger had a neck beard and lots of energy. He talked at us for a while, and used the verbs "evoke," "invoke," "shape," and "show" at least a dozen times apiece. "If you veer toward a cliché," he said, "try using an image cluster chart." I figured if I disappointed my father by not becoming an architect, I could at least write him a really short *Moby-Dick* in Mr. Berger's class, something he might actually have time to read.

When I tried to do the tech drawing homework that night, I discovered I couldn't draw a straight line. I spent hours at our kitchen table, attempting to get the T-square to align with the paper. "Practice makes perfect!" my mother said. But actually each time I practiced, each time I attempted a straight line and failed to make a straight line, I'd get a little bit more panicked and the next line would get a little bit worse. The first big assignment was to draw a floor plan of our home. But when I tried to draw the bird's eye view of the two bedrooms, the kitchen, the bathroom, everything looked off center and slanted.

"The borders are wrong," Mr. Hoffman wrote later in his red

ink. "Also, windows are too big (½" space). Also, WHERE ARE DOORS??????? B–."

He was right. Somehow I'd forgotten to draw doors.

. . .

As the semester went on, I spent most of tech drawing watching James, anticipating his reunion with the blue-haired girl. I'd heard him call her Disney. Maybe her parents had been trying to convince someone to give them all American citizenship. Or maybe they were just trying to be subversive in some way I didn't get. Since my locker was nearby, every day after tech drawing I continued to watch the two of them together, both envious of and enthralled by their synchronized make-out movements. They never were apart.

Finally, though, one day, I managed to catch James alone. During lunch, April had brought cupcakes for another AP World girl's birthday, and the sugar high made me bold. When I saw James leaning on his locker, waiting for Disney, I walked right up to him. He was holding *Moby-Dick*.

"Is that *Moby-Dick*?" I asked.

"Yeah," he said.

He scratched at one of the zits on his cheek.

"You know," I said, "whales have more developed brains than humans. Like the limbic system or something in the whale brain, like the part responsible for feeling and emotions and for socialness? That's bigger than a human being's."

I half-expected James to roll his eyes. But instead he nodded. He smiled this really huge, really real smile.

"Right on," he said. "Big fucking whale brains. Right *on*."

A bright burst of blue hair started coming down the hall.

"Well," James said to me, "see you, Whale Girl."

That nickname had not been my desired takeaway from the conversation, but at least it was something. I don't know if he finished *Moby-Dick* but after a while other books were visible through the kangaroo pocket's mesh. *Pale Fire. Infinite Jest.* For a few days, *War and Peace.* Part of me suspected that now he wasn't reading the books so much as picking out a different one to wear each day. But, at least during tech drawing, he would sometimes make a show of flipping a book's pages under his desk while Hoffman talked. Once Hoffman said, "James, put that book away. You can't do work for other classes in *my* class. This is your education passing right before your eyes. Whoooosh."

James looked up. Then James and me, we locked eyes. He gave this little shrug—not to Hoffman but to me. "Sorry if I'm busy learning how to be a human being," James said.

Hoffman sent James to the dean. As James slumped out, he winked at me.

．．．

That same day, in English class, Mr. Berger announced we were taking a break from writing analysis papers on sample college admission essays. Instead we were starting on a poetry unit. Mr. Berger asked, "Where does poetry come from?"

A girl wearing a flowing floral-printed skirt—even though it was November at this point, and cold—raised her hand and said, "I like to write poems about the dreams I have. The subconscious is so pure, you know?"

Mr. Berger stroked his neck beard. He said that although he appreciated the subconscious's role in the creative process and although our college admissions essays and poems and stories were all in some sense about our dreams, writing about our actual nightly dreams within these contexts could point to a callow imagination and might suggest a failure on the part of our higher faculties. "The key," he said, "is the way your waking mind generates analogy."

That afternoon, on the subway ride home, MTA musk emanating from everything around me, I wrote a love poem full of analogy. It was a sonnet in which an unnamed party (James) begged me to design him the best and biggest house possible, a house made entirely out of green locker doors, "verdured scrap metal." The unnamed party said if I could build a house like that, we might live there together, haunted always by our love. I thought the poem was very romantic and handed it in the next day to Mr. Berger. Mr. Berger, however, decided that poem was about academic and parental pressure. When he handed the poems back, I saw he'd written a mildly concerned note to me in his green ink. "Analogy," he wrote, "is defined as 'a comparison between two things, typically on the basis of their structure and for the purpose of explanation or clarification.' I am not sure what this poem is clarifying, but it seems to point to the narrative that high school is designed to help 'build' you a home. Is this narrative worrying you now? How can you guide the reader to unexpected places instead of swerving? How, through analogy, can your poems CLARIFY your emotional intent???"

I didn't tear up my love poem to James. I didn't show it to him either. I buried it in the bottom of my backpack where it got shuffled up with other papers and was, eventually, lost.

. . .

That Saturday, after I'd just gotten out of bed, the world swerved. In the kitchen, my mother stood over me and my milk-soaked wads of Mini-Wheats. She showed me the newspaper and asked me if I knew him.

Great, I thought. Another Nobel Prize. But then I saw the picture.

What I felt in my stomach and my heart and my brain was not like anything I'd felt before. There is no analogy for it that I can find, even now.

My mother: "It says this boy here went to school with you. Did you know him?"

There were three photographs of three different boys in the article. One was James. All three boys had drowned together after setting forth in a boat late at night.

No, I told my mother. I hadn't known him. Not really.

I don't remember too much about what I felt or thought in those next few hours.

I do remember that, later, I looked around our kitchen, labeling the things I saw. A window. A sink. Some walls. I remembered Hoffman's comment: WHERE ARE DOORS???? It was a good question. I didn't see any doors, just the open space in the wall that led back to the dead end of the living room.

On Sunday, instead of doing homework, I Googled articles about the drowning. Most people speculated that the kids had been headed for Hart Island (those quoted in interviews always called the victims "kids," although James had seemed older to me in his James Deanishness). I looked up Hart Island. It was a restricted area at the western end of Long Island Sound, which had once housed yellow fever victims in quarantine and also a women's lunatic asylum. Now it contained defunct missile silos from the Cold War, and mass graves. Over 850,000 dead were buried there. Mostly they were people whose bodies hadn't been claimed or whose families couldn't afford burials. James would not be buried on Hart Island but when I closed my eyes, I kept picturing him on his way there.

In tech drawing on Monday, James's chair remained empty. We all pretended not to see the empty chair, but the chair was watching us.

This was my first encounter with the supernatural on public school grounds. The chair had on either side of its top large silvery screws, which I easily read as shiny eyeball sockets. I frequently saw human faces in inanimate objects, in warped wood and rucked dresses. As a child, I requested a nightlight not for the illumination, but because I wanted the prongs to cover the outlet's eyes.

Hoffman said, "I've been teaching forty years. And it's always like a personal tragedy when one of my students dies." He studied his feet for a second.

But it shouldn't have just been *like* a personal tragedy.

Then he explained our next assignment. We would be designing a roller coaster. "Remember," he said, "2-D graphical representations will simply not be sufficient. You must determine how to represent the 3-D aspects of the system, too, in order to construct."

All I was able to complete that class were the borders that would surround my roller coaster. When the bell rang, I stood in the hall for a minute, wondering if I would see Disney. I didn't.

In English class, we were supposed to describe a person, the first step in designing a character. I described a boat on tumultuous waters. It was a small boat, a plunker of fiber glass and polymers, not designed for furious weather—or so the clueless reader would think. I evoked in my description a setting, obsidian waves that dashed the boat to and fro, leaving its shivering occupants in growing despair as they gazed up at the cold, sharp, unseeing eyes (i.e., stars) of the black January night.

But when the first bit of estuarial water wormed its way inside the boat, a beam that all of Long Island Sound could see shot up like a divine flashlight from the boat's center, alerting the city of the occupants' danger.

Mr. Berger handed my story back the next day. "Boat=person??"

he wrote. "How does the boat do this trick? Is this fantasy/sci-fi??? Remember what I said day the first: No genre fiction in this class. STILL, I'm thrilled you're letting your imagination run not only free, but wild! B–."

. . .

None of the AP World girls mentioned James's death, not on that first Monday after the boat accident, or that Tuesday or Wednesday, so finally on Thursday I brought it up myself. "That kid who drowned a few days ago was in my tech drawing class," I said.

The AP World girls got very quiet for a minute. Some of them muttered, "That's so sad," and "Are you okay?" But then Caitlin said, "Actually, I think it was hypothermia. Not drowning. It's the cold of the water that usually kills you."

Dina said, "Did you know one of the other kids who died in the water went here too? He couldn't take it, though, and transferred."

I didn't see how that was relevant, but I kept eating my cheese sandwich.

"Transferring's a little like dying," said April, and they all tittered.

"I read an article about the whole drowning thing," Dina said. "Apparently, they were trying to get to some island with this old graveyard on it. Stereotypical teenage *ahngst*." She waved her plastic spork around. "Who decides to sneak off to some forbidden Long Island heap in November, is what I want to know. Let's see, tiny dinghy, freezing cold water, strong current, nighttime . . . Stupid."

Stupid, they all agreed, with total confidence. As if "stupid" was the right answer to the question of death, of grief.

I decided that day to stop eating lunch with the AP World girls.

The next morning, on my subway ride to school, Disney sat next to me. At first, just looking at her out of the corner of my eye,

I didn't totally recognize her, separate from James. But then she said, "Hey."

I'd been sleepy before, but now I was fully awake.

She said, "You're the crazy girl who always used to watch me and James."

"Huh?" I squinted. "No, I'm not."

"Oh, we noticed. I thought you were incredibly creepy. But James said once you were kind of cute."

I turned away. The reflective subway pole in front of me was covered with fingerprints.

"Don't get too excited," Disney said. "I think he just wanted to get a reaction out of me."

The doors opened and closed and people with briefcases rushed onboard, pressed close to our knees. For a while we were silent. Then Disney said, very quietly, "I have something to tell you."

"Yeah?"

"I'm telling you this because you're weird enough that you won't try to make me feel better. Don't tell anyone, because they'd say I was crazy and maybe make me miss class."

"Okay."

"I've been seeing James everywhere."

I held my hands together, tightly, in my lap.

"On the subway, around the city, at school, in my bedroom. He just sort of looks at me and smiles. My mom doesn't even know I was seeing him. She's very strict about dating." Disney bit her lip. "I see him every night too. He's in all my dreams." Her voice sounded strange, oddly fluted. "You know, I was planning to break things off with him? I had written him a letter and everything. It said I wanted to stop seeing him. And then he got on that stupid boat and died. And now I can't stop seeing him."

"Oh."

"Do you think I'm going insane?"

"No," I said. And then, to make Disney feel better, less crazy, I lied. I said, "I think I saw him too."

She started laughing. "You wish." Her whole body trembled with her laugh. Then, shoulders still shaking, she turned her face away.

. . .

Mr. Berger told us he believed in sequential learning. So that day in English class, for homework, we were supposed to develop the character we had designed and maneuver it into some sort of plot, some sort of real story. This was problematic for me because my original character had been a boat. I decided I needed to bury my boat-with-the-ray-of-light idea. I created four characters, four boys, named Rob, Bill, Will, and Frank. I gave them a new boat, something simpler, sturdier, made out of indestructible steel. But the buoyant kind.

In my story for class, which I drafted on the back of a tech drawing plate, the boat miraculously reached Hart Island, just as a huge wave nearly overturned it. The four boys found refuge from the storm in some silos, so I wrote very long descriptive passages in which I evoked the old military silos the boys hid in, silos I had searched Google Images for extensively. In these silos, all night long, they heard a ghost woman from the old asylum, laughing. The loon laughter was like a siren song, and they each fell in love with the voice alone. Deciding never to leave their island, they planted a false story with a newspaper saying they'd drowned. But really they just wanted to skip class, skip pre-college prep, skip college apps, skip jobs, skip it all. They wanted to devote their entire lives to listening to that woman laugh.

Mr. Berger wrote in the typed-out story's margins, "Hmmmmm,

some of the details here seem a little too familiar. Do you need to see a grief counselor, Elena?" He also wrote, "While you've obviously done your research (I think you might be the class silo expert!!), some confusion remains. Where do point A and point B connect? Also remember, nautical ghost stories=genre. What is the crazy woman doing there? What does she mean? Fear of death, burgeoning sexuality, ETC.? A lot happening. Think about shaping the symbolism of the story. Have you created an image cluster chart?"

. . .

Instead of eating lunch with the AP World girls, I'd started to spend the first half of lunch reading the books I'd seen James wearing (beginning with *Moby-Dick*) and the second half of lunch wandering around the hallways. I was looking for James's ghost so my lie to Disney could transform into the truth, a right answer. I strolled past bulletin boards, some devoted to student achievement ("Six students have been named Intel semifinalists!"), some devoted to lists of procedures to follow in case of a terrorist attack or fire ("File out of the building in a single line!").

About a week into these lunchtime wanderings, I began to wonder: What if the school itself was a ghost? After all, the things we most believed in here—the numbers in a percentage point, the grade—were not concrete or tangible. But we consumed the intangible as the stuff that fueled us, and so we became intangible ourselves. At first I felt very profound, thinking that, and kind of sociological. But then I felt scared. Shortly after I started having these thoughts, I stopped going to tech drawing and English and AP World. During those classes I just read in the library, blending in with the other kids who had free periods.

April found me there once. She pushed her round worried face close to mine.

"Where have you been?" she whispered. "Elena, everybody is extremely, extremely concerned. We think you're on meth, basically. Are you mad at us?"

"No."

"If you're mad at us, say something. This passive-aggressive behavior is so immature."

"You're really not supposed to talk in the library." And I stared down at my book. I could feel April glaring at me. But then she said, "Here. I made a bunch of these for Andrea's birthday."

She put a brown paper bag down on the desk. I smelled frosting. Then April headed for the door. After a minute, I went after her, holding the bag. But she was gone. I stood in the hallway, in front of the picture of the Nobel Prize–winning alum, and stared into the pixels of his eyes. Then, without looking away, I reached into the paper bag, pulled out a cupcake, and wolfed the thing down almost whole.

Eventually, the school sent a notice home about all the classes I was missing. My parents sat me down at the kitchen table one evening before dinner. I buried my head in my arms.

My mother said, "She needs Prozac."

My father said, "She needs iron. I told you, you cook too much carbs. It's an iron deficiency."

"It's emotional!"

"Look at the girl. She's anemic."

"She's not going to graduate." Although I couldn't see her with my head in my arms, I knew my mother was looking up at my father, knew they were communicating in their special eyebrow language. "If she racks up more absences," my mother said, like I wasn't there, "it's going to show on her record. Forever."

"What do we do?"

"This woman from the school called me. She asked had there been a trauma."

"Well," my father said, "has there been a trauma?"

My mother moved her chair in. "Tell me right now, Elena. Has there been a trauma?"

"Not really," I said.

"No, she says! Well, so, what do we do if there's been no trauma to tell the school about?"

"It doesn't matter, okay?" I lifted my head. "They don't want me to be human at that place. And I want to be a human being. Is that so much to ask?"

"What does that even mean?" My father put his hand on my shoulder. His clean, pink fingernails were cut in neat, perfect squares. "An F and a copy of *Moby-Dick* will do your human life no good, Elena."

"Elena," said my mother. "What would your grandparents say? If I told you what your great-grandmother went through coming to this country, on that boat."

Then my mother started to cry.

The sound made me rise from my chair without thinking. I walked to where my mother sat, on the other side of the table. She grabbed me, pulled me toward her, pressed my dry cheek against her wet one. I put my hand on her back and felt her body juddering back and forth.

James now was a ghost thing. Grades were a ghost thing. But my mother's wet cheek—that was a very real thing. Her hurt, her panic for my future—real feeling. I thought about the cupcake April gave me, its thoughtful, cloying sweetness. And how fast I swallowed it down.

"Sweetie," my father said.

Being a human being meant, now, making it so my mother would stop crying.

. . .

I started going to class again. I caught up in what I had missed, used my money from working at the laundromat to pay this really smart girl to do my plates for me by hand, and passed tech drawing. I even asked my father if I could take Sunday off, and I went to the shelter to volunteer with April. It turned out to be the kind of shelter for animals. The puppies were very cute.

In Mr. Berger's class, too, I did okay. I started writing stories about landlocked people, who lived in states I'd never seen. They spent a lot of time driving around in sedans, thinking. Mr. Berger didn't love these stories, but he also didn't hate them. "Your work has acquired a greater sense of clarity," he wrote me.

Disney, however, didn't do so well. She transferred out, I heard, though I never heard to where.

Although I passed my classes, I'm still not sure whether, ultimately, I succeeded or failed that year. I didn't become either of the things I dreamed of becoming when I was fifteen. I'm not an architect, I'm not the author of an abbreviated *Moby-Dick*. I guess I'll be an educator, eventually. Right now I'm finishing up my student teaching. I enlighten first graders about vowels, Native Americans, and manatees, all in the same day. I teach them, too, how to distinguish between living and nonliving things. That's part of the actual science curriculum.

I like the first graders because of the things they chase: not dreams, not numbers, not letter grades. When I open the door for them, when I let them out into the playground during recess, they chase leaves. They chase squirrels. They chase one another, all the time, across the rubbery Kid Kushion playground tile. "You're it, you're it!" they laugh, even when they haven't managed to touch each other yet. Just laughing wildly like that without accidentally peeing in their pants is, for them, a real success.

The funny thing is, even now I do have this one dream, all the time, where I'm back in high school, and I'm graduating in an auditorium in Lincoln Center. I'm in a nice green robe (in reality, I think, our robes were blue). Our principal is there, still bald and beaming. And then the dream goes one of two ways:

In the first way, right before he calls all our names, the principal announces he has just received news from the Swedes that I have somehow miraculously won the Nobel Prize, the youngest winner ever. I have won purely for being a human being. Nobody saw it coming! Everybody gasps and looks at me and notices me. AP World girls gape. My parents cry, but in a thrilled way.

In the second version of this dream, though, I hold my breath throughout the whole graduation ceremony, waiting for them to call my name. They never do. Then I realize that I haven't actually breathed in hours. I'm a ghost, a pretty neat accomplishment. Scrambling from my seat, I defy physics: I fly through walls, fly rapidly to the Sound to meet James. He waits for me in a glass bottom boat that we both pretend is headed to Hart Island. It's the perfect boat for us, all straight lines, rigid right angles. It's made to sink in a slow, leisurely manner, so that you can see the bottom of the harbor the whole way down. There's all sorts of goopy broken wreckage down there, weird fish and shelled creatures that no one else knows exist, beings that live on the margins, outside of any logical dimension, any successful design.

Both of these dreams, in their own ways, are happy ones.

Recuerdo

During the winter of 1985, Stephen's job was to listen for sounds of intrusion. A lamp rested near his elbow, a space heater hummed near his feet, and a small radio exhaled steady static, sometimes with undertones of synthpop, sometimes with undertones of Iran-Contra news. From four in the afternoon until midnight he would sit at his desk in a dark building on Prince Street and protect the former garment factory's emptiness—its high ceilings, its gutted insides of plywood and sheetrock. The factory had been bought by someone wealthy, and that person had hired the security company Stephen worked for to make sure the building didn't get vandalized before renovation began. Stephen had taken this job as a security guard primarily because it offered health insurance for both himself and Kathleen, his wife, who was pregnant. He had no prior security experience. But he had thick shoulders. Which counted for something.

He never encountered any real trouble at the empty factory until one night in late December, after he'd worked the job for a few weeks. He was standing outside the building, talking with Kathleen on the payphone just across the street. He called her, usually, right before she fell asleep, exhausted from her waitressing shifts and night classes. Tonight she said, after a long yawn, "I'm going to call the doctor tomorrow to schedule the first visit about the baby. Hopefully he won't get me all hyper-neurotic about nutrition. I ate maybe five hot dogs today."

Kathleen must have met a few pretentious people as a part-time student, because she often described things as hyper-whatever these days. From most anyone else, Stephen would find this irritating. But the way Kathleen spoke, he could tell she was just trying out the prefix, like a woman slipping into a beautiful dress she was not sure she could afford, spinning around inside the department store's changing room so she could get a sense of the garment's grammatical buoyancy.

Stephen was just about to reassure Kathleen about the hot dog thing and the doctor visit when a bulky figure approached the factory. The figure looked in both directions. Then he or she lifted the lower vent grate beside Stephen's building and dropped down. The figure's legs and belly and chest and shoulders and head disappeared in one swift second. If he hadn't known the vent was there, Stephen would have guessed the sidewalk was eating people whole.

"I'm going to give Miranda a call," Kathleen was saying. "She left a message about how Mom was asking her all these questions about our financial stability. Can you believe that? I mean, she could call us, you know? She doesn't have to go through my sister. But it's always been this way."

Stephen stared at the spot in the sidewalk through which the figure had vanished.

"Stephen?"

"Sorry, babe," Stephen said. "I've got to go."

"Everything okay?"

"Just fine. Don't worry. I'll see you later."

Stephen hung up the phone, and walked over to the grate. A glint of light flickered there. Voices drifted up.

People were passing through the vent, into the building, under his feet.

His building. His feet.

Okay. And this was his job. His job was to keep this building secure. His job was to go down to the basement and see who was there, see if there was a Situation.

But instead he pictured his wife across the water, on Staten Island where they lived, in St. George. He saw Kathleen hanging up the phone, then lying on her back in bed, legs splayed out. Kathleen, falling asleep, her face lost beneath her dark hair, dreaming about the lions. That was her new dream now: to get a job inside the library with the lions. The library lions sat like guards themselves, day and night, protecting all those words, all those poems Kathleen knew by heart. And wasn't Stephen's job, ultimately, to protect Kathleen? What if the men sneaking into the building had weapons and he tried to chase them out and got hurt? Too hurt to keep working, to keep their insurance? Although they hardly spent any cash, they had little money saved.

Stephen had never really been one to get into fights, but getting married last year had made him hesitate even more when it came to taking risks. Getting married, also, had made his life seem more real, more *good*. And had made other people treat it as more real and more good, too. One day his mother was railing about how he should get some ambition and try to become an electrician and do something more with his life, and the next day he was married and his mother was saying only, "Congratulations!" And his friends, who usually just complained about their lives, were also saying only, "Congratulations!" And even his father, whom he hadn't seen in years, was calling to say "Congratulations!"—like suddenly he'd remembered Stephen existed. It was as if an invisible force had validated Stephen by recognizing what he'd already been doing since high school, doing for years: loving Kathleen.

Kathleen didn't see why getting married was such a big deal. "Nothing's changed. It's not like my father gave you goats or anything. We just have a piece of paper now, is all. And I love you the same amount, which is the most."

Just a piece of paper. This from a woman taking out loans to study how to protect pieces of paper, this from a woman who memorized old poems. Well, Stephen felt the difference. Not only in the expected places, like in his heart or in his bones, but in his lungs. The years they'd been together before, he'd been pretty much holding his breath, and now, now he could let loose, exhale deep, and feel Kathleen wouldn't disappear. But the contract was this: he shouldn't disappear, either, or get hurt, if he could help it. Especially with the baby on the way.

If there was anybody in the basement, they weren't hurting anybody. Probably. And it was safer for Stephen to ignore them, to avoid a confrontation.

So Stephen walked into the building, sat back at his desk, took out a paperback—he was making his way through *The Lord of the Rings* because Rocky, the day guard, had recommended it—and read for another hour. From where he sat he encountered no more disturbances. No one sneaking in under his feet. Just orcs and elves and long-winded descriptions of various fictional ravines.

Finally the night guard showed up. Bill was an ancient silent man with white hair and a thin face and a large mole on his right temple. His shoulders were very small.

"Hi," Stephen said. Bill nodded in his ancient silent way. He hardly ever spoke. The young man and the old changed places.

Then Stephen headed toward the ferry.

When he got home, Kathleen was asleep, not splayed out like he'd imagined, but curled up. She had left the nightstand lamp on for Stephen. He kicked off his shoes and socks. He wriggled free of his uniform—dark pants with a skinny stripe up their side, a light blue shirt so densely polyester that when he threw it on the floor it retained his shoulders' shape. At last he slipped into bed and slung his arm over Kathleen's hip.

"Hi, goodnight," she mumbled. Her voice at night seemed to travel differently, to go deeper once the sun had set, like the dark slowed down the sound waves of her speech. Stephen kissed her neck, put his hand on her stomach, thought about the doctor who would listen to his wife's stomach, listen for signs of life.

. . .

The next night on Prince, Stephen tried to read. But the lamp was flickering. If people were sneaking around under his feet, they remained very quiet. Around eleven, Stephen stepped out of the building and walked to the payphone again. Kathleen would have made her doctor's appointment. She would tell him about the receptionist, she would impersonate the receptionist's voice, probably. He turned into the phone's shelter, so he wouldn't have a view of the street or the vent. Kathleen usually picked up on the third ring, but this time she picked up halfway into the very first.

"Stephen?"

She had the hollowed-out voice she got after crying.

"What's wrong?" Stephen asked. "Is it the baby?"

The baby was okay, she said. The problem was their insurance. That afternoon, when she'd called the doctor and given the receptionist her insurance ID number, the receptionist had informed her the pregnancy was not covered. It turned out the insurance company would not cover pregnancy until she and Stephen had been enrolled with them for a whole year.

"Do you know how much getting the care we need is going to cost?" Kathleen said. "We don't have the money, Stephen." Kathleen's breathing went weird and jagged.

"Go to bed," Stephen said. "Make some tea, watch TV, go to bed. I'll be home soon. We'll figure it out."

"Stephen—" she began.

But he couldn't stand it, her hollow voice, the unspoken sense that he'd failed his small family in some way. He hung up the phone. The street was empty. Had someone snuck inside? He walked to the heating vent. Darkness. No glint. He spat into the grate, listened for the sound. There. The sound of his own spit. He spat again.

Back in the building he turned the radio's volume even higher. Its FM static soared up multiple stories of empty space. Soon Bill arrived and Stephen went to catch the ferry home.

The night ferry was not like the ferry ride in the afternoon. During the afternoon ferry, white gulls occasionally skimmed over the gray waves. But this late, he saw no birds on the water. It was past midnight and still very cold and why couldn't the boat move a little faster and why was he living on the wrong island? Stephen and Kathleen had both grown up in a suburb in New Jersey. When they'd made the decision to move to New York, they wound up on Staten Island because, through pure luck, they'd found a rent-stabilized apartment there. Originally they were excited about riding the ferry all the time. The first few weeks in New York, Kathleen would whisper this poem into Stephen's ear before bed:

We were very tired, we were very merry—
We had gone back and forth all night on the ferry;

And you ate an apple, and I ate a pear,
From a dozen of each we had bought somewhere.

"Did you write that?" he asked the first time she recited the poem.

"No. It's "Recuerdo" by Edna St. Vincent Millay."

"Well, obviously."

She laughed. She leaned into him. "I just can't believe we're here. Living here, I mean."

Of course, over the next few weeks they'd learned how freezing cold it got out on the water at night, how dirty the ferry could be, and the early sense of lyricism gave way to the boat's sticky floors. It didn't help that rarely were Stephen and Kathleen together as "we" on the ferry: their schedules aligned only on weekends. Traveling on the boat alone was a different sort of poem. A poem without rhyme, maybe, but not entirely without pleasure. At least the ferry sold pretzels and coke. Beer, too. And the views were something else. There was the Statue of Liberty, her crown jeweled with windows, so people could look out. There was the dark harbor, the skyline, the buildings of Manhattan, many of them bright as candles now as Stephen crossed the water toward his home. The maintenance guys kept the electricity burning to give the illusion that the skyscrapers, full of light, were occupied with more than glow—with people, with families, too.

When Stephen got back to the apartment, the TV was flickering in the living room, but on mute. Tiny people talked, shouted, laughed silently at each other. Kathleen was home and wide awake, sitting up in bed, cross-legged. She drew the sheets up, now, over her knees. Stephen sat down on the bed. He put his arm around her. He said, "We're going to figure this insurance thing out. Okay? I'll find something new. We won't go bankrupt. I'll take care of it, I'll figure it out."

She looked small. She said, "I have figured it out."

"You have?"

"Stephen," Kathleen said. She spoke in the dog-tired monotone of someone who has exhausted her daily quotient of hysteria. "I called my sister and she thinks we're going to have to get a divorce."

His brain felt hot. For some reason, he grinned at her. "What?"

"She said this happened to a friend of hers. If the government's looking at just my income alone, I should be able to get on Medicaid. Especially since soon enough I'll have to quit at the Midway anyway, right?" She pulled the sheets up higher, brought her knees closer to her chest. "Anyway, that's just what Miranda thinks."

Stephen's head was filled with a buzzing sound, a sound like the radio at work made when you walked directly in front of it. "I'll call the insurance people," Stephen said. Was his voice still steady? He should try to keep it steady. "You didn't talk to the right person."

"I talked to a whole chain of people. It's hard to get a straight answer. It's layers and layers of bureaucracy."

"Kathleen. I just think Miranda's suggestion is a little—"

"I talked to the right people, Stephen." Kathleen tucked her chin over her right knee. "You can't fix this."

Someone upstairs was taking a shower. Water gurgled through the pipes.

"You left the TV on," Stephen said then. "You should turn it off, okay, Kathleen? You leave the TV on, you leave the lamp burning, no wonder we don't have much saved."

"I leave the lamp on because I know you get in late."

"Still, it's wasteful."

"It would only be a divorce on paper. We could get married again, down the road."

Down the road. Stephen wanted to spit on the floor. Instead he said, "I'll talk to Rocky tomorrow."

"The day guard guy? Why would he know anything?"

"He's been in the city forever. He'll know what to do."

"Stephen."

"Just let me talk to him."

"Listen, Stephen."

But she didn't say anything else. He shifted away from her to turn off the lamp.

. . .

The next night it was freezing again. Stephen usually went outside for at least part of the ferry ride to Manhattan, but this time he stayed indoors, on a bench full of people in puffy coats. When he finally reached his building on Prince, Rocky took one look at him and said, "What's wrong, Stevie?"

Stephen explained the insurance crisis to Rocky, trying again to keep his voice very steady. "Should I maybe talk to someone?" he asked. "I should call someone, right? I mean, this isn't our fault. I could probably just call someone. Right?"

"Call who, Stevie? The mayor? The president? Do you know how lucky you are, to have what you have? For a job like this? You shouldn't complain. Who knows what they'll do to you then. They might fire you. Or worse. They're insane. They're psycho."

"Who?"

"All of them. Every last one." Rocky stuck his hand into his beard and scratched at his chin. "Anyway, I gotta go. I'll leave you some beer."

Then Stephen was alone. But he needed to do something. So he had a beer. Rocky had left him four.

Maybe when Kathleen had called the insurance company before, she hadn't been convincing enough. Her voice, he loved her voice, but it had a tendency to waver around in its pitch when she was under stress. Stephen rose from his chair, left the building, walked to the payphone, and called the number on the back of his insurance card. Two rings, followed by Muzak on a loop. He looked over his shoulder, back at the factory. Wind raced down the street and rattled the Styrofoam cups sheltered in the gutter.

Then, just yards away, it happened again. A figure, all in shadow, lifted the grate on the heat vent and dropped into it.

The rush of hot fear should come now, right? But instead, when the adrenaline flooded his body, Stephen's brain tagged it as anger. It felt the same, the heat, but somehow now his brain called it some other emotion. Did the people under his feet even care that the building wasn't their own? Did they think it was funny, a security guard who had not found them out? Did they laugh about him while they traded around whatever it was they traded around? Did they think they were invisible?

They were not invisible.

The Muzak was still going, but it did not matter. Stephen hung up the phone and went back inside. He grabbed a flashlight from the desk. The stairs to the basement were uneven stone slabs. The air was wet. A rat ran past his feet, but not such a big rat.

When he reached the last step, he took a deep breath and looked down the basement's empty hallway. Sounds traveled toward him, voices maybe. There were a few doors down here, leading to rooms that held nothing—so he'd thought.

Another rat ran past. A bigger one. Spunkier, too. It stopped and looked at him, then ran on. Did it sense the upcoming confrontation? What if this was a wrong-place-wrong-time situation? Maybe he should pray, something like "God, please no knives or guns?" But when he tried to pray, what came was his wife's voice, reciting the beginning of that stupid poem.

We were very tired, we were very merry,
We had gone back and forth all night on the ferry.

He crept up to one of the doors, flung it open. An empty room with a sink. Nothing. No voices. Just the sound of the poem rushing like wind in his head.

We hailed, "Good morrow, mother!" to a shawl-covered head,
And bought a morning paper, which neither of us read;

Next he crept to the door that led to the old boiler room. The boiler was still in there, but it wasn't operational. He pressed his ear to the door. Something else was in there now. He heard a noise like crying.

And she wept, "God bless you!" for the apples and pears,
And we gave her all our money but our subway fares.

The noise kept going. His heart kept going. The poem running through his head had stopped, thankfully. Yes, whatever was here was behind this door. He closed his eyes. He did not want to do this. But this was his space. His job. He could do his job. He opened his eyes and the door at the same time. The door's hinges sang out. He shone his flashlight in the direction of the crying sound.

A couple.

A man and a woman.

It was hard to tell their exact ages. The guy was scrawny and the woman was scrawny too, but they each wore layers of bulky sweaters. Stephen could tell from all the different colors and textures of collars poking out around their necks. Although they had on many sweaters, neither the man nor the woman wore pants. The gooseflesh of the woman's thighs glowed under Stephen's flashlight's beam. She had her legs wrapped around the man's back and the man was against the wall. Her pink cotton underwear looped around one of her ankles. She had long dark hair, longer even than Kathleen's.

Piles of clear garbage bags surrounded them. Stephen shone his light on the bags. They were full of clothes. This couple had been living here, storing their stuff in this forgotten room.

He shone his flashlight on the pair again. The woman's green sweater—the final one she wore over all the rest—said "MERRY CHRISTMAS" on its back in white script, and was patterned with snowmen wearing Santa hats. Their snow bodies kept moving, unmelting, with the regular rhythm of the woman's thrusting hips.

The couple had seen him, but hadn't ceased.

Stephen turned off the flashlight. A ray of streetlamp light slanted in from the heat vent. It was still freezing out. They were still going at it. Didn't they have enough shame, even, to stop? He cleared his throat. They *should* be embarrassed. They were not supposed to be doing that here. This was not a designated area for doing that. They should stop or get out. Even now they weren't stopping.

"You guys gotta leave here," Stephen said, finally, into the dark.

The woman turned. She looked at Stephen. He felt her look more than he saw it—like someone grabbing his arm and shaking him.

"Fuck you," she panted.

"You guys gotta leave here."

"Fuck you."

He spoke calmly now, reasonably. "I'm going to call the cops in an hour if you and all your stuff aren't out of here. Okay?"

At last he had mastered that steady voice. But it made him feel less steady inside now, like someone else had started speaking through his mouth. A big rat slinked by, not in a spunky way.

"I'm serious," Stephen said, still with that new voice. "I'll call the cops. Would you like me to do that?"

The man didn't say anything. The woman had her face in the

man's neck now. Stephen turned away. He knew from the man's silence, from the way the woman finally hid her face, that they were going to leave. His stomach hurt. He left the room.

The three remaining beers were still there when he went up-stairs. He drank two of them. The woman's face in the gloom, her eyes. He started on the last beer. Well, he'd been doing his job. He could get fired if he didn't do his job. Keeping the empty spaces empty. You couldn't beat yourself up about some woman having sex in an oversized snowman sweater, anyway. It was actually re-ally funny. It would make a funny story one day, when he was more successful. And the couple would find another place to go. They were experts, probably, at finding places to go, places where they could seem invisible. This city had special people designated to help them find a place, right?

Stephen turned up the radio and went back to his book. Lots of strange creatures were looking for a ring. The ring was evil. Or maybe it was good. It was hard to tell. It was hard to focus now. His polyester shirt was itchy. There were just so many characters. Also a lot of landscapes and landscape words. A shit-ton of ravines. Dales. He drank beer six and rested his head in his arms. Lakes. Islands.

Before his shift was up, he stumbled downstairs. Silence. He checked the room. The couple was gone. Their bags were gone too. Like magic. As if he had dreamed the thing. They had moved very fast.

Stephen staggered back upstairs, listening for the radio. He'd definitely left it on. But now he couldn't hear any music at all. He only heard his own heart. Which meant someone else had turned off the radio. Someone else had snuck into the building, without Stephen seeing. He ran up the rest of the stairs, flashlight wobbling across the walls, ready to catch this new invader.

Silent ancient Bill was sitting at the desk, surrounded by Stephen's empty bottles. Stephen breathed out and realized it wasn't his shift any longer. That was why Bill had shown up. Stephen's shift had ended.

"Shit, Bill," Stephen panted. Sweat dripped over his eyes, caught on his eyelashes.

Bill stared at Stephen. The mole on Bill's face seemed to shiver with the small pulsing movements of Bill's temples. Then Bill said, very softly, "You okay?"

Stephen didn't know the answer. So he didn't say anything. He wiped his brow. Bill kept staring Stephen down, waiting for Stephen's to respond. Finally Stephen nodded at Bill and wandered from the building.

Next he was on the ferry, moving over the water, under the sky. He tried to locate the bathroom but he couldn't figure out where it was. Which didn't make sense, he'd been on this boat many, many times, he couldn't get lost on the ferry itself. He found the women's bathroom, and went there. It was empty. But when he exited the stall, an old lady was at the sink. Her fingers were twisted, arthritic-looking, and bright under the running water. She looked up, smiled at Stephen.

"Oh!" she said. "Am I in the wrong one again?"

"Yeah," Stephen said.

He walked out of the bathroom. But then he turned back. "No," he said to the lady. "You're in the right place. This is the women's room. You're okay."

"Whew!" she said.

"I was the one in the wrong place."

"Okay!"

How easy it had been, to make them disappear into the cold. A magic act with words. "I'll call the police." He wanted to tell Kathleen about this, about what he'd seen and done, about how easily someone here could do just that to them, if they used the right voice and the right words. But he couldn't speak.

He would quit. He'd find a new job, one with real health insurance, and everything would be fine. They would not need to track down invisible people on the corporate ladder. They would not need to get a divorce. Maybe he'd figure out how to become an electrician. Anyway, they would find another path. They had been taken by surprise the day before with the insurance news, that was all, startled and scared out of using their imaginations.

We were very happy. We were very merry.
We were cold as shit on top of this shit ferry.

He'd got the rhythm right, at least! Stephen grinned to himself. The beer had warmed him enough that he could step outside now, onto the ferry's deck. He was alone out here. But alone with what must be pretty much everything. The skyline. The city. The Statue of Liberty, her face in the gloom. The water was dark blue and the sky was dark blue, and Manhattan's million lit-up windows seemed the luminous tiny threads stitching the two types of dark—the water and sky—together into a single world. Beautiful, he thought. Then he vomited over the ferry's side.

When he got home, he would look around their apartment and imagine it empty: the lamp left on the curb, the bed dropped off at Goodwill, Kathleen's books donated to the library with the lions. Kathleen needed to quit school. They needed to leave the city. They should stay together, stay married, move away. He would give her a firm look and tell her so. She would try to argue. But Stephen would square his thick shoulders and tell her what he'd seen and tell her, too, what he'd learned he could make disappear.

The Afterlife of Turtles

On good days we talk about science fiction and soup. On bad days we talk about turtle heaven and hell.

Today is a bad day. "I saw their shells all piled up on a rock in Golden Gate Park," my uncle says to me over the phone, speaking fast, his voice projecting itself over thousands of miles into my ear. I am walking back to my dorm room from the dining hall, crossing over the small bridge that spans the green pond. "My question is: Do they go to hell?" My uncle's voice gets even faster. "Do they go to a special turtle heaven? The water at Golden Gate is going really green. What happens to their shells? Erica? Do they get split off from their shells? I saw seven turtles."

"You know, I just reread *The Martian Chronicles*," I say, to try to turn this bad day into a good one.

"Their head flabs sticking out of the shells like they knew something was coming. I'm worried," my uncle says, "that I'm regressing into a Buddhist world." Yesterday he extolled the virtues of minestrone soup and snow cones. The day before he crooned, "I want to be a rock star."

Uncle Miles's condition has gotten worse since my grandfather's death. He's in perpetual need of other people's ears, constantly calling not only me, but also my father, my mother, my aunt, my cousins. I always pick up my uncle's calls, even though I'm busy with my first year at college. Often I don't know what to say. I only know we don't want him talking to himself. He needs to hear a voice outside his head. So I better answer the phone. Even if I don't speak much, I better answer.

"I have two split minds," my uncle says today. "I worry when I die, I'll be split. All the time. Split. Erica?"

The longer I'm quiet, the more rapid and scared his breathing gets. At last I tell him that certain turtles have special brains. They're able to sense the earth's magnetic field over vast oceans, eventually finding their way back to land, even after years at sea.

"How do you know that?" he asks.

"TV," I say. "Where else?"

I don't add that the magnetic field drifts, and that according to the somber-voiced Discovery Channel narrator, plenty of turtles never make it. I just listen to my uncle's breathing on the other end of the phone. Finally he says, "Okay. I'm going to make some soup now." He adds, "Call you later."

I've seen Uncle Miles in person, though not often, since flying's expensive and my uncle doesn't travel well. I saw him once when I was four, once when I was nine, once when I was fifteen, and once last year. He lives in San Francisco, with the rest of my father's family. Each time I see him, he looks different than I remember. His brown eyes seem too dark and his skin too pale. His face shape, though, is always the biggest surprise. Squashier than I imagine it to be when we talk on the phone. Fatter. The medications he takes are known to cause weight gain, but on the phone his voice doesn't reveal these extra pounds. His voice is full of hard angles. Lean, I mean. All ribs. Yet in person his belly is too soft, and his voice seems too soft as well, I guess because I'm so used to his voice being directly in my ear. Somehow, in person, he seems farther away than on the phone.

Uncle Miles's brain started going weird when he was exactly my age, eighteen. Also, we share the same birthday. I try not to read into this too much, because reading into things too much seems unbalanced. Miles sends me birthday presents like no one else's. Watches meant for old men. Piles of yellowing pulpish paperbacks. Huge stacks of *National Geographic*. When I began to pack up for college, I didn't pack these gifts. I packed light and sensible: clothes, toiletries, a few notebooks. I'd gotten this pretty large academic scholarship, which made my father put his hand on my shoulder the night before I moved. He said, "I'm proud of you." But later, when he thought I was asleep, I overheard him saying to my mother in the living room, "I'm glad I know exactly where she's going to be for four years. I'm glad she can't just disappear." Miles, when he was eighteen and when his brain went weird, disappeared for a bit.

The truth is, although it sounds paranoid, I've always been a little scared that even though I'm a girl, I'm too much like my uncle and I'm also going to turn out to be an unbalanced person, which is a nice way of saying crazy. Here's why I think we're too alike:

1. Same birthday.
2. I don't know what I want to major in, English or chemistry, and my college counselor in high school said, "Huh, a right-brained AND left-brained person, you don't usually see someone split down the middle like that." That sounds like a casual comment, but I'm not so sure.
3. I like science fiction books. So does my uncle. Although, despite the fact that he reads so much science fiction, my uncle never talks about aliens. He talks mostly about the policies governing heaven, hell, turtles, and God. My father says their family wasn't religious, so it's funny that Miles worries about the state of his soul in a way intense enough to allow him to receive money from the state. But anyway. I'm digressing.

4. I digress a lot in conversation, and so does my uncle, and I actually really enjoy my conversations with my uncle, even (or especially?) the weird ones.

5. The fact that I'm paranoid enough about being like my uncle to make a list about ways I could be like my uncle suggests some inherent unbalance.

So anyway, those are a few of my reasons.

. . .

My uncle calls me again, a few hours after our conversation about the turtles, right after I get out of English class. When I pick up my phone, I'm outside, on a concrete path to my dorm. A green pond has been strategically placed alongside this path, the university's algae-gunked gesture toward landscaping. I stop and look at the water while pressing the phone to my ear. "Hi."

"How're classes going, Erica?" Before I can answer, Miles says, "I need to tell you something important. I found this thing in this book in this Salvation Army, this book's called *Renaissance Guitars*. A music book. But I found something about turtles in it. Like what we were talking about earlier? Do you remember? I'll read it to you. It goes . . . Are you ready, Erica? It goes, 'This lighthearted dance is taken from Testudo Gallo-Germanica.'" He stumbles over the dance's name, pauses, keeps reading. "'The word Testudo means lute, or more literally "tortoise shell," from the myth that the first lute was the result of a tortoise decaying. Its entrails were stretched across the shell, and when plucked they had a musical sound.'" He stops. "What do you make of that, Erica?"

I pretend to think. "Tortoises are different from turtles, right?"

"Not really," he says. "Okay. New topic. What class did you last have?"

"English."

"But you know English. Ha-ha. But so, okay, how was English class?"

I'm doing fine in the course, but it's not exactly fun. The best part of class, actually, occurs during the first five minutes when the professor makes us rearrange the seats from rows into a horseshoe shape. Chair legs squeak, table corners collide, students accidentally touch and say, "Oops, oops, sorry." The professor perspires a little as she pushes around a desk. For those few minutes, as the seat arrangement changes, I feel like I could really get around to understanding everyone in the class: the girls carrying their schoolbooks in small designer handbags, the boys with haircuts like lessons in geometry, the freshly formed couple with tribal tattoos. I feel like maybe I could talk to them directly as my uncle talks to me.

But then the seats are re-arranged and actual class begins and everyone's eyes go opaque. In high school, English was different. We wrote essays on themes like justice and tolerance. In this class, though, we analyze a bunch of symbols strung across the story like charms on a necklace. The idea is if we follow the string of symbols just right, they should tell us what the author was thinking, lead us directly to the author's own brain. All this effort, an entire course dedicated to ice-picking our way into a stranger's head. Talking to my uncle after English class is a relief. He lets me into his head right away, no questions asked. And I don't need to labor over symbolism much, don't have to ask, "What does the turtle mean to you, Uncle Miles?" All I need to do is acknowledge the turtle means something to him and then calm him down a little. Turn the day from a bad one into a good one. Ask him what kind of soup he's thinking of making for dinner. Lentil, chicken, barley? And what herbs, what spices does he plan to use?

. . .

Sometimes Miles calls me when I'm in my dorm, when my room-mate, Mallory, is around, and while I hear his voice, I look at her. She's a former swimmer or something, sleek. Weekends she goes to parties with lime-flavored Jell-O shots and loud music. Before she leaves our dorm room she always tries to get me to go out too, or at least do shots with her from the big bottle of vodka she keeps wrapped in a varsity sweatshirt under her desk. "It's good for you," she says, unfolding the sweatshirt's plush arms to reveal the bottle, her voice coaxing me like a mother trying to get a kid to drink down cough syrup. "Really, Erica, you're crazy to try and study all the time."

"I have to keep my scholarship," I tell her, knowing that will shut her up. She's rich and doesn't need a scholarship.

Still, she's nice. When my uncle calls, if she's in the room, she puts her earbuds in and bops her blond-streaked head to a beat I can't hear. She puts her earbuds in one night right before midterms, when, like usual in the evenings, my uncle calls. "I took the train to Palo Alto today," he tells me.

I close my chem textbook. "What'd you do there?"

"Walked around."

"Cool."

"Also, I saw former Vice President Dick Cheney jogging in Palo Alto."

"Oh."

"Later I saw the same guy, the same Cheney, beating up a home-less man in a park. I went over to help and four big guys in dark suits came over. So I left. Don't ever go to Palo Alto. Okay, Erica?"

He doesn't usually create whole characters like this. I wonder if I should be worried.

"Or if you do go to Palo Alto," my uncle says, "watch your back. Anyway. New topic. What have you been up to?"

"Just studying," I say.

After I hang up, I focus on the very real, very grounded details of the dorm room. The curling-in corners of Mallory's posters depicting singers with straightened hair. The "Fire Hazard!" tags that hang off the stems of our lamps. The one broken slat of our window shades, which won't flip up like the others. The way the fluorescent light of the hallway outside creeps under the door and slashes a bright diagonal wound of light into the tiles. The tiles, they all fit together, like pieces of turtle shells. Mallory bops her head.

Not long after that phone call, I receive an email from Miles. Weird, since he prefers the telephone. He already thinks someone's following his steps; he says he doesn't need advertisers / the government following his clicks.

The email is about a visit he has taken to a church not so far from where he lives. He says: *dear erica, hope things are good. i took a good walk to the church again. there was a beautiful statue of mary with palms turned out and a quote from Walt whitman on the stone beneath her feet that she stood on. here's the quote.*

"a child says what is the grass, fetching it to me with full hands.

i guess it must be the flag of my disposition out of hopeful green stuff woven.

or i guess it is the handkerchief of the Lord."

pretty cool. . ive been meaning to ask are there places to cook in the dorm? love uncle miles

The email is really all in italics, just like that.

The day I receive the message, my uncle doesn't call. Makes sense, I tell myself. He just emailed instead of calling. Except the next day he doesn't call. And the next day he doesn't call. But my father calls. My aunt, too, and my cousin. None of us have heard from him. When I try to reach him, an automated voice tells me the mailbox I am trying to reach is full.

My father calls my uncle's caseworker. She can't reach Miles. My father calls the coordinator of the support group my uncle attends. My uncle has not shown up to a meeting. My father tells me, trying to sound calm, "This happens. This is common for people like Miles. He'll show up again."

Without Miles's calls, a world closes off to me. The destinies of turtles, the menacing bureaucrats haunting wealthy suburbs, the statues in niches of cathedrals, Walt Whitman—all vanish.

. . .

When my uncle disappears, English class gets worse. Every grammatical quirk in a work becomes laden with significance, with what our professor calls "subjective sweet spots." You can say anything you want about the text, the professor says, just so long as you can back it up. But back it up with what, exactly? There is never anything concrete to "back up" our interpretations. No matter how fiction stretches to mirror the world, it's fantasy, a type of lunacy. Our labored in-class interpretations are based in clouds, dreams some dead guy made up in his dead guy head. What I mean to say is: I lose any lingering interest in English. Instead of interpretations based in clouds, I become more interested in studying the composition of clouds, the actual material bits hanging over us, the pieces that condense, then rain down hard. There's a science to certain mysteries. Next semester I want to take only science classes. Chemistry classes. There we go. A choice. A major.

No more split.

My father takes some time off from his job fixing elevators, and flies out to California to look for Miles himself. His boss says if he doesn't come back soon, he'll be fired. I stay in upstate New York, at school. There's nothing I can do, my father says. My mother thinks I should just try to keep up my grades, because if I lose my scholarship, we could really be in trouble.

One freezing Friday night, when my father is in California and Mallory is out at a party and I'm alone in my room—I tell myself I've stayed in to study—I end up looking for fifteen minutes at the tile of our dorm. I blow my nose on a wad of white napkins pocketed from the dining hall. And after that, in my head I keep hearing: "Or I guess it is the handkerchief of the Lord." The voice seems to come from outside myself, which could mean I'm turning either religious or unbalanced or both.

When Mallory comes home that night, her cheeks are drippy with lines of mascara. "Alexis is a bitch," she says, her voice wavering. She looks at my face. "Oh, sweetie," she sighs. "Want to do some shots?" She removes the varsity sweater wrapped around the vodka bottle and gives the sweater to me. I'm trembling a little. I put on the sweater.

We do shots. I warm up. "Finally," Mallory says. "I've been *waiting* on a little roomie bonding."

We start to laugh.

"You're so sweet," Mallory says, giggling. "Don't be so sad, Erica. I can tell lately, Erica, you've been so sad."

"It's true!" I say.

She kind of bops her head around and somehow I see my uncle's voice. And Mallory says something else about Alexis being a bitch and what a cold night it is, and Mallory and I, we cry together. Then we dry our eyes with white napkins and yawn and go each to our separate beds, pushed against separate walls. My father is the alarm that wakes me up. He calls. He says, "Nothing. We found nothing."

. . .

More weeks pass. At school, it's time to sign up for next semester's classes. Over half of my general education requirements have been knocked out. I sign up for chem classes and ecology classes and join a club for volunteer work where we mostly talk about who might want our volunteer work. Keeping busy keeps me from thinking about how, deep down, I'm waiting for some sort of resolution. I'm waiting for a phone call.

But one day I'm walking past the mucky green pond that snakes around the dining hall and there's a turtle sunning itself on the mucky brown bank.

I stop walking and I notice how hard the turtle's shell is, how protective, and I tell myself it's a sign, it means he's okay. This turtle is telling me that my uncle is just holed away somewhere with no reception, having a good day cooking soup, the steam moving over his body and mind like a warm shell. Why not just choose to believe he's fine, somewhere safe? Why not believe this is a sign? Why not say turtles, too, can be subjective sweet spots?

But then I tell myself no, that's crazy. It's crazy to see signs like that. It's crazy to think too much about how weird it is that this turtle is waiting around, on campus, where there usually are no turtles. Like someone has set it there for me. Like someone is trying to talk to me, trying to call out to me with a symbol, to tell me, "Interpret *this*!"

In my head I tell that someone: You can't fool me. That's no message about Miles. I have no delusions.

And I tell that someone: When this turtle disappears, it's not going to heaven or to hell, it's not going to make music or evolve into a lute or do anything else. It'll just be another piece of the silent earth's hard shell. I don't believe anything different. This turtle tells me nothing about my uncle. Nothing about who he was or where he is now. This turtle as resolution? I won't accept it.

I take measured breaths. If I start to read turtles like an alphabet, I turn into Miles. The trick is to keep my mind busy in other ways. It's Friday afternoon. Which means soon it will be Friday night. Maybe I'll finally go to a party with Mallory. The look on her face! Maybe I'll drink green drinks and allow the party's manic beat to fill every brain-bit.

Yes.

I will go with Mallory to a party that has music so loud, you can't even hear your own voice or the voices of people around you, you can't even hear yourself think. There I'll feel protected. There, for a short time, I will allow myself to disappear—to make today a good day, I tell myself.

Guardian

The afternoon Joan first spawned Cind, she was supposed to be helping her mother clean. Joan's father was due home from another business trip in the evening, and all day long Joan's mother had clung to a variety of scrub brushes and dusters. She had ordered Joan to her room, to pick up her shoes and dolls. But Joan was more interested in spending time in front of the forbidden TV. When she was sure her mother was fully occupied cleaning the bathroom and coordinating her scrub brushes, Joan crept to the living room, turned the dial, and watched a syndicated episode of *The Brady Bunch* come to glowing life.

In the episode, it was near Christmas and Cindy Brady asked a shopping mall Santa Claus to give laryngitis-stricken Mrs. Brady back her voice so Mrs. Brady might sing in church. Mrs. Brady's face on TV was a perfect equilateral triangle, a hunk of head displaying all the properties of a harmonious composition. Joan's mother's head was round and shapeless and her face was often frown-twisted and Joan wished very much for a mother more like Mrs. Brady, a mother who was beautiful and kind and super blonde, a mother without such a strong Long Island accent, a demure mother who sang in church. Joan's mother did not even go to church, although she did possess a serious love of cherubs. Their living room walls were covered in framed portraits of second-rate knock-off Raphaels, angels with polished apple cheeks and penitent saucer eyes. Nothing weird like that hung up in the Bradys' house, so far as Joan could see.

Joan must have gotten swept up in the show, or perhaps the laugh track blotted out the sound of footsteps, because suddenly there her mother was, marching forward toward the Bradys. She lifted up her arms, sheathed to the elbow in clammy blue latex cleaning gloves, and with her hands covered the faces on the screen (though Joan could still spy bits of Brady girl hair peeking blondely out between the webs of her fingers).

"I said no TV." Joan's mother frowned. "Didn't I say no TV? Joan. It's brain-rot. Do you know it'll rot your brain? There are *studies*." She stopped covering the TV with her hands in order to face Joan and cross her arms over her chest. Her cheeks puffed out, granting her already round face a cartoonish appearance. "What are you gawking at?" she asked Joan.

"Nothing."

"Keep your eyes to yourself. Aren't you supposed to be cleaning your room?"

Joan looked away, shrugged. Disobedience felt like a new toy, a brilliant baby doll that spoke words more wondrous than "Mama." After nearly a minute of tense inactivity, Joan's mother did not just turn the TV off but unplugged it altogether, the screen sizzling in static exhalation. She hoisted Joan up from the rug, dragged her down the hall to her room and shut the door. Her cleaning gloves had left their damp latex smell on Joan's skin. Joan covered her nose with her ponytail until she smelled her own self again. In other houses, she knew, *The Brady Bunch* continued. Somewhere problems were solved. Long hair was swung. An invisible audience laughed. Fell silent. Laughed again.

Out of boredom that day, and envy of those invisible audiences,

Joan created an invisible friend and named her Cind. The name came, of course, from the youngest, blondest, most ringleted Brady daughter, Cindy. Joan shortened the name because she didn't want to completely conflate the child she was imagining with the real TV one. She wanted to acknowledge from the start that hers was the lesser creation—a sort of compensation.

Although Cind was technically a spin-off, she quickly evolved into something very different from her television counterpart. Cind was cute like the Brady daughter, sure, with big blue eyes (much more charming than Joan's brown eyes), tufts of gold hair gathered into pigtails (Joan had dark hair always put in braids), and deep dimple dents (Joan's face was excessively freckled). But for all her cuteness, Cind was also kind of creepy. Joan had ended up imagining her into the three-dimensional space of her bedroom covered not in the skin of a small child, but the surface of the small screen. Cind's face crawled with what seemed a tight net of glimmering multicolored insects— oversized pixels instead of flesh. Her eyes, also, Joan had imagined too literally: they flickered with electricity and sometimes resembled kaleidoscopes, the lambent blue flecks of the irises swimming, flow- ing, moving constantly with strange symmetry. Because Cind was an imaginary child carved from another imaginary child, she seemed exponentially more phantasmic, spectral to the second power.

She was not TV-perfect, but she would have to do.

After introductions, Joan ordered Cind to hide with her under the bed because a monster was coming. Together they crawled beneath Joan's mattress, poking at the diamonds of its frame, breathing in the claustral under-the-bed stink. Once they were properly settled, Joan jabbered to her about how gross the monster was, booger-colored and slimy, too. Cind did not say a thing, but stayed close as Joan pictured the two of them running from the monster in the thick of the forest beyond the backyard. Joan shifted her arms a little under the bed, and kicked her legs to simulate their flight. They stayed there, twitching together like dreaming dogs, right up until Joan's mother opened the door to Joan's room and sighed at the mess and announced Joan's father's arrival.

When Joan went to hug him, he smelled like another family's fabric softener. He moved in with that other family a few weeks later. Other than occasional weekend dinners in the city, she saw him rarely. However, Cind, unlike Joan's father, kept up her regular appearances all summer, until school began and Joan forgot about her entirely. Cind, too, eventually vanished.

But she showed up again, decades later, in the hospital—right next to the machinery measuring Joan's unconscious mother's heart.

■ ■ ■

Of course, Joan did not know what to say to her at first.

Cind—still blond, still pigtailed—was breathing hard, as if she had just run a great distance. Her exhalations sounded like a snowy TV that had lost a transmission. Her inhalations just sounded kind of wheezy. She wore overalls and a pink shirt and pink sneakers, and she still looked like a five-year-old girl, although by this point, technically, she was in her thirties, like Joan, who sat there in slacks and a sweater the color of split pea soup.

A whole minute passed between Joan and Cind in silence. At last, Joan cleared her throat, which was very dry. "Wow, Cind!" Joan's voice wobbled from her great effort at enthusiasm. "Wow, wow, wow. You haven't aged a bit!"

Cind tilted her head. "You *definitely* have."

Joan had not thought to imagine what Cind's voice might sound like now, after so many years. If someone had asked her to guess what an invisible child's voice resembled to an adult, she would have gone with the lyrical. Wind chimes in a suburban spring, maybe, or birds singing on a summer morning. But, at least in this hospital room, Cind's voice was actually closer to the laugh track from a sitcom going off in an empty room. Joan could sense the static at its core, a sound designating her as nothing more than signal, electrical output. Should she treat this Cind like so much white noise? Should she treat her as a symptom, a preemptive sign of grief? The doctors had told her that her mother might not wake up, and that must be why Cind was here, of course. It was simple, it was grossly Freudian, yes, just a sign of grief. But how do you interact with a sign of grief, when it approaches you so audaciously? What do you say to a branch in a thicket of the brain's figments and fictions?

"Want a Coke or something?" Joan tried. She lowered her voice. "From the cafeteria?"

" 'Kay," Cind said.

Joan rose to her feet. Her legs, to her own surprise, were steady. She and Cind walked together into the hallway.

. . .

Not long before Joan's mother had been hospitalized, she had called up Joan and they'd had a pretty shitty conversation. Joan had told her mother she'd ended things with Jeff and her mother had said, "What, honey?" and before Joan could say more, her mother had said, "Joan, you're getting older, what about kids?"

And Joan had told her mother what she herself had known for some time: she did not want children.

Silence. On the phone, Joan could not see her mother, but she could imagine an array of facial expressions that might pair with the breathy sound of her speechlessness. A sneer. A smirk. A pout. Joan imagined her invisible mother shaking her head, mouthing a curse to the fleet of kid-angels hanging on the walls.

At last, her mother had said, "You'll regret that choice."

"I won't regret it, Mom."

"Later on, you'll regret it."

"I've thought it over."

"Me, I wanted a big family, always. I wanted lots more kids besides you. But your father didn't feel the same way. And of course, then he left."

"I know, Mom."

"And so I thought grandchildren, yes, those will do. Lots of those."

"I know, Mom."

"I just don't understand. It's a woman's privilege."

"So because I don't want kids, I'm not a woman?"

"I am saying you *are* a woman. And it's your privilege."

Joan hung up the phone and breathed into the quiet of her apartment.

Since her mother had lost consciousness, Joan had thought over the conversation again and again, and each time she imagined that silence, it seemed different in her memory. Newly final.

. . .

But now, here, in the hospital hallway, walking beside her: the only child Joan had ever created. She seemed more real, more vivid, than Joan's mother, who was pale and unconscious, stretched out, not speaking.

. . .

The line in the cafeteria consisted of a bald man, a large woman, a silent couple in button-up shirts. None of them seemed to see Cind. But then none of them seemed to see Joan, either.

Joan bought only a coffee, a Coke, and some M&Ms. At the long white cafeteria table, Cind ran her thumbnail over the candy wrapper. One of her overall straps looked ready to fall off her shoulder.

The shoulder's flesh shimmered like the scales of a rainbow trout; the pixels that covered her had acquired, with the years, a new iridescence. Joan couldn't bring herself to reach forward and readjust the strap. Instead she poured another packet of half-and-half into her coffee and watched the cream dissolve, melding with the greater mass around it.

Joan and Cind sat without speaking. They sat for a long time. The woman ahead of Joan on the cafeteria line had finished her food and was placing her empty tray on top of a flat trashcan. The bald man who had been behind Joan in line was wiping his mouth with a napkin. Also, he was looking at Joan. When Joan caught his eye, he shifted his gaze and his forehead crinkled. He appeared, now, to be looking at Cind. Straight at Cind.

Which was impossible. Wasn't it? Only what if, over the years, Cind had acquired new skills, like visibility? What if, when invisible children went through their adolescence, they did not grow hips and breasts, but just matured enough so that they could in fact be seen? And if the man saw Cind, what must he think of her? Perhaps that she was Joan's slightly strange-looking child. *Was* he really seeing her? He definitely did seem to be staring at Cind, although after a minute he grew bold enough to look at Joan again, to stare back at her. His eyes were pink.

Her mother, if she were here and awake, would say, "Joan, don't look at strangers." No, no, that wasn't right. Her mother would say, "Joan, keep your eyes to yourself." How could Joan forget that line, even for a moment? She repeated it again and again under her breath, like a prayer. Keep your eyes to yourself, Joan, keep your eyes to yourself, keep your eyes. All her mother had wanted was a grandchild with whom she could share such a warning. All her mother had wanted was a big family, noise, children playing together, underfoot, shouting. It was not an extravagant desire, but it was not something Joan had been willing to fulfill. She was not that obedient. Still, right now she was sorry. She was sorry she had not been able to give her mother the family she had wanted.

The bald man was staring at Cind again. Was he? She wanted to get up and ask him but she was nervous he would look at her funny. If she knew for sure that he didn't see Cind, Joan would begin to feel crazy. But the way he was looking—it seemed possible that he was staring at more than empty space. After another minute, he finally got to his feet and left the cafeteria. Joan looked around. Nobody was watching her. All the same, she covered her mouth partway with her hand when she muttered, "Cind?"

Cind was contemplating her Coke.

"Cind." Joan's breath was hot on her palm. "I've got a question for you. Are you listening?"

"I guess," said Cind.

"It's a very, very important question, so I want you to be entirely honest. Can you be entirely honest?"

"I guess," said Cind.

Joan took a deep breath. "Can other people see you now? I mean, people besides me?"

"Yes. Sometimes."

"Sometimes?"

"When I want them to."

A new idea formed then, and although Joan's ideas, too, were mostly invisible, this one had such a weight that for a second Joan bowed her head a little, so that her nose nearly grazed the Styrofoam rim of her coffee cup.

She recovered herself, lifted her head again. Glanced across the cafeteria table.

Pretending to examine the nutritional information on the Coke, she whispered, "Listen. Are you listening, Cind?"

"I guess."

"It's a real long shot, but I have a plan. If my mother wakes up and notices you, I want you to act like you're my daughter."

"Huh?"

"Make her see you, and act like you're mine. Okay? Call her grandma or something. Can you do all that?"

When Joan had been a child, Cind had obeyed her every word. She ran through woods full of sludge monsters. She scaled castle walls in pursuit of mythical birds. She built with Joan little cities out of clumps of under-the-bed dust. But now Joan was a changed person and Cind was a changed sort of imagining.

"Why should I?" she asked.

"She's drugged up, she's dying." Joan glanced down again at the coffee. "There's a chance she'll accept you as reality. And if she does, she'll be really happy. She'll think I obeyed her. She'll think I had a kid, just like she wanted."

Cind stared at Joan with such directness, Joan was taken aback. She had looked at Joan before, but this was a different look, as if someone behind a TV screen had reached out and grazed Joan's face with the back of their hand and left a buzzing electron-y feeling all across Joan's skin.

At last Cind said, "Don't you have a real child to pretend with?"

"That's none of your business, Cind."

"Okay."

"But no. I don't have kids."

"Is that because you only take imaginary lovers?"

"What?"

"You know you can't have children with imaginary lovers, right? Some women don't know this." Cind smiled with a strange triumph. "It's their sperm."

"*What?*"

"Imaginary sperm have this weird texture. Like silk thread. Not sticky enough to make a baby. Just sort of spools around in you. All gyre-y."

"All…"

"I may not look like I've gotten any older," said Cind, "but I *have* gotten older." She slurped up the rest of the Coke noisily through the straw.

Joan took another measured breath. "But will you do it? If she regains consciousness? Will you make her see you?"

Maybe it was all the sugar in her soda, but there was a new gleam to Cind's eye now. "We'll see," she said. She stood up, headed toward the elevator.

Joan followed.

. . .

When they got back to the hospital room, Joan's mother remained unconscious. Equipment continued to monitor her with a trill of beeps, an elaborate soundtrack of alerts and chimes, indicators of invisible dangers that rose and fell and seemed still only half-real. Joan sat down beside her bed once more. She said to Cind, "Let's wait here a little longer. She might wake up."

Cind sat down in a folding chair. "Okay."

"Don't go anywhere, Cind."

"I'll go where I want," Cind said, but she didn't move.

From the hall came the sound of rushing, of small efficient metal wheels clicking and clacking like sets of metallic teeth. It was getting late. Joan looked at Cind, who was still alert as ever, her weird eyes trained on Joan's mother.

"Okay," Joan said. "Okay. It's time to be leaving. We can try tomorrow. She may wake up tomorrow and then we can see if she sees you. Okay? We can try tomorrow. She may wake up tomorrow. We don't know. Okay, Cind?"

And Joan's mother's eyelids fluttered.

Joan grasped the edges of her chair so hard, even the little bones in her wrist seemed to acquire a timorous heartbeat.

Her mother's eyes slowly opened. It was a miracle on the scale of a made-for-TV Christmas movie special, beyond the Bradys, even. It was a wonder. Her eyes were very dark.

"Hi," Joan said once she'd caught her breath. "Mom. Oh, God."

Joan's mother stared hard. Then her gaze traveled to the space next to Joan, the folding chair occupied at the moment by Cind. Did she see her? Joan tried to read the expression on her mother's face. She appeared, staring at Cind, bewildered, her eyes asking, "Who is this?"

So Joan turned to Cind. But Cind seemed changed. She looked now like the cherubs that hung on the walls of Joan's mother's house, her eyes bright, her ringlets extra golden. Perhaps Cind was not just an old imaginary friend, but also a guardian angel, an external guide who had arrived to lead Joan through the hospital wings, to give Joan the chance to lie sweetly to her mother, to offer her mother a sense of peace by assuring her that her genetics would trundle on.

"That's my child," Joan said in a very loud voice, pointing at Cind, but looking at her mother. "I have a daughter. It happened after all! See?"

Joan waited for a thin smile, or a look of amazement to dispel the confusion on her mother's face. Instead she blinked and Joan saw her eyes say again, "Who is this?"

She was looking at Joan. Cind looked Joan's way too.

"Oh," Joan said.

"Who is this?" said the eyes of Joan's mother, and Joan realized that it was Joan herself that her mother could not place, Joan who she could not recognize.

After another minute her mother's eyes closed again.

Joan got to her feet. She needed to leave. She did not want someone to come in and tell her to leave. She would go before then.

"Come on, Cind," Joan said. "Let's get out of here."

But Cind didn't move. She stayed beside Joan's mother's bed, swinging her legs, waiting for some new game to begin, maybe, or some old monster to appear. So Joan left the room without her and took the elevator downstairs. The bald man was exiting the hospital too. He looked at Joan and she had the sudden awful sense that he was working up the courage to give her his number. She rushed past him before he could speak to her. She did not want to know the sound of his voice.

An empty plastic bag swooped bat-like around the hospital parking lot, displaying the red supermarket logo on its front. Joan was shivering. It took her a minute to find and recognize her car, and another minute to make her feet move toward it. Had that happened? Had her mother woken up? Had she looked at Joan, with no recognition? As Joan drove out of the lot, she glanced back at the white bulk of hospital. Some of its windows seemed to stare back at her and other windows blinked. A few windows were dark.

The Cind inside that hospital was not Joan's Cind. She was not her old friend. And she was not a guardian angel. She was a prophet, foretelling what Joan's mother would become to Joan: A half made-up being without real breath. A person whose image shifted in Joan's mind like shadows on a screen. "She'll live on in your memory." Wasn't that what people would say, once it was all over? But Joan's mother would not be preserved solely in memory. She would also be preserved in imagination, and that was the scarier place by far.

A thick fog was gathering under the streetlamps and Joan's hands were shaking. She pulled over into an empty lot just to be safe. There she breathed deeply into the special quiet generated by locked-up strip mall stores. She leaned her head for a moment against the car window. When she lifted it again, she saw the smudged print of her left temple glow in a burst of passing headlights, taking on its own life.

Ghost Train

Nik and I first met in a used bookstore in downtown Manhattan. This was about three weeks after his arrival in New York from Germany. I was looking through paperbacks by Henry James because the over-ambitious book club I belonged to was about to start *The Portrait of a Lady*. Nik was looking through paperbacks by Henry James because he felt James was good for his English. He turned to me and his eyes were gray and clear. I remember trying to earnestly discuss the thematic treatment of personal responsibility in *Daisy Miller* while also silently calculating when I'd last washed the faded blue dress I was wearing, the dress I'd pulled from the hamper that morning, because I hadn't known I'd meet someone like Nik. We ended up leaving the bookstore together, walking for a long while. It was a drizzly, sleepy Sunday in March and the trees looked ready to yawn green from all their buds.

We walked across the Williamsburg Bridge, raising our voices whenever the train passed. Nik did something with computers and the cloud, could write code, which made him essentially trilingual, I told him. I told him, too, that I could say maybe three French words and three Yiddish phrases and that was it. He said, "It's okay. It's normal here. You are American." I couldn't argue with that. We found a bar on the other side of the bridge, in a place that had once been some kind of warehouse and could now sell overpriced beer precisely because it had once been some kind of warehouse. Nik said, "It is the same in Berlin." The bar was dark and didn't smell too bad. When our drinks arrived, I said, "So do you want to move to New York for good or something? Are you looking to transfer branches permanently?"

"No, no. This is fun, being here now, for the next few months. I love New York. When I was a teenager, you know, I loved Woody Allen movies." He gave me a significant look. "Very much."

"Sure," I said. "Me, too."

"Yes. He is very funny. But I could never live here permanently. Not in the United States."

"Why not?"

"I can't picture it. Besides, my mother thinks I'll get robbed and mugged and shot here. Everyone carries guns."

"Not me," I said.

"It's not you I'm worried about. You're an editorial assistant."

Nik treated me to my first drink, and my second drink, and my third. He bought me foreign beers with names I quickly forgot. We talked more about books and then more about one another.

"You're so tall," I said after a while of drinking. "You're so blond."

"I'm not blond," he said. "I have brown hair."

"It's blond." I seized his arm. "It's definitely blond."

"It's brown," he said. "You just don't know what actual blond hair looks like."

"Maybe you're dirty blond," I said. "But I don't even know about that."

He smiled, shook his head. "It's brown."

We were pressed together against the bar.

"What do you like best about New York?" I looked him right in the eye, so the question wouldn't just sound like a native's casual small talk, but would instead seem vested with real concern. "How does it compare to Berlin?"

"Berlin is full of New Yorkers, too." He shrugged. "I guess the biggest difference is you can sense the age here. The lack of age here. It's new. Your city, I mean, your city is new. It is called *New York*, after all!"

"Ha-ha."

"Of course, many of the buildings in Berlin are not so old. Because much of the city had to be rebuilt. Still, Berlin has been around in one form or another since the thirteenth century."

"But the river is old," I said, gesturing in what I guessed might be the direction of the East River. "The pigeons are old. At least biologically speaking. Species-wise. The place itself is as old as any other planet earth place. Right? In one form or another? Its past is just less documented."

"That is a good, deep point you make," Nik said.

"Well, I'm not sure about that."

"No, it is a very good, very deep point you make."

"You just have to imagine it. I mean, imagine how old this place really is. Sometimes as a kid I'd look out the window and I'd look at the grocery store or the Borders bookstore, and I'd imagine what had stood where those stores stood, long before they were built. Of course, now all the Borders are gone, too, so maybe what I'm getting at doesn't make much sense."

"Right," Nik said. "I do understand what you mean. There were people here, after all, is what you mean."

"Undocumented," I said.

"People here once. And then . . ."

"Right," I said.

"Like in *The Last of the Mohicans*! Have you seen that film? Is that what you mean?"

"That's what I mean. I mean I think that's what I mean, I mean."

"You are drunk!" he said.

"Just tipsy!" I said. "I haven't seen that film."

"You should see that film. Daniel Day-Lewis has very long hair in it."

I touched Nik's hair with the tips of my fingers. Before I could stop myself I said, "You know, I had relatives in Germany. On my mother's side."

"Yes?"

"Most got out before the war. But not all."

"Oh, Jenna," Nik said.

"Not to be a buzz kill." I tried smiling at him.

"Your hair," he said then, palming the back of my head, "is beautiful. Nice and thick."

"Dark brown."

"Yes," he said. "This we agree on."

I almost asked him then about his own family's past, where they were during World War II. But the question sounded like something some old interviewer on PBS might ask an even older interviewee with shaking hands. An accusatory question posing as benign public television. Anyway, the answer wouldn't matter, it wouldn't change anything, I told myself. Still, maybe it was something we should talk about?

But the first date didn't seem like the best time to ask. And the second didn't either—still too early. I wasn't sure what the official timeline was for querying your boyfriend about Nazis in his family. All I knew was, as things progressed, it soon seemed too late to ask. Embarrassing to ask, somehow. Like admitting you've forgotten the name of someone you've been bantering with at work for weeks, someone you laugh hard with, even, sometimes at lunch. I reminded myself that in the textbook materials I helped collate, there were always lots of references to the global village. Nik and I were both a part of the global village. Whatever that meant. It had something to do with Coca-Cola and the Internet. Anyway, what mattered was that Nik was easy to talk to and intelligent and taller than I was, and he was not unkind. He spoke softly but with great precision. For example, if you asked him to say, "Coca-Cola and the Internet," each consonant would have its own distinct click-clack sound.

• • •

In New York, Nik was always taking photos. His two favorite subjects were the squirrels in the park, and me. Once, he took a photo of me *with* a squirrel in the park, and had the photo printed and framed. In the photo, I kneel on one of the park's gravel pathways, with some peanuts in my palm. About a yard away, a squirrel stands on its hind legs, inspecting me intently. My hair is a curly mess, my lips are chapped, but Nik said, when I saw the framed picture on his nightstand, "You look beautiful here in this photograph."

"Well," I said, "at least the squirrel looks okay."

"I love your expression and the squirrel's expression. But especially your expression, Jenna. You look so open and so curious, like this is the first squirrel you have seen in the universe. That openness." He put his arms around me. "It is rare and nice."

"What you're calling my open expression is actually my 'I-hope-you-don't-have-rabies' expression."

"Funny. But no. That is an open expression on your face."

Did Nik really speak as woodenly as that? No. Probably no. Probably I am forgetting to include the more real, lively moments between us. And that is a disservice to our history. I should make space for the other things: how I would make fun of his fear of birds, how he thrilled over the chopped salad kits the supermarket sold, the way we would stay up for hours talking about the authors we'd only discovered in college but who felt like they'd been talking to us for ages. But maybe that list, also, is disingenuous. Maybe the liveliest moments were when I was showing him the city and we weren't talking, we were just looking together. The way Nik saw my city *new*—that maybe was the thing that really excited me. A surprised glance from him at an unexpected fountain or a beautiful street could be enough to make me forget all my own history with that fountain (wading there with Jake in sophomore year) or with that street (crying at my mother as a child when she refused to get me ice cream at the shop on the corner). When he took my empty hand, my mind went empty, a tabula rasa sort of thing. Nobody had done that to me before, stripped my mind of memory so that I felt naked even before we went to bed.

We went to more bookstores while Nik was in New York, more parks. We went to museums and examined the different bones of different dinosaurs: cervical vertebrae, a fragmented femur. I pointed to the new luxury high rises going up and said, with disgust, "This city's changing," which made Nik nod very solemnly. We dated just long enough to decide we were in love. In May he was transferred back to his company's Berlin office.

"You should visit me in the summer," he said before he left, taking both my hands in his as we stood on the Brooklyn Bridge. "Visit me. When you're not collating PDFs or what have you."

"I can get maybe a week off?"

"So get maybe a week off." He reached out to touch my hair. "Stay with me for a few days in Berlin and then I'll take a few days off work and then we'll go somewhere else. A different place." Cars streamed past us, people eager to get home. "That way," Nik went on, "it can be like we're both on vacation together. You know? We've never had that. And then you can fly back to New York directly from wherever we go together."

"And then?" I said.

And then we had fallen silent. We both knew we should talk

about what we would do after my trip, if we'd break up or not, but neither of us seemed up for conversing much about the future.

. . .

Before I'd left for Berlin to visit Nik, my mother met me for coffee and gave me a brand new camera. She said, "It has a crazy zoom!" She said, also, "Have a wonderful time with Nik! He seems very polite and he has a job!" But then she took a long sip of coffee, thunked the mug on the table, and added, "But me myself, personally?" Her face flushed pink. "Me? I wouldn't feel safe there. I mean I wouldn't be able to go there."

"Mom."

"You don't have a sense," she said, "of how the past and the present fit together or jumble up. Of how those timelines overlap. For me, at least, it'd feel haunted."

I thought she was being a little melodramatic. All of that was a couple of generations removed from me and it wasn't like we ever went to synagogue or anything like that. All we did was celebrate Hanukkah, and we did that mostly so I wouldn't feel left out about not celebrating Christmas. Still, I was sure when I stepped off the plane in Germany, I'd sense something of what she mentioned. A twinge, at least, of history. A great-grand-aunt had lived in Berlin and then had been taken away on a train. There was documentation of her getting on a train to one of the camps, but no documentation of her getting off or entering the camps. She had disappeared. In school, I'd given several reports on her, but she seemed so distant from me I felt I was telling a made-up story about a made-up person. "It's tragic," my teachers always said at the end of my report. "Jenna, it's truly tragic." Their shoulders would slump, their heads would bow, as if an immense weight had been laid across their shoulders.

"I know," I'd say, in front of the whole class. "It's tragic."

Then I'd try to bow my head, too, pretending I felt the far-off past fragmenting the present moment, pretending to feel that same weight on my shoulders.

In JFK, running late for my flight to Berlin, I anticipated finally feeling that weight, that history. I thought I'd sense the past on my skin, like some sort of denser air, like a ghost. I raced to my gate and got stuck in a winding line at the security checkpoint. Signs told me it was time to take off my shoes, and to empty my carry-on of liquid and razors. A third sign said, in big black capital letters, "Please be advised, snow globes are not allowed through the security checkpoint. Your safety is our priority." The sign slowed me down for a moment. Was there a hall of confiscated snow globes somewhere in JFK?

I picked up my pace again and made it to the plane. The flight attendants smiled wide and spoke a fast, clipped English. They gave me tea and small dark chocolates. I had a window seat and looked down on the blue sky. Across the sea, Nik was waiting. Across the sea! Lyrical as hell. Nik, waiting for me, maybe with a copy of *The Ambassadors*. Maybe I wouldn't feel the past at all when I landed. Maybe I'd just feel the future. Maybe I'd move there, to Berlin, or something. People my age did that. It was cheaper in Berlin, they said. I wouldn't need to have so many roommates.

Nik met me at the gate with coffee. We hadn't seen each other in three weeks. He'd brought a big umbrella, since it was raining out. The train taking us from the airport was clean, the seats upholstered, the people quiet. I tried to look outside the window dripping with rain, but I kept falling asleep. I felt no danger anywhere. Certainly I didn't feel haunted. I felt sleepy and excited that I was going to have sex again. We got off the train at a stop surrounded by kebab shops. Then we were in Nik's apartment. He guided me toward his bedroom. The picture of the squirrel and me sat on his desk. He took off my shoes and my socks and my shirt and my pants and my bra and my underwear, then said, "I'm going to get you some water first. I don't want you to be dehydrated."

I followed him, naked, into the kitchen. He had the same Brita filter he'd used in New York, the same filter that had purified water for me in his apartment there.

. . .

The day after I arrived in Berlin, Nik had to go to work. He woke me up before he left and said, "The jet-lag will be easier if you just go through the day like normal. Experience the city. Trust me."

"Okay," I mumbled, half asleep. He gave me a detailed map, and then he went to work. While he was in the office, I wandered around the memorials Nik had told me about. I'd decided I would wander from nine to five, like it was my job. "The memorials are very tasteful," Nik had said. "I've been very many times on class trips. And it will be easy for you. Everyone speaks English. It's muggy out, but bring a small sweater, as it will be air-conditioned if you go to a museum."

I went to a museum called the Topography of Terror, built on the site that had once housed the headquarters of the Gestapo and the SS, and I looked at all the poster displays until my legs started to ache, to wobble. I went to the memorial by the Tiergarten: big stone slabs, around which children played hide and seek and teenagers tanned and tourists took pictures. I took a picture of the tourists taking pictures of the Holocaust memorial and then I felt kind of sick, like I was trying to make some statement or like I was trying to separate my own touristing self from these people. My legs still hurt. Across from the memorial was a Dunkin' Donuts. I thought about going into the Dunkin' Donuts to sit down in the air-conditioned cool, but then decided that was not in the spirit of travel abroad. A guy stepped forward, asked me in English if I might want a beer special. I said no. Nik was right: everybody spoke to me in English. There was even a sign about a new building being constructed and someone had scrawled on it, in English, "Stop gentrification!!"

I walked a little more. Only a block away from the Holocaust memorial was Hitler's bunker, where he'd married Eva Braun and killed himself as the Allies closed in. A plaque explained this history. It *was* muggy out. I was sweating. Behind the plaque were a housing complex and a spa that offered something called "Biocosmetic Massage." I didn't fully comprehend not only what had happened here in the past, but what was happening here now, in the present. What was a biocosmetic massage? I turned around and retraced my steps. I was asked again about beer specials, and again I shook my head. After a while, I sat down in the green park beside the Holocaust memorial, a park dense with trees.

I couldn't imagine any of it. Any of the history that had happened here. I couldn't feel the weight my mother had told me she'd feel. I could just feel the heat of the day. I closed my eyes. Still jet-lagged, I ended up falling asleep and only started awake, heart beating hard, when a clatter of stroller wheels passed by my park bench. I checked for my bag: still there. Wallet: still there.

But where was my camera?

I dug through my shoulder bag and could not find it. I almost began to cry. But then, then, there! Something boxy between the ribs of the umbrella I had stashed in the bag, just in case the rain started up again. I breathed out. The camera felt like some extra layer of protection.

At five o'clock I followed Nik's directions and took the train to the Turkish market, a series of stands along the Landwehr Canal, parallel to the Spree River. I met him by a stand selling bright fabrics by the meter. Nik and I bought hummus and pita bread and feta and small nut-filled desserts neither of us had ever eaten before, desserts we didn't know the names for. Behind the stands ran the canal, its bank muddy from the rain the night before. We walked down there, our sneakers leaving tracks. Despite the rain, lovers lined up along the bank, sitting on one another's sweatshirts, kissing or sharing bottles of wine. We sat down with our food and looked at the water and the swans and, spanning the canal, a bridge brightened with loud blue graffiti and swan shit.

Nik asked, "Did you have fun today?"

"You know I went to the Holocaust memorial, right? And a museum called Topography of Terror?"

"Well, I did not mean fun as in *fun*. Are you still jet-lagged? You know—"

The couple next to us, two teenagers speaking French, screamed out. I jerked away from Nik. The yellow yolk of an egg dripped just to the right of the French girl's flip-flop. Giggles behind us. Another cracking sound, this one right beside Nik. I turned. Two children, two boys, grinning. The kids were throwing eggs at the lovers on the bank.

"I want to move," I said to Nik. Even though the eggs hadn't hit me, I felt a sudden slimy coolness on the back of my neck. "Nik," I said.

"Jenna, really, it's fine, it's fine."

I knew he was right. But I still felt the coolness. I shook my head. "No, let's just move."

"They don't have the courage to hit us. The game's all in near misses, you see? You are overreacting."

"Please."

"It will give them satisfaction. They want you to react. Don't give into them. Enjoy yourself. The view."

"Nik."

He squinted at me. "I was thinking we can go to a club tonight, if you want. There's this club in an abandoned power plant, which Americans like. Though I have to get up early for work."

More giggles behind us.

"Nik."

"And then, this weekend, Vienna!"

"Nik."

"They're just the children of the men who own the stands. Jenna. Is it that they're Muslim?"

"What?" I said.

"I thought you were anti-occupation."

"I am!" I said. "I just don't want to be egged." I closed my eyes. "Jesus, Nik."

"They're just children. Harmless. We're staying."

And for a moment he held me there. He encircled his fingers around my wrist and held me there and I felt colder than ever. I pulled away. "No," I said, "let's move. Look, Nik, it's about to rain anyway."

. . .

It poured all the rest of that week. Historic floods, washed-out roads. By the morning of our trip to Vienna, the Elbe River, swollen from heavy rainfall, had spilled over its banks, wrecking homes and causing significant train delays. But Nik and I had already bought our Deutsche Bahn tickets from Berlin, reserved our room in a hostel, made a list of things to see. We didn't want to cancel our trip, especially since soon I would be heading back to New York, and who knew when we'd get a chance to do this again, to travel as a couple. We got up very early, went to the Berlin Hauptbahnhof, bought croissants, found our track. Almost as soon as we were on the train, I fell asleep.

When I woke up again, hours later, and looked out the window, ducks were swimming past a partially submerged streetlamp.

"Good morning," Nik said and handed me a piece of chocolate.

Our train click-clacked forward across the elevated tracks at such a sleepy speed that I was able to not only closely inspect the damage from the recent flood, but to photograph it with my mother's camera. I took a photo of people paddling in boats around their backyards. I took a photo of windows boarded with wood to keep out water. I took a photo of the gray river surging forward, and a photo of that same river in the tangled tops of trees. I took a photo of a bag of Euro-Cheetos floating past.

Nik took my hand. "Jenna."

His blond hair, in the afternoon sun, looked nearly white, and his eyebrows were so pale as to seem invisible. I freed my hand from his and turned the camera on him. He squinted, his eyes reduced to nacreous slivers. Someone who didn't know Nik might guess that he was facing an overwhelming light, but his squinting expression was actually how he expressed disapproval. Instead of frowning, he acted like he couldn't quite believe what was before him, acted like there must be something wrong with his vision. Without saying a word, he told me via squint that he was surprised I would think this moment the right time to take a picture of my lover, with all those wrecked homes just outside the train. What about their trauma, his squint asked me, and what about all the implications of global warming behind their trauma, of bigger worldwide issues, and was I trying to steal some of the solemnity from this tragedy?

I saw his point. I put the camera down. Our books rested closed on our laps.

The uniformed man who had earlier inspected our tickets passed by and inspected our window's contents. He and Nik exchanged fast words in German, back and forth. Then a little boy on the train, American like me, started to screech, "Look outside, look outside! That swing set is almost underwater!" He sounded happy about the weirdness of it all, too happy, and perhaps he caught some significant look from one of his parents, because next he added, very seriously, "It's so sad. It's so sad."

Yet he sounded even happier when he said those words—pleased, I guessed, with his own gravity. I imagined his nose pressed to the window. Nik's hand pressed into mine.

. . .

Eventually, as our train to Vienna moved farther south, as the geography changed, the flooding went down. Nik and I made it to our destination, four hours late. The train station was pretty dry, only a few puddles. We got almost immediately onto another train, a city train, and told each other to look at different buildings out the window. "It looks so old," we said, almost together. I pointed out some especially pretty mullioned windows and said, "Maybe Mozart looked out of one of those windows while he took a shit in the toilet."

"Chamber pots," said Nik. "Actually, they used chamber pots, I think."

Then we were at our hostel, located right next to the Wurstel-prater amusement park. We grabbed some brochures from the front desk, and then we went upstairs. Nik had gotten us a private room with a skylight that showed the rotating tips of the park's famous Ferris wheel.

"It was in the movie *The Third Man*, Nik," I said. "It's the Ferris wheel Orson Welles rides, and gives his famous speech about people below just being little dots to squash."

"I know. It says so in this enthused little brochure." Nik rolled up one of the brochures and tapped me on the head with it. I grabbed it and unrolled it. "Highlights and History!" it was titled. The brochure from the hostel's front desk said, "The Prater was once imperial hunting ground and only accessible for the aristocracy, until the Austrian

Emperor Josef II donated the area to the Viennese in 1766 as a public leisure center!" It said, "In 1913, Adolf Hitler, Leon Trotsky, Josip Tito, Sigmund Freud, and Joseph Stalin all lived within a few miles of each other in central Vienna!!!!"

Nik really wanted to check out the vineyards surrounding the city and I really wanted to go to this snow globe museum the brochure mentioned, mostly because its name was insane: "Original Wiener Schneekugelmanufaktur," I read to Nik. " 'In the museum you will see where the very first snow globes have been invented by the current owner's grandfather.' " Nik kissed my neck. Outside the skylight rose the important-looking tips of important-looking buildings. I kept reading: " 'In the pleasant atmosphere of our 250-year-old building you will see both historic and current themes produced in the snow globes.' Nik!" I cried. "It's run by this guy named Erwin Perzy III!"

We decided for tonight we'd just ride the famous Ferris wheel, since it was right outside our window. Nik suggested that, before we got on the Ferris wheel, we should first explore the amusement park as a whole.

"It will make it more impressive," he said, "when we're suddenly above everything we've just walked through."

. . .

There was no charge to get into the amusement park in Vienna—different rides were owned by different families—and so we wandered freely. I took pictures of people and now Nik didn't reprimand me. I took a photo of a woman in a white hijab holding the hand of a blond little girl face-painted like a tiger. I took a photo of a skinny guy feeding his dog fried dough. I took a photo of a balloon man, selling helium-filled versions of Hello Kitty, Dora the Explorer, a seriously off-blue Smurf.

"Look at that," Nik and I said together.

"Look at that."

And we got even more excited when we both pointed to the same thing at the same time and said those words in the same way, because that sameness felt like love.

I took photos of some of the rides, too. There was a carousel but the ponies weren't plastic, they were real, huffing out horsey breaths as they rotated round and round in sawdust. There were bumper cars, of course, and a mural on the ride's walls: paintings of sloe-eyed yellow-haired women in denim cut-offs and red-and-white-striped blue-star-spangled bras, their bodies draped over the hoods of cars.

Nik was looking beneath the mural at the actual bumper cars, which contained no women at all. Just tiny children, screaming and smiling at the same time, calling out to each other in different languages, joyfully crashing into one another. They were cheered on by mothers in baggy blouses and flower-printed jean shorts.

"Jorts," said Nik, pointing to one of the mothers' shorts.

"Jorts are definitely not in Henry James." I elbowed him in the ribs. "Your English really is excellent."

"Now it's up to you to learn some excellent German. Here. We'll start today."

In front of one of the Prater's haunted house rides, Nik told me that the German term for this ride translates in English to "ghost train." *Geisterbahn*. A feminine noun.

"A feminine noun," I repeated. Then I looked at the haunted house before us: a façade of fake dungeon-ish stones, out of which projected plastic grinning demon creatures that seemed more genetically tied to garden gnomes than genuine devils. Written near the haunted house's top, in bubble letters was, indeed, "*Geisterbahn*."

Nik put his arm around me. "We use this same term, too, for the tunnel of love. In German, *Geisterbahn* also means tunnel of love."

"So both the haunted houses *and* the tunnel of love count as ghost trains? The rides are called the exact same thing?"

"Yes."

"Swans versus serial killers? You wouldn't call those by the same term. Are you sure it's the same term?"

Nik squinted, his eyebrows slanting toward each other. At last he said, "Yes, they're both called ghost trains."

Mechanical howls wafted from the haunted house beside us.

Nik turned to me. He rubbed my back. He said, "Would you ever want to live here?"

The guy who had fed his dog fried dough passed us. The dog barked.

Would I ever want to live here.

I looked very intensely at one of the plastic garden gnomes/demons. Where was *here*? Did he mean the haunted house? Sweeping up the fake cobwebs. Falling asleep among skeletons. Waking up next to a screaming automaton. Making breakfast and some monster pops out at you just as the Pop-Tarts leap out of the toaster.

Would you ever want to live here?

Almost definitely he didn't mean the haunted house. Maybe he meant would I ever want to live in Vienna. Or Europe more generally. No, what he meant, really, was would I be able to live with him back in Berlin. I must have guessed this question would be coming, but it was like my mind going blank on a test. I couldn't remember the answer I had planned, or if I had even planned an answer.

"I'd never want to live in a haunted house," I said, pretending to misunderstand. Then I shrugged. But I still had my arms around his neck so the shrug read more like a jerky attempt to pull him to me, even closer. There was a funny thrumming in my ears. I smelled fried dough, cotton candy and elephant ears, all around us.

"What do you say we ride the famous Ferris wheel now?" I asked.

"Okay," Nik said. "Okay."

. . .

Staring up from below the Ferris wheel, the bright red cars swinging back and forth looked like they might shake themselves loose. Inside the ride's entrance there was a very small museum devoted to the wheel, a series of low-tech dioramas featuring Vienna and the Ferris wheel at different times. One diorama took place during a snowy season, tiny diorama people in sleighs skidding around the Ferris wheel. Another diorama depicted the wheel in some old timey time, more tiny diorama people in homunculus hoop skirts and hats, strolling arm in arm.

Among the merry dioramas was an extremely depressing one of the Ferris wheel post–World War II. All the bright red cars were gone. The only thing standing was the Ferris wheel's skeleton, its rim, its spokes, unmoving and unpopulated. A couple of bare gray trees surrounded it, and next to the wheel was a gray building with a red-orange bulb shining through its window—a diorama representation of fire from a bombing, I guessed. It was like seeing a children's dollhouse with death and destruction inhabiting the room in lieu of Barbies. I thought about the American boy on the train, looking out at the flood: "It's so sad. It's so sad." The text beside this diorama said—in German, in English, in Italian, in Chinese—"After the destruction of World War II, the reconstruction of the Prater was a priority for the Viennese and a symbol of recovery. And still the Giant Ferris Wheel turns....."

"All those ellipses are pretty intense," I told Nik, but he was not by my side anymore. I wanted him next to me, I wanted very much to talk about those ellipses. Never before had punctuation thrown me into such a panic and I wasn't sure why. But Nik had already rushed past the diorama and now he was at the door leading out of the entrance hall, to the Ferris wheel itself, and he was gesturing to me. I wanted to grab his hand and pull him back. Instead I took a picture of the diorama and then I followed Nik, who was following an attendant. The attendant pointed us to a red car. It was paneled with an orangey wood and big glass windows. We shared this space with several old men and a couple with a baby in a stroller. Declarations of love in language upon language were scratched onto the wood panels. The attendant closed the door to our car. We gripped the metal bar that ran along the window as the wheel began to move and our car began to ascend.

When the wheel started rotating, Nik and I stood close together and looked out. There were hardly any high rises in sight: strict zoning legislation here, said Nick, due to all the UNESCO World Heritage business. We were able to see so far when we looked straight ahead. The green of the park, the slants of the buildings, red roofs, glimpses of train tracks, blue hills in the near distance. When I looked down, I saw the amusement park and the shadow of the turning wheel. Everything was diorama-small.

"That's us." I pointed to the shadow. "There we are."

Nik was still looking straight ahead, at the city's skyline. "Take a picture," he said. I assumed he just meant a picture of the skyline, but then he turned around and grinned at me, a camera-grin. He wanted to be in the picture, too. I raised my camera and got a photo of Vienna and of Nik. He stood with his arms at his side, easy and relaxed, his eyes wide open, looking directly into the lens.

"It's a beautiful city," I said, once the picture was taken.

Nik answered, like I'd asked him a question, "It's how Berlin would look if it hadn't been bombed as much as it was." Matter-of-factly.

I touched the back of his neck. He put his arms around my waist and rested his chin on my shoulder. The sun was going down as the car went up. Nik turned his head and said, into my ear, "I think we had a little bit of a misunderstanding before."

"What?"

"I asked if you would ever live here. And you said not in a haunted house. Do you remember?"

We stood in silence while the men beside us talked in their language.

"Anyway," Nik said, "I meant Berlin. I was wondering. Would you live in Berlin?"

I wanted to say, "Yes." I said, "I don't know. Maybe we should talk about it."

"Well, yes. That is what I am trying to do now. If you're worried about jobs," he said, "I'm sure the government would give you some kind of grant. I have met other girls in Berlin from New York who have received government grants. One is studying the history of Yiddish theater troupes. Another is studying the architectural influence of synagogues."

"Other girls from New York," I said.

"Yes."

I moved away from him a little bit. "Why not say Jewish girls?"

He leaned against our car's railing and shrugged. "Well, they *are* from New York, too."

"But what you mean is they're Jewish."

"Well, they happen to be Jewish."

"If you're asking me to move here, don't you think maybe you should be a little more direct? Don't you think you should say what you mean?"

He blinked at me. "I do say whatever I mean."

"What did your grandfather do?"

"What?" He was too surprised even to squint. He shifted away from the railing and his cheeks went pink.

"It's just not something we've talked about ever."

"It comes out of nowhere."

"I was just wondering." I tried to smile. "I was looking at that crazy diorama below, the one of the Prater after the bombing? And I just started wondering."

"My grandfather worked in a factory."

"What kind of factory?

"Just different kind of factories."

"And your great-grandfather? Where did he work?"

"I don't know. I guess also a factory. What about yours?"

"I'm not sure," I said. "Probably also a factory."

"So the same."

"I guess."

"The same."

We were higher and higher, almost at the wheel's apex.

"What is the question you actually want to ask?" Nik said. "It's not where did they work. It's other things about them. Things that have nothing to do with them, but with circumstances. So? Ask it. Ask it. Because I have asked my question. Twice. Down below and now up here. Twice."

"Your question?"

"Have you forgotten again? Could you live here. Twice. And neither time did you answer. You have neither answered my question nor asked yours. You just stand and watch and take pictures and gape like a child."

He delivered the words very gently. But then he stepped forward and encircled my wrist with his hand.

"There are just certain histories we leave behind," he said. "Enough is enough, right? At some point we are so far away from the past, it is not ours exactly to hold onto."

"That's a good, deep point," I said.

His fingers tightened around my wrist. It was the same way he'd held onto me a few days before at the canal, when the children were throwing their eggs. We're staying, he'd said. His grip had been very firm, and his grip was even firmer now. He couldn't understand why I'd wanted to move.

The wheel was descending again, which meant we were more than halfway through up here, if not too many more people were waiting to get on below us. I was suddenly scared. I was scared I'd always feel haunted by how I was not properly haunted.

I pulled my wrist away, out of Nik's grip. I didn't speak.

"You're right," Nik said at last. "It's a beautiful city."

Just before we reached the bottom, he put his arms around me again, but not as tightly. I leaned into him.

After we got off the wheel, we wandered around the gift shop, each of us in separate corners. I bought postcards for my parents and my friends back home, and some chocolate for myself. When I headed to the cash register, Nik was already heading out of the door of the gift shop, clutching a small bag. The woman at the register said something to me in German. I pushed my purchases mutely across the counter. When I left the gift shop, Nik was standing just outside.

He handed me the little bag. Inside of it was a snow globe of the Ferris wheel. "Vienna" it said at the snow globe's base.

I took the snow globe and shook it and watched the fake snow fall over the wheel and its little red cars.

"I know it's very sentimental," Nik said. "And a little silly. And not actually properly symbolic. After all, it is June."

"That's true."

"I mean it's not like it is even snowing during your visit. Just lots and lots of rain. And I guess if we go to that snow globe museum, you might prefer to buy something like this there."

"No, I like it."

"It's to remember Vienna when you're back home."

A goodbye gift.

I shook the snow globe again, as if that was proof I wouldn't forget.

. . .

My mother said, before I left for Germany, "Enjoy yourself, I guess. Me, personally, I would not enjoy myself. You'll be able to tell, I would be able to tell, that for many people it had been hell."

But some moments it was like heaven, not all the time, but there was this one afternoon in Berlin that was like heaven, or at least like the loveliest of limbos. It was the day before our train trip to Vienna. We went to a bookstore near Alexanderplatz, a chain bookstore but one with a big English section. It was raining outside, and windy, and soon there would be bad floods. Despite our shared umbrella we entered the bookstore dripping wet and laughing at how our hair was plastered flat against our scalps. We were there to pick out books for our eight-hour voyage (which would end up, due to the floods, being over twelve hours). Nik and I headed upstairs, where the English section was. It was extensive, practically a whole bookstore itself, catering to the city's large number of English-speaking ex-pats.

Nik and I wandered around the shelves together. We wandered around the New Fiction, the Classics, past Memoir, past Science, past History, past New Age. We flipped through parallel books, we stood close, we shared random passages out loud.

I read: "The force exerted by the country lane varies according to whether one walks along it or flies over it in an aeroplane. Similarly, the force exerted by a text varies according to whether one is reading it or copying it out."

Nik read: "If you flip a dime a thousand times, you'll get approximately five hundred FDRs and five hundred torches; but you're unlikely to get exactly five hundred of either, because each flip is independent and random."

We tried to help one another determine which books would be best to buy for the train trip. We didn't kiss, we didn't touch, we didn't need to; it would somehow be like an exclamation mark ruining the gravity of a perfect sentence. I didn't want to leave that in-between place, where we were helping each other figure out what to read next.

Still, eventually we had to buy our books and exit the building and walk the street and board the trains and read the stories we had chosen, and think about the stories we decided to try to forget, to leave behind in that store, as we moved forward from that moment and further away from one another.

The Sextrology Woman

Aaron was stuck on the E train, wedged next to a woman who was making him nervous. She looked to be about forty, had long frizzy hair dyed bright red, and was reading a book with the word "Sextrology" on its cover. Ever since the train had stalled, she'd been making little humming sounds as she read, like, "Hmm," and "Huhhhhla." These sounds seemed to be part of a small-talk warm-up, similar to a singer practicing scales before venturing into a more extensive melody. Any second, Aaron suspected, the sextrology woman would turn her head and say something to him. And Aaron didn't feel like listening. He was busy planning his own speech for when his flight arrived in California, the lyrically charged things he'd say to Chloe about the power of love and mold.

We are still being held by the train's dispatcher. Please be patient.

Of course, if the train stayed stuck here much longer, if the suspicious package issue was not dealt with soon, he'd miss his flight out of JFK and wouldn't get to look Chloe in the eye at all, wouldn't get to deliver an in-person speech about why yes-duh an American studies PhD candidate and a mold removal guy could be, no, *should* be together. Tomorrow Chloe was flying to some tropical island for a vacation with her family who, according to Chloe, questioned Aaron's ambition, and would probably talk her into breaking up with him for good. But this whole spontaneously-taking-a-plane-to-California thing was a major point in his favor, even if this time around he'd only get to visit Chloe for about twenty-four hours. Chloe had been impressed with the way Aaron had splurged on the expensive last-minute flight to see her before her vacation. She'd been shocked and flattered that Aaron was acting with such determination. Aaron, too, had surprised himself. And he so rarely surprised himself that this decision to visit Chloe left him feeling expansive, almost buzzed, the same way he felt when he walked into a building that looked utterly ordinary only to discover an extensive fungal colony of the strangest living spores he'd ever laid eyes on. It was as if, although he looked the same as always, he had discovered through Chloe something new and astonishing within himself. A capacity for boldness, risk.

The train shuddered a little, but did not leap forward. Aaron sighed, inaudibly he'd thought, but the sextrology woman next to him must have perceived the sigh as the equivalent to a hearty "hello." She turned to Aaron and said, as if they'd already been talking a long while, "This is ridiculous. I mean, how long can they just trap us in here, like prisoners?"

Aaron gave what he hoped was both a sympathetic but also non-committal little shrug. He had a strong, broad back, though, and large shoulders, so when he shrugged, the movement always seemed more meaningful, more monumental, than it would have on a skinnier, smaller person. The woman certainly read the shrug that way, because she kept talking. "First they raise the fares every five seconds," she said. "Next they do track work that basically suffocates any borough that's not Manhattan or the yupster parts of Brooklyn. And now they delay the train for no good reason? Suspicious package, yeah, sure. My ass is a suspicious package. You know?" She rolled her eyes. "The MTA is disgusting. I mean don't you think it's disgusting? They treat us like dirt, yet they keep raising fares. You can't have it both ways. Even if you're middle class, you're made to feel like you've done something wrong, like you've really dropped the goddamn life-ball. We need some kind of revolution."

Everybody else on the subway had their headphones in or their heads down or a newspaper covering their faces. Across from Aaron sat a teenaged couple that hardly seemed to notice the train had halted. The pink-haired girl had her face buried in the boy's neck, in a manner that was somehow too sloppy to seem vampiric. Aaron looked away, stared down at the big backpack between his feet, containing clean T-shirts with buttons and nice crisp jeans, outfits to show Chloe he was taking himself seriously. He was going to tell her he loved the way she made him take himself more seriously and she would make that face where she was trying not to smile too big, and then she would smile anyway, real big, and the sextrology woman next to him was still talking, of course she was still talking.

"It's robbery, basically. The way the MTA operates." The woman shifted her book so that it was splayed, pages down, on her lap, suggesting that she had officially moved on from the illusion of small talk and was ready to engage Aaron in the full-on song of her opinions. "Not just robbery of our money. But robbery of our time."

Aaron couldn't figure out a way to politely not respond, so he said, "It's unbelievable."

"Right?" said the woman. "It's un-freaking-believable. You a college student?" The woman peered at him from small brown eyes. "Usually I can tell but I can't tell with you. You've got that big backpack like maybe you're a college student?"

Aaron, who had never gone to college, much to Chloe's chagrin (and her family's total shock), scanned the tube of fluorescent light above them. "I'm not in school."

"Oh, thank *God*," the sextrology woman said.

Then she told Aaron she worked as an alcohol and drug counselor for those enrolled at NYU. She despised the students there. That cheered Aaron up more than it should have—Chloe had gone to NYU, and a lot of her friends had gone there with her. While her friends weren't across the board *not* nice people, they were definitely always telling inside jokes that Aaron didn't get and when Aaron showed up at parties, they'd say, "The mold guy is here! Look who's here! It's the mold guy!" At those parties, Aaron often felt like a supporting character in a TV series about young people moving to New York. The weird native guy around for a few episodes to better illuminate the arc of the real star. Chloe's New York was like a televised New York, and a televised New York was a moldless New York. And a moldless New York? Was not Aaron's city. But there was no way to explain all this to the sextrology woman without sounding like he was an insecure little baby.

Anyway, the sextrology woman didn't care about Aaron's story. She was too busy complaining about the students she worked with. "I think all the time about what my forbearers would feel about my job," she said. "Jewish socialists, ree-vo-freaking-lutionaries, rushing away from Poland for the sake of their *lives*, of a better non-dead *future* for their kiddos, trying to find shelter, trying to sneak into a country over a whole goddamn ocean. And here I am, trying to clean up the blood streams of the wealthy quote-unquote elite with some watered-down talk therapy bullshit. No wonder Abe showed up and gave me that hard stare of his."

"Abe?" Aaron said. "Who's Abe? That your boyfriend?"

"No, no, no. My great-uncle, Abe. He's long dead. And he just showed up the one time. His ghost, I mean. Everyone always told me he was a real character."

A ghost. Right. The ghost of Great-Uncle Abe. Clearly this sextrology woman had psychological issues. Or maybe she had mold? Aaron's father had told him about university people doing research into "ghost mold." Little hallucinogenic spores, often found in old dilapidated buildings. People breathed them in, had psychotic episodes—that was the theory, anyway. Which meant mold was possibly the special effects team behind haunted houses stories.

"Anyway, the ghost of my great-uncle is not my point," the sextrology woman said. "What I'm getting at? Is it's all cycles. Revolution, suppression, revolution. Have you noticed that? Well, we all gotta serve somebody I guess."

Aaron looked at his watch. His flight would depart in under an hour. The train still was not moving.

"You bored?" the woman said. "Listen. I've got a fun game to pass the time. Name a discipline."

"Huh?"

"An academic discipline. Go ahead. You name a discipline and I'll tell you the type of substance abuse a student in that discipline is probably involved in. Give me a field of study. Like say, history or something. Go on."

He was interested in spite of himself. Stuck in a tunnel with this woman, Aaron might as well play along. "History," he said.

"Alcohol. History majors are definitely alcoholics."

Aaron didn't want to laugh, but he couldn't help it and the reaction caused the woman to bounce up and down in her seat with joy. "Another one!" she cried. "Try another one."

"Okay, okay. Philosophy."

"Alcohol.

"English?"

"Alcohol." The woman sighed. The spine of the splayed-out sextrology book, Aaron saw, was perfectly lined up with her thighs. "Get out of the liberal arts, will you? Take, say, MBA students."

"Okay. MBA students."

"MBA students," she said, "now that's alcohol *and* coke."

"Wow."

"Music and art, there's a lot of pot there, now, okay? It's all about the brain's reward system. Astronomy majors, a mix of pot and shrooms."

Aaron looked up at the subway lights again, pretended to think. "What about American studies?"

"American studies?" The woman paused. "I'd guess alcohol." She tugged on a long strand of hair. "I don't actually know what American studies is, really. Do you?"

"Of course I know," Aaron said, although really he wasn't one hundred percent sure. "It's interdisciplinary," he tried. Chloe mentioned that word a lot.

"Interdisciplinary." The sextrology woman nodded, like Aaron had really clarified something for her. "Interdisciplinary is almost always alcohol. I'm Rina, by the way."

The sextrology woman—no, Rina, he must think of her now as Rina—reached out to shake Aaron's hands. Rina's fingers felt a little damp. One of the first things Aaron ever learned from his father was that mold needed just two things to grow: moisture and organic matter. Now as he and Rina shook hands he visualized, out of nowhere, a white lacy spore-string wrapping up their fingers. The image was so vivid, so startling, he snatched his hand away again. Such visions were not healthy. What if Aaron was accidentally breathing in toxic mold during work, what if that was triggering psychosis, hallucinations? Possibly there was ghost mold right here, right on the E! More likely, though, being stuck on the subway like this just wasn't good for a person's psyche. Definitely the train needed to move. Was it going to move? It did not move.

Rina gestured to Aaron's big backpack, lodged between his feet. "If you're not a student, what's in the bag?" She let her eyes go wide. "Is it a bomb? Is *that* the suspicious package delaying our train?"

Some of the people around them blinked or shuffled their feet. Even the teenagers seemed to flinch a little.

"Ha-ha-ha," Rina said. "I'm only kidding."

"Don't joke about stuff like that. Jesus."

"I'll joke about whatever the hell I want." She glared at him, picked up the sextrology book again, and began to read. Aaron peeked at the pages. *Any planets impacting your fifth house will reveal your artistry and individual vision between the sheets!* Rina saw him looking and shifted the book away. Although Aaron had not wanted her to talk to him to begin with, now he felt a little bad for turning her sulky.

"Clothes and stuff," he said.

"What?"

"That's what's in my bag. I'm trying to get to JFK."

"Ooh-la-la-la-LA." Her huffiness vanished. "Not LaGuardia for you! J-F-Freaking-K! Vacation?"

"I'm flying to California to talk to my girlfriend. She just moved out there." As he said this, Rina smiled in a way that made Aaron think she was about to say something lewd. "I think she wants to break up with me," he quickly added. "So I'm trying to convince her that's a bad idea."

"Break up? With *you*? Why does she want to break up with you?"

"She says we're drifting apart. But I don't think it's that, really."

"Well, then what?"

"I think she's realized something." And he tried very hard not to hang his head. "I think she's realized she doesn't want to date a mold removal specialist long distance."

. . .

The sad thing was Aaron wasn't even a specialist. He was fairly new to mold. His father had started the business when Aaron was a teenager. "Finally, my own boss," he'd said. "Finally, I'll start to take up room in this city." Although he'd always expressed hope that his son would join him in his work, Aaron had resisted for years. Declaring a future in mold, as an adolescent, felt pretty much equivalent to declaring an interest in early death. Instead, Aaron had done construction jobs since high school, but he'd hurt his back one day, lifting some heavy beams, and decided that at twenty-eight, he was too young for all these aches. When he asked to join up with his father, his father fist-pumped the air. "Listen, Aaron," he'd said. "You'll love it. Don't look at me like that! You'll definitely like it."

His father had taken him to the house of an old lady on Staten Island, EdnaGladysEdith or whatever. The old lady had died a while back and her kids wanted the house fixed up so they could sell it. Aaron had pictured a place full of Hummel figurines and old sofas preserved in sofa-sized Ziploc bags and hard candy stuck to the bottom of bowls. He had pictured something boring.

But the furniture, all her crappy stuff, was secondary to what Aaron saw on that ceiling. Molds hanging down like stalactites inside a cave. Unbelievable molds in all sorts of shades of red, green, blue, black. "They didn't do proper cleanup in here after Hurricane Sandy," his father explained. And these colors, these weird shapes, were the result of that failure. Some fragment of a howling storm from years ago could crystallize into something else, take on this new form, become fuzzy and silent. A storm that had seemed to challenge a whole city to a duel could become a thing you could reach out your hand toward and actually pet. Aaron had looked up at the dead lady's ceiling the way some people might gaze up while inside a cathedral, as if serious Mystery was whooshing around a sacred vaulted space. The wildest, most exciting house he ever saw was this old lady's house. Standing there, gazing up—it was the closest Aaron had gotten to feeling like he had a calling.

This was not a belief to share with Chloe in his speech, of course. Chloe felt Aaron needed to give up mold and go to college as soon as possible. "I know your parents were broke ten years ago, but your father's business is starting to do okay now, right?" she'd said. "And you're smart! You're smart and you're still young and you're just going to let your brain go moldy with mold?"

"Thanks for saying I'm smart," Aaron had said.

So, rather than going on about the magic of mold in his speech, Aaron would instead try to convey to Chloe how steady the mold removal business was, much steadier than whatever business employed American studies PhD students like Chloe. Once he'd learned enough about mold from his father, he could move out to California. Even with all the drought, they certainly had mold in California. He could support Chloe as she studied the things she studied. He was happy to do so. She was beautiful, and very intelligent, and the fact that they were ever together to begin with seemed like a miracle. They had met a few months back during one of the first jobs Aaron had joined his father on, only a couple days after they'd seen the old lady's house on Staten Island. Chloe had recently graduated, moved out of the dorms into her own studio apartment, and she was concerned about a growth along her shower wall. "The super won't do a thing," she'd told Aaron and his father. "The landlord won't do a thing. And me, I've got basically a newborn to worry about." She'd gestured to the micro-dog doing laps around her ankles. "I don't want her developing asthma. Cecelia's super susceptible now, you know? Her lungs are still forming, practically."

The dog loved Aaron. It followed him around, staring up at him with eyes like lucent black marbles. When Aaron's father left the apartment to make a call, Chloe had sidled up to Aaron and given him her number. Her eyes were—Aaron couldn't help thinking of them this way—a fungal green. Which sounded disgusting, but which could be a good thing. Melanized fungi were healthier than non-melanized varieties, at least. Aaron wished he could tell Chloe this, but he knew it wouldn't sound as romantic to her as it did to him, so he just smiled and put her number into his phone. Then they had looked stupidly at one another. "It's hard to meet new people in New York, now that I'm not in college," Chloe said finally. "And even harder to meet men Cecelia approves of." She grinned down at the dog. "Cecelia hates men. She's tried to bite literally every guy I bring over here. Except for you. You must be special."

Nobody had ever called Aaron special in a good way before. He'd felt warm all over until, later that day, he discovered a chunk of pastrami sandwich he'd shoved into one of his pants' giant cargo pockets and forgotten. What puppy wouldn't follow him? But he never told Chloe about that discovery—better to think she'd witnessed a dog-sanctioned sign of his true specialness. The bread was besplotched with green and white patches when Aaron discovered it, mold patterns that seemed nearly feather-like, nearly beautiful. A kind of magic, definitely. He chucked the sandwich chunk, but reluctantly. Then he called Chloe.

The months that followed: making out with Chloe at ancient movie theaters, people-watching on the Staten Island Ferry, taking Cecelia for long walks that ended with hot strong coffee. Each date Aaron thought his role in the TV show of Chloe's life was nearing its end, but the next day he was always still recurring, invited back. Chloe believed in Aaron, in what Aaron could be, in Aaron's intelligence, and she wanted to channel that intelligence into a container that would make sense to her and to her family. A good university, a white-collar job, something that didn't involve dirty ducts and mold spores spraying from an air conditioner's grimy blower blades.

Aaron, Chloe. What creeping forces had let their lives grow together for nearly six months? Especially when they'd grown up very differently? Chloe came from money. Aaron did not. Chloe's dad was in finance. Aaron's dad was in mold. Chloe was hot. Aaron was just okay. He had the broad back thing at least. Of course, Chloe wasn't perfect. Who was? She wasn't always the easiest person to get along with, but like everyone, she had her reasons: her last boyfriend had cheated on her, and she would sometimes need reassurance if Aaron had a job in another young woman's home. Always he reassured her: "I would never do anything."

"You wouldn't," she'd admit. "I can tell. You're a good guy."

Maybe the unlikeliness of their pairing, in some ways, made Chloe feel safer. Of course he wouldn't leave her. Where would he go? Aaron had always lacked a certain aspirational impulse in school and work, but here that impulse was at last, showing up in his romantic life: Chloe was better than him and he wanted her for that. More than wanted. He loved her. Loved her more since she'd left New York for California, with the sort of clingy whole-heartedness that accompanies the possibility of total abandonment.

■ ■ ■

"Gross," Rina said after Aaron told her about his love for Chloe (leaving out the stuff about his growing sense of specialness). "All of that, everything you just said? Is totally gross."

Aaron scowled. "How is it gross?"

"It's just totally gross. What a story. Listen, if this suspicious package blows us all up, my real regret will be that the last love story I heard was that one. It's not even love. It's projection. You haven't really told me a thing about this woman beyond what she plans to study—which, you don't even really seem to grasp what that is—and the fact that you think she's better than you and also that she has a dog. It's as if she's some possession that you need to hold onto. Some *thing* that will elevate you. With her beauty, or worth, her whatever. It's a kind of high for you. Trust me, I recognize a sign of addiction." Rina shook her head. "A story about love at its grossest. At its most delusional."

"*I'm* delusional? You're the one seeing a ghost."

"Not just any ghost. My great-uncle. A *refugee*. A *revolutionary*. A *survivor*. And he only showed up the one time. To express his disappointment in me, mostly. That's how I know he was real."

"You probably have mold," Aaron said. Aaron's own great-grandparents on his mother's side had fled to America from Russia, and one set of his father's grandparents had come to New York from Mexico, but Aaron had never been haunted by the phantom of his ancestors' disappointment in him, not for one second. "You probably don't just have mold but *ghost* mold." And his eyes went wide as he told Rina what ghost mold was, like he was telling an actual ghost story. Little toxic spores in the air. Hallucinogenic. Studies were being conducted right now.

"That's a lot of bullshit," Rina said, but she was frowning. Because of her job, she was probably extra sensitive to the idea of toxins floating around in the air, sneaking in unannounced. "I don't have mold. I know I don't."

"Or so you think. People act all concerned over a patch of mold they spot on their wall, but the mold that's slowly murdering you is the stuff you usually can't see." Aaron raised his eyebrows. "The stuff you breathe. From your carpet. From your air conditioner."

Rina drew her shoulders in a little bit. "I don't have mold," she said again.

Aaron grinned. He was getting to her. "You should get an expert to check it out, is all I'm saying. You want my card?"

"I can't afford something like that," Rina said. "My rent's just gone up again. No experts are crossing my threshold. My landlord certainly won't pay for some mold big shot like *you*."

Her cheeks were flushed. Her voice had gotten very loud. Aaron wanted to get back on Rina's good side. He didn't like seeing her so upset. Plus, she seemed like the kind of customer who was reluctant at first, but who, if you made her paranoid enough, might pay up big. He should back off for now, change the subject. He gestured to the book on Rina's lap.

"What's your sign?" Aaron asked.

"Huh?"

"Your astrological sign."

"Oh. A Taurus, I think? But I'm on the edge or the cusp of something. I never remember."

"You don't know? I thought you'd be obsessed. What about that sextrology book?"

Rina shook her head. "It's my mother's book. She made me promise to read it because she said it'd help my love life. I guess it helped her out at the senior center. She met some Leo. But me, I don't believe any of that stuff. Celestial bodies, moons and planets roaming inside houses? Nope. Ghosts, though, traces of old things in different forms, that I'll believe in."

Aaron felt a quivery recognition, hearing this speech. The traces of old things in different forms. He thought about the flooded house in Staten Island. Yes. Yeah. *That.*

Then the train moved.

People looked up. People who never made eye contact made eye contact. The teenagers across from Aaron and Rina looked right at Aaron and Rina. No cheers, no smiles, but something close. The spores of smiles in the air. Aaron turned to Rina. She wasn't smiling. "Well," she said, "maybe you'll reach your princess after all."

Aaron glanced down at his watch. His flight departed in forty minutes. With security and the AirTrain, he still wasn't sure he'd get to his gate in time. But he would try his best and maybe with some luck—only then the announcement came.

They all had to get off the train at the next station. Service to and from this station would be suspended until further notice. A shuttle bus was not yet available.

Aaron put his face in his hands.

"You're not going to make it," Rina said.

"Thanks, Rina." He lifted his head. "Thanks, I hadn't realized." Aaron turned away. Then he turned back to Rina. "That's it. That's it. Chloe's going on her vacation and her parents are going to say 'Why date mold long distance, sweetie,' and 'He's not your intellectual peer, you'll get bored,' and 'Is he going to get a degree?,' and I'll never even get to hold her and remind her that we've got just this connection. Chemistry. You know?"

Rina sighed. She began to say something, stopped. The sounds she was making kind of seemed like the demented cousins of her earlier small-talk warm-up sounds, the strangled starts of sentences. Finally she got it out: she lived a few blocks away from the next station, the station just coming up, and if Aaron wanted, if he really did want, she could drive him to the airport. He might actually make his flight then. With no traffic, JFK was maybe fifteen minutes away. So what did he say?

Aaron said nothing, just stared at her.

"What? You suspicious? You're wondering why I'd do that for you?" He nodded.

"Oh, gosh, I don't know. Look, in principle I'm anti-delusion, but in practice it's hard for me to resist the romance of it all." And she smiled. The smile lit up her face, and Aaron saw that her brown eyes were speckled with green. "Rushing to the airport for true love. True delusional love, but still true enough, right?"

Aaron scratched the back of his neck.

"Would it be easier to accept if I made it an exchange? Maybe when you get back from California, you could just check my apartment out for any toxic ghost mold, spore spirits, whatever the things are. Not that I believe in them."

"You'll believe in ghosts but not ghost spores?"

"I believe in Great-Uncle Abe."

The train pulled into the station. They rose to their feet, stepped off the train. Aaron half expected the whole place to blow up, or maybe masked men with guns would show, but nothing like that happened. There were just cops. Lots of cops. Although he and Rina had done nothing wrong, they were quiet walking through the station, didn't make eye contact with each other or anyone else.

. . .

When Aaron sat down in the passenger seat of Rina's car, she reached into the glove compartment and offered him a bag of Cheetos. "Go crazy!" Rina said. She turned the radio to a classical station and they were moving forward. "We're going to make it!"

"How do you know?"

"I've got a good feeling about the open road today."

It was only as she began to drive that Aaron's phone buzzed with newfound reception. He had many messages, all from Chloe. *Are you at the airport? You said would text me when at the airport. Are you there? cleared out day so could pick you up from airport. . . . Switched around Cici's date to visit vet . . . Packed for vacation earlier than would have otherwise. You there? So uhh this is pretty rude . . . Are you NOT there? Guess you are on your way? See you soon I guess. . . . OK.*

He read the individual messages through again. Aaron hated when Chloe wrote "uhh" in a text, as if she were talking out loud, struggling for words, when actually the "uhh" was the most premeditated part of her stupid messages. But okay. She believed in him. Believed in him in a new expansive way, different from the way others believed in him.

"Do you mind if I make a quick phone call?" he asked Rina.

She waved toward his phone, swerved a little. "Make your call. I'm Zen-focused as hell."

Chloe picked up right away. "Aaron! There you are!" Cecelia's persistent yap-bark in the background. "I've been kind of waiting for a confirmation that you were still coming."

"Yeah. Yes. I'm on my way. I'm almost at the airport."

"Isn't your flight about to leave?"

He explained about getting stuck on the E train. He explained about the suspicious package. He explained about service being suspended and about how it was okay now, it was definitely okay now, he really was almost there, he had gotten a ride, it was awesome, it was excellent.

"And if you miss the flight?"

"I'll buy a new ticket."

"Aaron, I don't want you to get all broke and martyr-y over a visit."

"Tell her you're making this flight," Rina said. She raised her voice. "He's making his flight."

"Who's that?"

"My driver."

"Who's she?"

"Just this woman," he said. "A woman I met on the train."

"Just this woman?"

"I met her on the train."

"And she's giving a ride to a total stranger?"

"Well, we talked on the train. For a while. We were stuck. On the train."

"Who's this woman?"

"Just a woman I met—"

"Right. You met her on the train. Is she attractive?"

"Listen. Don't do the jealousy thing." He lowered his voice. "She's not even, like, young."

He bit his lip, glanced at Rina, but she gave a thumbs up. "It's true!" she mouthed.

"Ah," Chloe said, "an older woman."

"No! I mean, yes. But—"

"Wow. So basically it's like you're Dustin Hoffman in *The Graduate*. If you were, you know, an actual college graduate."

Aaron pressed the phone against his ear so that his ear felt hot. He could taste the Cheetos in his mouth. Artificial cheese. Real cheese had mold. Useful mold, they called it.

"I'm kidding," Chloe said when he was silent. "That was a joke about *The Graduate*. Aaron?"

Aaron closed his eyes. Pictured Chloe's fungal eyes. Also the rest of Chloe. He opened his eyes, looked over at Rina. She was bopping her head to the symphony on the radio as though she were listening to a pop song. Her hair frizzed out in horizontal ways, little tendrils curling toward the sun like plants jonesing for light. A big gigantic bassoon thing started having some kind of a solo and Aaron, surprising himself even more, said quietly into the phone, "I think we should break up."

"Aaron!" Chloe laughed. "I was *kidding*. You know I just love that movie. I love Dustin Hoffman. Don't go crazy out of nowhere."

Well, and that was another thing about mold that Chloe would never appreciate—mold was always out-of-nowhere. Like it could be growing away behind a wall or in the ceiling and not causing any harm to the air, sealed up, sealed away, but once a wall came down, whoops, you were breathing in toxins, you were in real danger! All of a sudden! All of a sudden he saw. Their love story *had* turned gross, toxic. It was done. It was over. "It's done," Aaron said. "It's over. I'm not coming to California."

A suspicious package exploding would sound softer than the silence on the other side of the phone.

Finally Chloe said, "You were supposed to be different than Alex. That was the whole *point* of you."

"I'm sorry, Chloe. I just can't date an American studies PhD student long distance," Aaron said. No, that was only what he imagined himself saying after he had said nothing, after Chloe had hung up, after he'd curled into a ball in Rina's car, trying not to sob/dry-heave into his arms, into his arm hair, and now Rina was saying so is that a no-go on the airport, because it's looking a helluva lot like a no-go on the airport and Aaron murmured to his arm hair that it was a no-go, and Rina turned the car around and Aaron was at Rina's apartment, definitely at Rina's apartment, which was small but clean, which was painted blue, and his eyes were pink but he'd stopped crying, there was that, at least there was that.

They sat for a few minutes in silence at Rina's kitchen table. Eventually Rina said, "I didn't get you all the way to the airport, so how about a drink instead? A drink in exchange for a mold search?" She stood up and pulled out from under her kitchen sink the most gigantic bottle of Jack Daniels he'd seen in a while. "Well?" Rina said. "Will this do?"

"That's a lot of booze."

"I," Rina said, "was an English major."

She did a shot of whiskey. So did he.

"Well!" Rina said. "Do you want to talk about the girl? Do you want to cry a little more or anything? When the addicted students are sent to my office, usually they cry. So I can handle tears."

"No. I don't want to cry more."

"Do you want to talk about astrology? I don't believe in it, but I've learned some things from my mom's book."

He turned the shot glass around in his hands. "I want to search your apartment for mold. I've got a feeling about this place. And that, coupled with your hallucination—"

"It was not a hallucination!" Rina leaned across the table, and whispered to Aaron, "You won't explain Abe out of existence with *mold*. Great-Uncle Abe has survived more than that. And Great-Uncle Abe came to me in a bona fide vision. Besides, there's no mold anywhere in this apartment. You won't find it."

"What about the bathroom?"

"Go on. Check."

He went to her bathroom, ducked his head behind her floral shower curtain, examined the inner workings of her toilet bowl, looked around the sill of the tiny window near the sink. He checked under her large shampoo bottles. He ran his hands over her towels. He wished he'd brought a moisture meter. He wanted to find something. A hint of something visible. Rina stood in the doorway, watching him. Finally he turned to her. "I'm sure there's mold around here. Maybe some rot you're not aware of."

"I told you," Rina said. "There's nothing."

The red of her hair did that curling plant tendril thing again. Aaron stepped forward and kissed her. Then he stepped back, his mouth open, oh, god, he should close his mouth, you shouldn't mouth-breathe after kissing anybody. But Rina mouth-breathed right back at him.

Then she took off her shirt.

. . .

The sex was very wet. Almost sudsy. And startlingly organic. In bed after, he imagined little spores settling on their damp skin, in a pretty way, like snow but greener, smaller, more intricate.

"Well, great," said a deep voice from the corner. "This is just lovely."

Rina was asleep. An old man stood by the bed.

"Just don't hurt her," the old man said. He wore a buttoned-up blue shirt and crisp jeans, a mockery of Aaron's take-me-seriously outfit. "I'm Abe," the old man said. He jabbed his finger at Rina. "Her great-uncle."

"Oh, shit." Aaron sat right up.

"She's a great girl." Abe raised up his quivering hands. "But what you should know is this: she seems quirky-manic like a middle-aged romantic comedy star, but really she's quirky-manic like a middle-aged manic person. So don't hurt her."

"You're mold," Aaron said. "There's ghost mold somewhere in here. In this place."

"I really like mold," the old man said. "Mold finds the rich folks and the poor folks and the middle folks alike, the few that are left in this city. It attacks LEED-certified buildings and housing projects. It's very democratic, mold. The idea of democracy is essentially a theory of spores. Right? Little spores causing massive dictators to decompose on the spot. America at its best." He gave two trembling thumbs up. "I like that you're in the mold business. I approve."

This swift approval softened Aaron up so much, he decided not to argue with Abe about his realness. "I didn't go to college," he said instead. "Do you think that's a problem?"

"That is in fact very smart," said Abe. "They always go after the intellectuals first."

In her sleep, Rina pulled Aaron close and Abe was gone. Aaron's phone was ringing. It was Chloe. He had missed a bunch of texts from her, all variations on "*call call call you fuckhead.*" He silenced his phone. Rina barely stirred.

Chloe had believed in a version of Aaron that did not exist. Great-Uncle Abe, who might not exist, believed in the version of Aaron that existed right now, right here, buck naked and present. And Rina? What did she believe? He didn't know yet, not completely.

An enormous exhaustion suddenly overtook Aaron. He fell asleep fast, his face buried in the small of Rina's back. And he woke up still wanting her. Moisture and organic matter. That was all it took for strange and surprising forms to grow, to break down the older forms you'd known and thought you wanted. He would not tell Rina he'd seen some version of Abe but a knowledge sprouted inside him: Unlikely as it seemed, he and Rina had somehow shared a vision. He knew that when Rina woke up, he would ask if he could see her again.

A Magic Trick for the Recently Unemployed

1. Acquire a hat. The hat should be expensive, brand new, preferably trimmed with velvet, and yes, I know, buying that expensive hat will probably not be easy, because if you are reading this manual, if you are considering doing this trick for public audiences at all, you probably have lost your job. Maybe you pulled money from thin air for your clients, until the economy downturned. Maybe you traded derivatives or analyzed risk or managed assets. Maybe you rhapsodized to potential lovers about your passion for game theory, or decision science, or your belief in rationality, or your skill in fast-paced environments, and sometimes you maybe deceived people, but weren't you told to do so, wasn't that part of the game? No one called you a professional magician in your former career, but that is what you were back then—you made cash appear where there was no cash, made something out of nothing. Until one day you yourself were made to vanish.

But were you ever the magician, actually? Weren't you always told that getting where you were in the first place was someone else's trick? First in your family to go to college. Your mother working nights. Well-meaning people have held you up as their greatest piece of prestidigitation: Your high school teachers. Your guidance counselor. Your wealthy friends at university who took you in and took you to their country homes and presented you before their families. The company you worked for, too, sometimes, treated you that way: at your boss's Memorial Day barbecue, your higher-ups would maybe say well well well look how far you've come, but what they meant to say is look how far we've come as a company, and when they said these words and patted you on the back, it did not seem like justice, it seemed like magic, your being here, like you were the rabbit pulled from the expensive hat, and you sometimes even blushed as they patted your back, which just made the trick that much more convincing.

. . .

2. Acquire a rabbit. Pet stores are okay, but you probably haven't been exercising much, so in the spirit of cardiovascular health and adventure, you should go to your local green space. If you are still located in or close to New York City, head for Central Park. Central Park, as you probably know, is filled up with the abandoned doves of failed magicians. What you probably don't know, though, is the park has rabbits, too. There are a few wild cottontails that you can chase, but your best bet is to go in search of your rabbit shortly after Easter, when enough fed-up parents have set the creatures free to fend for themselves.

Try to find a grassy place by some hedges, an area unfrequented by too many tourists or dog walkers. Bring some carrots and bananas and alfalfa hay. Sit in the grass for a while and watch and wait. Don't assume you'll be successful on your first try. Catching a rabbit requires a great deal of patience. Cultivate a great deal of patience in all things.

When you finally see your rabbit, talk to it. Rabbits don't have good close-range vision, they're farsighted creatures, which means that from a distance they can see the world laid out before them, but from close up things blur and become much harder to navigate. Your best bet, when the rabbit starts to come close to you, is to talk to it for a while, so it becomes acclimated to your voice. Tell it your life story. Tell it about what you had and what you lost, though don't sound too sorry for yourself, because a rabbit, like everyone else, is repelled by self-pity.

If you are out in the park long enough, you may see someone you know. Possibly even your former boss on a jog, wearing tapered track pants. When he sees you, he will probably avert his eyes. He will probably pretend not to see you at all. He will definitely not stop. Don't be fazed. He will keep running. You should keep talking. Allow the rabbit to grow comfortable with the rhythms of your storytelling. Maybe, after a while, chew on a carrot. The rabbit knows the sound of chomping means something tasty lies ahead, and it will come even closer. It will advance and retreat and advance again and eventually it will allow you to pat its head. Pat its head. Then scoop the rabbit up.

When you hold the animal to your chest, don't feel like you are stealing or displacing anything. You are rescuing something lost. You are making sure this creature doesn't disappear.

. . .

3. Pull the rabbit out of the hat in front of an audience. What kind of an audience? Maybe a crowd of strangers on a subway. Maybe a group of tourists in Times Square. Or maybe you should perform your trick in front of people you know. Maybe even in front of your former coworkers at your boss's Memorial Day barbecue. Maybe you will get an old cat carrier and line it with newspaper and maybe you will place the rabbit in the carrier and get on the Metro-North, giving yourself the necessary pep talks on the way. Wear your velvet trimmed hat, even if people on the train stare. Let them stare. Their stares should mean just one thing to you: You haven't vanished yet! Congratulations.

Arrive at your destination. Everyone will pretend you've been invited. Someone, perhaps the boss's wife, will try to give you a plate heaped with grilled meat and potato salad. Although you are hungry, don't take the food. You are here to work. Politely ask your hosts if you can do a magic trick. They will magically say yes—guilt, it turns out, is an effective form of enchantment.

The actual details—how you do the trick, the method you use to pull the rabbit out of the hat—are not what matter here. You didn't need this manual to learn *that*. You're not an idiot, you know how to Google, the Internet is full of people eager to break down all illusions. So research the various techniques on your own. Maybe you set up a table or maybe you have a secret pouch where the rabbit is hiding or maybe you have a colorful scarf that you wave in the air to serve as a diversion while you get the rabbit into the hat with your other hand. All that matters, here, now, really, at step 3, is that you have the rabbit and the hat and your audience's undivided attention.

For this last step to work, I mean for it to *really work*, you'll need to convince yourself that the hat is empty, that there is nothing warm or animal or scared inside of it. That way, when you reach in, when you discover there is still life and heat and something that wants to keep breathing hidden away in a place where nobody expected it to be, the look on your face will be truly astounding, so astounding that your audience, including your boss, will not avert their eyes from you, not even for a second, not even for a millisecond.

No, they will not dare.

Mutant at the Pierre Hotel

Melinda and her mother took off their high heels to walk the four flights downstairs. Their apartment building had no elevator. But that afternoon in March, Melinda didn't mind. The stairs felt cool and smooth against the soles of her feet. In fact, everything—the air, her purple dress, her mother's papery hand on her shoulder—felt cool and smooth. Her shoes dangled from her fingertips. Her eyes, behind her glasses, were heavy with mascara.

Unfortunately, the mascara and the dress and the shoes couldn't mask the dowdiness of Melinda's glasses. The frames, the gray color of a dead tooth, were also very round, robbing Melinda's long oval face of any sense of definition. At school, a couple of girls had started a rumor that Melinda had bought her glasses from Goodwill, which somehow transmuted into a grade-wide joke about how she got her underwear from Goodwill too ("Dead people panties!" Fat Alex would shout at her across the hall. "The shit streaks of the spirit world!"). Even Ella, a junior who Melinda had briefly dated, once asked Melinda if she'd considered saving up for frames that were a little bit more sophisticated. Ella had claimed the glasses made Melinda look senile, not in an old-lady chic way, but in a way that was sad and decrepit and cheap. When Melinda had argued that she liked her glasses, Ella told Melinda she was blinder than she thought and maybe an idiot.

"The other students are just jealous," Ms. Naylor said to Melinda after class, when Melinda had told Ms. Naylor that she'd been having a difficult time with her peers. "Once you're in a top college next fall, you'll see who has the last laugh."

Ms. Naylor was a fine-featured, wholesome-looking woman who taught at Melinda's school through some sort of young professionals fellowship program. She looked like she should not be teaching public school at all, but maybe instead modeling sleek winter sweaters for some sustainably minded sweater designer. Yet while Melinda's mother was telling Melinda not to bother applying to all those universities, Ms. Naylor was gathering brochures from the college fair, stuffing them into Melinda's hands. "I couldn't believe in myself, in what I'm doing as an educator, if I didn't believe so fiercely in you," Ms. Naylor said.

And Ms. Naylor had been proven right. Melinda was accepted into a whole slew of good schools. Now, to celebrate, Melinda and her mother were going from their apartment in Queens to the Pierre Hotel on Fifth Avenue. The Pierre offered an afternoon tea, which cost way too much money. But Melinda's mother, surprisingly, didn't care. "All those acceptances," her mother said. "You deserve a real treat."

Melinda's mother's idea of a real treat typically meant bringing home whatever coupon-discounted cake at the grocery store was most densely sprinkled. It was her mother who had insisted that Melinda buy the cheapest frames at the optometrist ("The lenses already are so expensive, Sweet Blind Mel") and her mother who had insisted that they stay in their walk-up apartment despite her own bad knees ("The stairs keep rent affordable, baby"). That was just the way Melinda's mother was. She'd had to be like that, at one point, to survive. When Melinda was in middle school, her mother was laid off from her job as an administrative assistant in an office that helped other offices outsource their administrative work. "Don't worry about me," she'd said to Melinda after she'd lost her position. Her thin lips pressed into a smile. "Just do *your* job, okay? Just stay focused on school stuff."

School stuff was easy for Melinda to focus on because school stuff always stayed pretty much the same: screaming kids, scummy lunches, sighing teachers, right answers, wrong answers, hulking boys with hyena laughs, girls who smelled like sweat and mango. It was the world outside of school that had seemed irrevocably changed. The day after her mother was laid off, on Melinda's after-school walk to her grandmother's, the stores struck her as unreal, not like places of employment but like movie sets. The Dunkin' Donuts, the bodega, the Happy Suds Laundromat, the eternally closed-down Xerox shop—none of them seemed to contain real insides and Melinda's insides hurt, just imagining her mother wandering inside those doors, asking for work.

But that was five years ago. Her mother now had a decent job as an office manager. Maybe this fancy tea meant Melinda's mother finally really understood things were okay.

Normally if they wanted to get into the city from their home, the trip would take several subway transfers, long waits in underground stations that reeked of beer-sweet pee. But today was a different sort of day. Today Melinda and her mother got on an express bus that smelled like Lysol. In happy, solemn silence, in their sparkly heeled shoes, Melinda and her mother passed light bulb factories, tire warehouses, truck and auto repair shops. Melinda tapped her right foot, like she was listening to a song.

"It's going to be *fancy*," her mother said, folding her hands together, unfolding, refolding. "At the hotel. It's going to be very fancy there."

"I know. I read all about it last night." Melinda linked her arm with her mother's. "It sounds delightful."

As the bus trundled along Melinda delighted over that word—

"delightful"—the way it cast both a real earnestness and a sunny elegance on any noun to which it might fuse. A delightful hat. A delightful smile. A delightful concept. Ms. Naylor used the word all the time. "This thesis sentence, Melinda, is truly delightful." "What a delightful contribution you made to our classroom environment." "I think it's delightful that you got into so many amazing schools, but I can't say I'm surprised."

This moment, too, on the bus, was delightful and so were the other people on the express, the people Melinda might soon be leaving behind: An old woman wearing Barbie pink headphones. A boy and his dad, both wearing Mets caps. A girl Melinda's age, in high heels that made her look like an art installation, sipping small sips from a flask. Two guys Melinda's age, watching the girl and her small sips and not even glancing Melinda's way. Another mother and another daughter, the daughter much younger than Melinda and clinging to her own mother's wrist with all her might.

"I don't want to go," the little girl chanted. "I don't want to go. I do not want to go. I do not want to go."

Melinda and her mother looked at each other and laughed. Their laughs were so similar in that instant, the sound seemed to come from a single person whose voice scattered prism-like through the room, casting its laugh-light against the bus's large laminated glass windows and aluminum walls.

"Anyways," Melinda's mother said, when the laugh was done and they were both just smiling again, "I thought while we were there, at the hotel, maybe we could talk a little bit about next steps. Like where, school-wise, you might actually want to go. I know there are some impressive names on your list. But some of the colleges, the ones closer to home, they're pretty good too, right?"

Melinda unlinked her arm from her mother's. "But less good, is the thing."

"But still good." Her mother took Melinda's arm again. "And closer by? And with better aid packages?"

Melinda squinted at her mother, as if she had taken off her glasses. "But with less end value."

"Ah. Yes. The end value." Melinda's mother raised her eyebrows high. "The good ole end value. You sound like someone on a management team."

It was a day of celebration, not a day for scorn, and so Melinda did not respond to her mother's quiet teasing. Instead she pushed her face close to the window. The bus was stopped near a fruit and vegetable stand. The vendor, a small woman in a puffy coat, strutted proudly before her pears, apples, broccoli, and onions.

"You could save so much by just living at home, Mel, is all I'm getting at."

Melinda closed her eyes for a moment. Then she turned so that she was facing her mother again. "I can't wait for this tea, Mom," she said. "I can't wait to see the hotel." And before her mother could change the topic back to tuition expenses, Melinda began to recite everything she had researched about the hotel the night before. Big-deal celebrities used to live at the hotel, she told her mother. And then, too, there was the robbery, the biggest hotel robbery in history. "It made the Guinness Book of World Records," Melinda said.

Her mother must have known she was changing the topic. But she just shrugged in a tired way. "Okay, Ms. Melinda," she said. "Ms. Melinda" was a childhood nickname, one her mother used to use whenever Melinda started to talk like a teacher. Hearing it again, Melinda felt like her mother had just thrown a heavy, itchy sweater over Melinda's head—a non-sustainable wool sweater, the kind Ms. Naylor would never wear. Was it possible for your brain to break out in hives? Maybe Melinda's mother noticed Melinda's irritation because she leaned into her daughter. "What's wrong, sweetie?"

"I just have always hated that nickname," Melinda said. " 'Ms. Melinda.' You only use it when you're making fun of me."

"I wasn't making fun of you. I was being, what's the word, nostalgic." Melinda's mother kissed Melinda on the forehead. "I swear. Now tell me. What stars lived there? At the hotel?"

This was a question for which Melinda had an answer, and that cheered her up and made the brain-hives feeling go away. Egyptian business magnates, she told her mother. Heads of entertainment conglomerates. Famous fashion designers. And the great actress of Hollywood's golden age—Elizabeth Taylor.

"Wow," her mother said. "Really? You know, your grandmother loved Elizabeth Taylor."

Of course Melinda knew. Every time she went to her grandmother's apartment after school, they would watch Elizabeth Taylor movies. The day her mother was laid off, Melinda had gone to her grandmother's and her grandmother had pointed at the VCR perched on top of her small TV. So Melinda pressed the big green button on the VCR (her grandmother had duct-taped the word "POWER" beneath the power button, because she was always accidentally pressing "rewind" or "fast-forward"). Then they were together with Elizabeth Taylor in high-society Chicago. The week before it had been England, the week before Egypt.

Without fail, after they'd finished an Elizabeth Taylor movie, Melinda's grandmother would give a long review of the actress's performance. These reviews, despite Melinda's grandmother's love for Elizabeth Taylor, were generally critical. "She did not look so beautiful in that scene," or "Those lines were wooden, like she was a doll."

On the day Melinda's mother lost her job, Melinda's grandmother had said, "Liz did not seem to really so *entirely* mean the love scene in this one, actually, but this is okay, this is not her fault, she was very young, because Hollywood in these times was like blood slavery."

Before Melinda could ask what "blood slavery" was, her grandmother's evaluation of Elizabeth Taylor's performance evolved to an evaluation of Melinda's own mother.

"She made a mess of things," her grandmother said. "Don't tell her I say that to you, my Melinda, though she knows what I think. Bad choices in work and love. She means well. She wishes to be liked. You, though, you will be different. I can see it. Pay attention."

"Okay."

"Stay in school, stay away from men."

"Okay."

"And go to college."

"Okay."

"And pay attention. Promise."

The express bus made a burping noise. Melinda's mother sat now, still and quiet, beside her. Her grandmother lay now, still and quiet, in a grave in New Jersey.

"She loved reading about Elizabeth Taylor's love life, too," Melinda's mother said then. "Your grandmother. Did you know she learned English from the tabloids?" Her mother's voice seemed to merge real fondness with a hushed mockery. "We had piles and piles of them, when I was growing up. It was the only thing she read. The sex lives of the stars."

Her mother smiled. Melinda did not. She thought the story was not funny but noble and sad, her grandmother heroically trying to hew knowledge of grammatical rules from the ruleless lives of rich celebrities. The bus turned a sharp corner, sliding Melinda against her mother.

"Did you know, Mom," Melinda said then, "what else I found out yesterday? Elizabeth Taylor was a mutant."

"A mutant?"

"She had two rows of eyelashes." Melinda held up two fingers as though her mother needed clarification. "That's why her eyes looked so incredible. I was reading about it."

"Why on earth were you reading about that?"

"I don't know. I saw that she had lived at the hotel and I just clicked around, one thing led to another." Melinda reached out her index finger and drew an invisible squiggly line onto the back of the seat in front of her. "I couldn't sleep."

Her mother tilted her head. "You were nervous about the fanciness of the tea, maybe?"

"I wasn't nervous," Melinda said. "I was just awake. There was a mutation on this gene that's supposed to kind of make everything normal for tissue development in embryos. For unborn babies."

"Huh." Her mother gazed over Melinda's shoulder at a Key Foods, then a passing Panda Garden. "Maybe you should major in something science-y."

"I'm thinking eighteenth- or seventeenth-century literature, actually. Nicola lent me this anthology of seventeenth-century stuff and it's really fascinating. That's what she studied in college too. From this same anthology."

"Is Nicola a lit mag girl?"

"No, my English teacher. I'm talking about my English teacher."

"I thought your English teacher was Ms. Naylor?"

"Yes. Ms. Naylor. But her first name is Nicola. I call her Nicola now." Which was sort of true. Out loud, Melinda carefully and proudly called Ms. Naylor "Nicola." In her own mind, though, Melinda still called her Ms. Naylor, as much as she had tried to change her way of thinking.

"Nicola." The mockery in her mother's voice was not even hushed up now. "Nicola. Isn't that the name of a type of cough drop?"

"No."

"Or are they breath mints? There's that ad where that man screams from the mountaintops, right? Ni-co-la. Isn't that what he screams?"

A reaction. Her mother just wanted a reaction. Well, Melinda would give her nothing. The bus passed under a tunnel. When Melinda looked out the window, she saw only her darkened eyes, her upper lip, the parts of her face the bus's fluorescent bulbs hit. Then the tunnel ended and cool light flooded the bus again. The little girl sitting near them was still chanting, but under her breath.

Melinda cleared her throat. "What's really fascinating about Elizabeth Taylor's mutant eyelash thing," she said, "is that she was actually lucky. Sometimes the eyelash mutation is really bad, because the extra row of eyelashes turn inward. Like the extra row of eyelashes grow actually *into* the eye and they mess up the cornea."

Her mother pushed back a loose strand of Melinda's hair. "You sound so happy about it, Mel."

"I'm not happy about it. It's just gene stuff. It's just cool."

But secretly she was kind of happy about it. Two sets of eyelashes! Who needed two sets of eyelashes? Nature, too, could be surprisingly extravagant. It could be careless with its own resources, for the sake of beauty.

They passed yet another Key Foods, yet another fruit and vegetable stand, a 99-cent store, without talking. They were getting closer and closer to the hotel. Now Melinda dreamed about herself and her mother stepping into an elevator gilded all in gold, the buttons gleaming, the white-gloved operator smiling sort of facelessly, but not in a creepy way. The white-gloved operator would be from Russia like her grandmother, probably, would speak beautifully but brokenly, would ask Melinda very kindly where she and her mother would like to go, and then imagine! All of them there rising so fast, all together, flying up with their hearts in their throats.

"It's too nice of you," Melinda said after a few long minutes of silence. She touched her mother's hand. "Tea at a luxury hotel. It's too expensive."

"Oh." Her mother brightened. "It actually wasn't *too*-too expensive. It was an online coupon thing. Have you heard of Groupon? I got a great deal."

A shameful bitterness suddenly submerged all Melinda's prior feelings of gratitude. She felt a sharp pain in her head, which happened to her sometimes when some new stress arose. A Groupon. Of course. Immediately, the whole excursion made sense. This had not been a change in behavior to commemorate Melinda's accomplishment against the odds, but her mother's same usual cheapness. A deal. Just a deal, the same as the gross cake deals at the supermarket, only masked this time in true fanciness, in celebration. And Melinda knew she must act in turn like it did not matter. She must not think about how if *she* had a daughter who had done what Melinda had done, she would splurge for real, would take her to tea in a fancy hotel with no discount, would open her heart up to a day of excessiveness.

But that was not the situation. Melinda must act like a very grateful daughter, girl, young woman, etcetera. She must act like the most delightful etcetera on the planet.

"I knew yoga studios did Groupons," her mother was saying, "and Asian fusion restaurants, and deep-fried cheesecake kinds of places, but I didn't know luxury hotels like the Pierre *did* the Groupon thing, but I guess so, I guess they do!"

Melinda's eyes traveled from her own hands to her mother's scarf. Its rainbow colors clashed horribly with her mother's red dress.

"The hotel robbery," Melinda told her mother then, "occurred on January 2nd, 1972." She smiled, very sweetly. "It was brilliant timing, because the guests were all hungover from New Year's, so they were deep asleep, and also they had all their best jewels in the hotel safes, because you wear your best jewels on New Year's Eve. The robbers all wore disguises. Fake noses. Glasses. Wigs."

Her mother gave Melinda a long, hard stare. Melinda stared right back. At last her mother looked away and said, "You *really* couldn't sleep last night, huh?"

Melinda took off her glasses. The frames, in her lap, looked especially fragile. "One of the robbers was even dressed as a chauffeur."

"Well," her mother said. "Well. Okay."

The pounding at her temples worsened. Melinda leaned her head against the window of the bus, suddenly exhausted. She exhaled onto the window so that the glass fogged and she could see nothing but the powerful proof of her own life force. She peered into her self-made steam and fell asleep, awaking again just as the bus began to inch its way through Midtown. Soon, Central Park would bloom before them in bursts of brand-new green. She had wanted to be awake as they went over the river, but at least her head felt a little better. She managed to smile at her mother, to take her arm as together they stepped off the bus.

. . .

The Pierre's lobby was decorated in "elegant neutrals," just as its website promised. Melinda and her mother moved over black and white marble, alongside the bank of elevators and all-white flower arrangements. Their heels clacked more loudly here than in other places, audible over the soft violin music playing. Yet no one seemed to hear or see Melinda. It wasn't that people were looking snobbishly away. The lobby was simply a distracting place of tourist limbo. Everyone Melinda saw seemed like they were waiting to be picked up, pacing back and forth. The stillest things were the pictures on the walls. "Look at that elephant!" Melinda's mother said, pointing to a framed painting that showed an elephant, wild-eyed, with a man and woman on its back.

"Maybe that's because of India," Melinda said. "A few years ago, India bought this hotel."

"India?"

"Well. A multinational conglomerate company with headquarters in India."

"I bet that company has great end value."

More teasing. But Melinda was only half-listening to her mother because she had spotted, at last, a very still and very breathtaking person: a girl, slumped in a leather armchair with a giant book. Her dark hair hung down one side of the chair, her long legs hung over the other. She wore black boots that laced up in labyrinthine ways. The boots were what first grabbed Melinda's attention, but as they walked by her, Melinda saw the girl's eyelashes were extremely dark and heavy and multileveled. For a second she wondered if this girl, like Elizabeth Taylor, had a genetic mutation. The girl looked directly at Melinda. Melinda's stomach dropped. She was much more beautiful than Ella. She was more beautiful even than Ms. Naylor. The girl smiled. The girl mouthed, "Hi." *Did* the girl mouth "hi"? Melinda couldn't believe anyone so lovely would move her mouth in that daydream way—at Melinda. A joke, maybe. The girl must be somehow laughing at Melinda.

Melinda's mother already had her back turned, was headed into the tea lounge, and Melinda ducked her head and followed her. She felt the heat of the girl's eyes on her back but she was too nervous to turn around.

The tea lounge was loud, full of chattering and clinking cups.

Neon blue lights ran up and down the room's stately columns. Leather couches, striped chairs, velvety pillows. The music piping from invisible speakers sounded like regular classical music at first, but after a moment Melinda realized it was actually an instrumental reinterpretation of Michael Jackson's "Smooth Criminal," played with cellos and flutes and violins.

Her mother announced to a man in a suit jacket that she and her daughter had made reservations, they were with Groupon, just so he knew, they had already paid in advance, so was that fine?

The man in the suit jacket smiled at them, the kind of smile straining not to seem strained.

"We ordered the sweets and tea option," Melinda's mother added. "Not the sandwich option. Make sure they don't bring us the sandwich option, okay? That wasn't the Groupon I chose. As far as tea blends go, I would like the Pierre special blend. Melinda?"

"Why don't you have a seat," the man said, "and we'll send a waiter over to you. You'll give your blend choice to him."

The table was low and the chairs were high-backed. The next song was an instrumental version of something from *Phantom of the Opera*. Melinda was seated against the wall, so she looked out on the whole lounge. The other guests having tea were also very dressed up, in ways similar to Melinda's mother: satiny fabrics full of color, giant floral motifs. There were many mothers and daughters here, the mothers examining the small cookies on their plate, brushing off a little of the sugar, the daughters lifting their phones high to photograph the tiered towers of treats.

Her mother's view was just of the wall, and of Melinda.

"Do you want to switch seats?" Melinda asked.

"No, no. I can sense the fanciness just fine." And it was true, her mother seemed perfectly happy. Melinda wanted her to look more annoyed. She wanted her mother to demand they switch seats. But she just sat there, smiling.

The tea blend the waiter brought was smoky, Melinda thought, but her mother said, "Hmmm, it has notes of plum, doesn't it?" Notes of plum? Her mother's imitation of a woman at a wine tasting, maybe. Melinda's mother raised her cup of tea and said, "To the future."

So Melinda raised her cup of tea too.

"Now, maybe let's talk a little bit about that future," her mother said. She was still smiling, but in a more crooked way.

"If you mean where I'm thinking of going for school," Melinda said, "I'm going to talk it over with Nicola on Monday."

"Nicola again. What does Ole Cough Drops want?"

"I told you this last week. We've set up an appointment. Nicola and I. And we're going to talk over the decision process."

"You should talk it over a little with me too." *Still* smiling. "I mean, I'm going to be paying for some part of it, right? And co-signing loans?"

"You wouldn't know about it, exactly, but the decision process is just really tricky, Mom. You have to look at the whole package. It's not just who gives you the most money. You have to develop your own personalized criteria."

"I'm only worried, sweetie, that your criteria is whatever school looks the most like Hogwarts."

Melinda gripped the edge of the table and glared.

"Don't *give* me that death stare, Mel. Jesus. I'm kidding about Hogwarts. That was a joke."

Melinda let go of the table. "I'm going to talk it over with Nicola."

"Ole Cough Drops is also the woman who told you not to write about your grandmother for your personal statement, right? Not that the piece about the community library didn't turn out nice."

"Nicola's dad's a college president. She knows about these things."

"But it's your story, Mel. Not hers." And her mother took a measured sip of tea.

"Everyone writes about their grandparents. You don't stand out if you write about your grandparents. She was right to give me that advice."

"I'm not criticizing. I'm just saying."

A little girl at the table next to them started singing a pop song Melinda didn't know.

"*Everyone* writes about grandparents," said Melinda. "Alyssa from Key Club. Emily from Lit Mag. Maybe if you had immigrated here instead of your parents, maybe the American Dream card would work in a personal statement. But you didn't. You were born in New Jersey."

"Well, I'm sorry that's inconvenienced you so much, Melinda." Her mother put down the teacup a little too hard. "I'm truly, deeply sorry."

The waiter came by with hot water. He smiled at Melinda and her mother. "The cookies are on their way!" He refilled their teacups. Then the waiter was at the next table, smiling at the parallel mother-daughter pair.

"It's just some of those universities, Melinda." Her mother lifted her teacup, but did not sip from it. "Some of those schools with those ridiculous price tags. Their students must have tea at the Pierre all the time. Some of them might be here right now. Do you really think you'd even fit in?"

"All the people here are on Groupons, Mom."

"I don't know if you're right about that." Her mother glanced around. "They all look perfectly fancied up to me."

Melinda poured a lump of sugar into her tea and watched it dissolve. *Did* she think she'd fit in at a prestigious, expensive college? She wasn't sure. If the kids at school made fun of her glasses now, what would the college people do? But she shouldn't worry about that yet. There was a more immediate battle happening right here, right now. She looked up from her tea, looked as calmly as she could at her mother. "Just be happy for me. Okay? What's normal is for you to just be happy for me. What's normal is for you to support me in whatever I want to do, whatever loans I choose to take out, all of it. It's my choice. I did all the work here, right?"

Melinda's mother stared. Then her eyes rolled up to the ceiling and she started to laugh. She laughed very, very loudly. Melinda's mother's laugh launched itself against an instrumental rendition of something from Les Misérables, it launched itself against the gentle sounds of scone-and-sandwich consumption, it launched itself against the silverware, it launched itself against the light fixtures pointing down at the patrons.

Melinda's face turned hot. She sensed that people were looking at her, people not even in that room. She felt angry and ashamed and then angrier because she hated that her mother was trying to make her feel ashamed, and that it was working. She rose from the table and immediately, her mother stopped laughing. "Mel. Where are you going?"

"I've got to use the restroom."

"That's not true. You just don't want to finish our conversation. You stay here until we've worked this out."

"Do you want me to get a UTI, Mom? You can get a UTI from holding your pee."

"Don't talk like that, Melinda. We're at a nice restaurant."

"I'm going to take a real serious piss, Mother." And Melinda walked away. She pretended to head to the ladies room, but then she left the tea lounge. She only planned to leave for a second, only wanted a little air to cool down. She stepped back into the chill of the hotel lobby.

No music was playing in the lobby, no overdressed mother-daughter pairs were attempting stubbornly to bond. Melinda could breathe again. This was where the people actually of the hotel were waiting—waiting for their taxis, for their rides, for their friends who lived near Central Park, for the next things in their lives.

The beautiful girl with the nice boots and with maybe two sets of eyelashes was still there, sprawled out, her legs still swung over the armchair's arm. What was she reading? Melinda tried to see the book's spine. The girl looked up.

She had noticed Melinda staring. And now, now she was staring back at Melinda.

"Ohhh," the girl breathed.

"What?" Melinda lifted a hand to her own face, worried the girl was horrified by her glasses or by the acne she'd thought she'd successfully covered up.

"I just really like your little collar," the girl said. "The collar on your dress."

"Oh." Melinda walked closer. Something about her mother's laugh had made her feel, in her hot anger, newly bold. "Thanks."

"You staying here with your parents too?"

"Yeah." She lied before she even had time to decide she was going to lie—it was as natural as breathing. Melinda needed this girl to believe that she was here on no discount at all. "I'm staying here with my mom."

"Where is she?"

"The gym."

"The gym is kind of *small*," the girl said. "Don't you think?"

"Micro-sized."

"Miniature."

The girl sighed heavily, closed her eyes. Melinda tried to get a good look at the lashes. But then the girl opened her eyes again. "I'm here with my parents and sister," she said. "We're supposed to be having a 'family weekend,' since I'm on break. But I ate the wrong pancakes at breakfast. The ones with gluten. So I've opted to stay here while they tour the city." She shrugged. "Not to give you my life story or anything. What do your parents do?"

"Huh?"

"For a living."

It was a rude question but Melinda already felt too flushed to pretend to take offense. "Stocks," she said. "They do stocks." She added, "They're extremely rich."

"Oh, yeah? Extremely?" The girl smiled wickedly. "Mine, too. Hey, you okay? Your face is red. Do you need to go to your room or something?"

"No, I'm fine." Melinda pointed to the book, mostly to get the girl to look somewhere else. "What are you reading?"

The girl waved her book the way some might wave their hand, so that the pages flopped back and forth. "*Paradise Lost.*"

Paradise Lost! That was seventeenth-century literature. Wasn't it? Melinda was pretty sure it was seventeenth-century literature. Here was Elizabeth Taylor (essentially), reading seventeenth-century literature. Melinda did not believe in ghosts but she did hear a voice like her grandmother's rushing around in her brain, saying, "*Pay attention. Melinda, pay attention.*"

She tried to sound casual: "What are you reading that for?"

"I have an exam on it. Quote identification. Very high school. But the professor is the most beautiful man. And on NPR sometimes. You should hear the way he talks about Milton."

"Yeah?"

"I mean, just really, it'll make you swoon. His discussion of the power plays, and theories of work, and reconceptualizations of sin."

Melinda didn't even know what *one* reconceptualization of sin would be, and this girl had used the word in plural—suggesting a whole hidden cosmos of reconceptualizations that might emerge at any second.

To the girl she said only, "That sounds delightful."

They both fell silent and looked at one another. Something like impatience moved across the girl's face.

"I'm going to head back to my room, I think," said the girl. "It's hard to do work in the lobby. It's noisy. I should go upstairs."

More than anything in the world, Melinda wanted to go upstairs too. The sudden curiosity felt as warm as her earlier anger. If this girl got into an elevator, Melinda could get in one as well, slip in behind her, no questions asked.

And maybe the girl would even invite Melinda to her room. Which was not the kind of thing that happened to Melinda. But her life *was* changing. Or would change, soon. And this girl was still smiling at her in a certain way, this beautiful and wealthy and educated girl.

"Yeah, me too," Melinda said, trying to keep the hope out of her voice. "I'm upstairs too. I'm going there."

The girl got out of her chair and they strolled together to the elevator bank. Nobody else got into the elevator with them. They were alone except for an operator in the elevator, a living, breathing elevator operator wearing white gloves. Melinda couldn't bring herself to look at the operator's face. If she did so, she was sure she would reveal herself in an instant. She must act natural, like she did this sort of thing all the time. The operator asked, "Where to?" His English was not broken in the least, but absolutely smooth. Melinda waited for the girl to respond—she knew she would need to say a floor the girl wasn't staying on, or risk getting caught—but the girl said nothing. She was looking at Melinda. Was the girl suspicious? Of course she was suspicious. She wasn't blind.

The operator said, "Ladies?"

"Fifteen," said the girl at last.

"Eighteen," Melinda said.

They began their ascent.

The non-mahogany parts of the elevator were paneled with mirrors, mirrors offering up images of Melinda's body in parts—there an elbow sticking out awkwardly, there a slightly quaky ankle, there a too-thick knee. The right kind of small talk would serve as the perfect disguise for her own intrusion. Melinda tried to think of something to say. She thought of Elizabeth Taylor, keeping her mutancy a secret, even when she was very young. What an actress. If only Melinda could start speaking to this girl about reconceptualizations. But she could hardly hold that whole word in her head, much less say it.

Someday soon, though, that word and all its attendant meanings would be Melinda's. In Melinda's own possession. She simply needed to try to go where this girl was going now and that was easy enough—she was being propelled alongside her by the same complex machinery. The decision ahead was clear. She would ignore her mother's fears. She would take out the necessary loans for whatever school Ms. Naylor said was the best. After all, she did not know what kind of place she might arrive at if she did anything else, if she didn't follow this girl. If she didn't go up in the direction she was traveling, Melinda guessed she could only go down. Wasn't that how elevators worked?

Right now, at least, that was how elevators worked.

But what if someday she might be able to invent a different elevator? An invisible elevator so sleek and so smooth and so modern that it went sideways, moving through the Pierre's walls, first through individual well-lit rooms, through moments of squabbles and post-sex moments, past the angry people and tired people and the people in possession of their own discontents. Then this new elevator would glide diagonally into dark, dark rooms, lit up not by chandeliers but by the stars of countries Melinda had never seen, constellations her grandmother, maybe, had known.

"Are you okay?" asked the girl. Just like that, Melinda was back in the elevator that went up and down, torn away from her brief invention. "You look pale. Do you need me to come to your room with you to make sure you don't, like, die?"

"I'm okay," Melinda said. "Sorry."

"I mean, don't apologize. Maybe you accidentally ate the wrong pancakes too."

Melinda looked more closely at the girl.

"Just a joke," said the girl.

Those weren't double eyelashes. Of course, any idiot could see that. The girl, like Melinda, just had on heavy mascara. Melinda would have known that right away, if she'd looked closer earlier, if she hadn't been so flustered.

Then the elevator doors opened. Floor fifteen. The girl put her hand in her right pocket and then said, "Oh, no. Oh, crap crap crap. I forgot my room key."

"What?" Melinda said.

"I forgot my room key. I always do this. I left it in the room. Do you think I could just hang out with you in your room until my family gets back?"

"Um." Melinda looked to the elevator operator as if expecting him to help her, but he didn't even glance her way.

"I'm too embarrassed to ask at the desk. I already lost my key and they charged my parents, which, no big deal, except my mother said it was a *sign* of my basic incompetence and went off on this whole rant about my quote-unquote savage immaturity. It's fine if I just hang with you, right?"

Melinda took a deep breath.

The operator must have taken that as a "yes" because the doors closed. Sixteen, seventeen. Melinda couldn't think of what to do. When the doors opened for her at floor eighteen, she stumbled out, staring down at a complex rug design that seemed to shift under her feet like a kaleidoscope crushed into carpet. Lanterns hung from the ceiling, casting gold light onto the white walls. The girl was right behind her. "Thank you soso much for letting me tag along," the girl said. "I'm Pia, by the way."

What now? What steps should she take? Melinda took off her glasses, trying to take the edge off the sudden keen pain around her temples. Without her glasses on, the lanterns looked like luminous globes. She tried to count her breaths.

"Let me try them," Pia said, taking first Melinda's hand, and then, before Melinda realized what she was doing, Melinda's glasses, which Pia put on immediately. "It's like being drunk! All tilt-a-whirl." She pushed the glasses further up her nose. "You aren't getting these back until you let me into your room!" Her voice had gone husky. She was flirting. "Well, and which room is it?" Pia asked.

So. Okay. Here Melinda was. And where was she supposed to go next? She wondered if she should call the elevator back, if she should make a break for it. Was it too late to claim that she, also, had forgotten her key? Maybe it was too late. Her brain wasn't working right. She felt especially blinded now, maybe from staring at the bright globes of lantern light. "Can I have my glasses back?" she asked.

Pia elbowed her lightly in the ribs. "Not until you let me into your room. I told you. Come on. While your parents are at the gym. Maybe we can order room service. They leave their credit cards in the room?"

Melinda swallowed. She went up to a door and stood before it. She saw herself as a child again, passing the stores that seemed empty, imagining her mother working in those stores. Sweeping up donut dust, being nice to the rude people who had just moved into the neighborhood. Her mother, right now, downstairs, with the tea. Waiting. What was behind this door? Nothing. Nothing meant for Melinda.

"Well," said Pia, "are we going into this room or not?"

"There's someone in my room, actually," Melinda said. "My mother."

"So why did you tell me your mother was at the gym?"

"I don't know."

"What do you mean, you don't know?"

Pia was onto her. She knew she was lying. Melinda could not see anything at all now. Just the globes of light. Her heart was pounding so hard, she feared it would abrade her rib cage, burst through her lungs, block all intake of air. *Pay attention, pay attention.* Melinda forced herself to look Pia directly in the eye, pushed her face close to Pia's. With Melinda's glasses on, Pia did not look so different, really, from Melinda. Her foundation looked cheap and chalky. And then, on a sudden courageous impulse, her heart still going crazy, Melinda said, "Why are you interrogating me like this?"

Pia actually staggered back, as if Melinda had slapped her.

Well, that was something to pay attention to. And she had nothing to lose. Pia's face was sweaty. Her eyes, wide. And Melinda had a wild idea. Lowering her voice, Melinda said, "I don't think you're a guest here at all."

Pia began to cry.

It happened very quickly. Her sobs soft, her tears heavy. Her mascara ran—dark goo-paths down her face. "How did you know?" she said. "How could you tell?"

Melinda stayed silent. She really hadn't been able to tell. She had only been able to guess.

Pia hurled herself into a teary confession, her eyes made huge by Melinda's glasses. No, she was not a guest at the Pierre. She lived in Staten Island. It was her first time doing something like this. Her parents weren't rich and plus they had cut her off to teach her a lesson, so she was paying for school all on her own and plus trying to become an actor. She was in a massive amount of debt.

Melinda chewed on her lower lip. Her heartbeat had slowed to a steady loud thud. Hearing Pia make this confession in Melinda's own dull glasses—Melinda did not feel anywhere close to triumphant.

"I figured I'd find a middle-aged rich man," Pia continued. "I'd steal a wallet, maybe. Or some cash. Or the man would offer it. I was going to play it by ear. That's how good improv works, my friend Beth says. My friend Beth does this kind of thing all the time. Beth says it's the easiest money you could imagine and that I just needed to walk in, be confident, play up the college girl thing, and make eye contact with the loneliest person I could find." Pia took off Melinda's glasses but did not give them back to Melinda. She just looked at the glasses in her hand as if her confession were meant for them, not Melinda. "Beth said it can even be fun if you meet the right person."

"But I don't look rich," Melinda said, her voice wobbling. "And I'm not a man."

"You look lonely, though. And you're kind of cute. And you were staring at me super hard. And you're staying here, so you must be rich. Your parents are in stocks. Right? Look, I just need . . . Seriously, anything. If you can just give me *something*. Even, like, forty bucks. It'll help. It really will."

"I don't have money."

"Why do you keep lying to me?" A new menacing heat in Pia's voice as she raised her left hand. The wires of Melinda's glasses looked like bird legs, sticking out of her palm. "Give me money or I'll stomp on your glasses."

"I don't have money," Melinda repeated.

"You do. You have money. You're staying here."

"I'm not staying here," Melinda said, finally, softly. The words hurt to say. "I'm just here for the fancy tea." For good measure, she added, "On a Groupon."

"A Groupon?" Pia shook her head. "What do you mean?"

"A Groupon is a combination of the words 'group' and 'coupon.' It's an online discount and—"

"I know what a Groupon is," Pia said.

In the long silence that followed, Melinda hoped Pia might laugh. And then Melinda would laugh. And then their laughs would move together and it would be beautiful, a sonic explosion, it would be like when she laughed with her mother on the bus. Two laughs mirroring one another. A funny and luminous twist.

But Pia didn't laugh. Rather, she let loose a string of curses. Then she dropped Melinda's glasses on the ground and crushed them under her boot.

Melinda exhaled, hard, with something like astonishment and something, strangely, like relief.

A door opened. A guest staying in the hotel. A blur of pink, a man's voice. "Is everything okay?" the man asked them. Imposters, imposters. They would be found out. The man looked down at the crushed glasses. Suspicious now: "Is everything okay, ladies?"

Both girls bolted at the same time for the stairs. Melinda stumbled and Pia, surprisingly, reached back, grabbed Melinda's hand to steady her. "Take off your shoes," Pia said.

Melinda took off her high heels and rushed with Pia toward the stairwell. Eighteen flights—not *so* far, although without her glasses, Melinda had to be more cautious. The border of each step was blurry but Pia held Melinda's hand, helping her keep her balance. By the time they were on the ninth floor, Pia had turned sweet and penitent, even as she gasped for air. "Crap crap crap," she said. "I'm sorry. I'm sorry about your glasses."

"It's okay," Melinda said. "I hated my glasses."

. . .

Melinda's mother was in the lobby, a long large blob of red. And her mother was screaming. She was screaming about someone abducting Melinda. *She is underage, you scumbags, she is still seventeen.* People stared. People smirked. Behind the desk, a woman picked up a telephone. She muttered something about security. The police would come, Melinda imagined. They would take her mother away. For a second, Melinda couldn't move. She felt she was watching something on her grandmother's little TV.

Pia was still beside Melinda. On the remaining floors downward, she had jabbered away like she and Melinda were new best friends. Now she gripped Melinda's wrist. In a way, they had become thieves together. When Melinda went to college far away, but before she graduated overloaded with debt, she would of course tell everyone that Ms. Naylor had been her mentor. Still, secretly—even though once she left the hotel, the two girls would never meet again—Melinda would think of Pia as her true teacher. You could wear ease and charm and fake wealth like a hat over your real self, your real brain. Wearing cheap and hideous glasses, you could still hide where you came from with a smile, a coy look, the right book, even as your debts grew. You could, for a time, fool people. At least, you could fool people like Melinda. And Melinda really only needed to fool herself to be happy in life. She was smart enough to know that.

"Who *is* she?" Pia asked, pointing to Melinda's mother, who was now flailing before the reception desk. "Is she some celebrity nutcase?" But despite all she had admitted to Pia, Melinda didn't claim her mother as her own. Instead, nervously, she laughed. It was the laugh Melinda's mother heard and recognized, somehow, through her flailing. She looked up, she stopped screaming, she said, "My baby. There. There."

And she headed straight toward Melinda, as if she thought she had the strength to pull her out of the hotel, as if she thought she had the power to drag her daughter by the arm out the door, across the East River, and all the way home.

Acknowledgments

I am grateful to the editors of the journals where many of these stories, some in slightly altered forms, appeared:

American Short Fiction online, "A Guide to Sirens"
The Chicago Tribune, "The Lock Factory"
The Collagist, "Guardian"
Glimmer Train, "The Afterlife of Turtles"
Guernica, "Subcortical"
Indiana Review, "*Recuerdo*"
Kenyon Review online, "Unit Cell"
The Masters Review, "A Suggestion"
Memorious, "My Four Stomachs"
The Normal School, "A Magic Trick for the Recently Unemployed"
The Sewanee Review, "Hart Island"

The quote on pages 189–190 ("The force exerted...") is from Walter Benjamin's *One-Way Street and Other Writings*, translated by J. A. Underwood, published by Penguin Classics, 2009. The quote on page 190 ("If you flip a dime...") is from Sam Kean's *The Violinist's Thumb: And Other Lost Tales of Love, War, and Genius, as Written by Our Genetic Code*, published by Back Bay Books, 2013.

Thank you, also, to the following people:

Wyatt Prunty, Catherine Goldstead, Hilary Jacqmin, and everyone at Johns Hopkins University Press for believing in this book and making it better.

Lorraine López for your humor, guidance, and incredible intelligence. Lorrie Moore, Tony Earley, Nancy Reisman, Kate Daniels, Peter Guralnik, Rick Hilles, Mark Jarman: Thank you for letting me learn from you. I am grateful to Vanderbilt University and to the English department at SUNY New Paltz for support and funding.

Marysa LaRowe for your friendship and editorial brilliance. Claire Jimenez for your smart and hilarious insight, on and off the page. Sara Renberg for poetry (and for that fact about turtles and lutes). Ellice Litwak for rail trail walks. Justin Quarry for taking me to Flannery's Andalusia and for all of your kindness. Simon Han and Anna Silverstein, for giving many of these stories first or extra looks. Laura Birdsall, Rita Bullwinkel, Reid Douglass, D. J. Thielke, and Maggie Zebracka, for your guiding thoughts on some of these characters in their beginnings.

My students, especially the teen writers at StudioNPL, for inspiring me with your words to be ever kinder, ever braver.

My father for teaching me how to look more closely at the world. My mother for your comic timing, for giving the best feedback, for showing me what it means to be a woman with creative daring.

Garrett Warren for letting me interview you about crystallography and atomic structures, and for making me laugh, and for being my home.